A TOUCH OF SHADOWS

BOOKS BY JESSICA THORNE

THE QUEEN'S WING SERIES

The Queen's Wing

The Stone's Heart

THE HOLLOW KING SERIES

Mageborn

Nightborn

The Lost Girls of Foxfield Hall

The Bookbinder's Daughter

The Water Witch

A Touch of Shadows

JESSICA THORNE

SECOND SKY

Published by Second Sky in 2024

An imprint of Storyfire Ltd.
Carmelite House
50 Victoria Embankment
London EC4Y 0DZ

www.secondskybooks.com

ISBN: 978-1-83790-910-0
eBook ISBN: 978-1-83790-909-4

For Pat, still my hero, always my hero.

GLOSSARY

Asteroth (country) [Ass-te-ROTH], Asterothian (adjective), capital Pelias – currently ruled by a regents' council in the absence of Aeryn, Queen of Asteroth, Chosen of the Aurum, 'The Lost Queen'
Aurum, the [OR-um] – one of two powers formed from old magic in the cataclysm, the Aurum represents light. It sits in opposition to the Nox and takes the form of flames. The centre of its power is held in the Sacrum in Pelias. In each generation it selects a woman from the royal family of Asteroth as its Chosen and she becomes the queen
Aurum-forged steel – metal forged with the power of the Aurum, the opposite of shadow-wrought but the same thing
Cellandre – forest in the northwest of Asteroth/southeast of Ilanthus
Darkwoods – parts of wild forest infected with traces of the Nox where bargains can be struck and shadow kin roam
Hedge witch – a witch living in a rural setting, administering to the needs of a village or small local community, generally unaligned, regarded as lesser by the College of Winter, the maidens and the sisterhood

Ilanthus [Ill-AN-thus] (country), Ilanthian (adjective and inhabitant), capital Sidonia – currently ruled by Alessander of the line of Sidon, King of Ilanthus

Knightsford – fortified town on the edge of Cellandre with a garrison of knights

Knights of the Aurum – sworn warriors in the service of the Aurum. Once the power (or light) of the Aurum runs through them they become Paladins

Line of Sidon [Sid-ON] – bloodline of the royal family of Ilanthus.

Maidens of the Aurum – society of witches dedicated to serving the Aurum – currently led by Sister Maryn. By law in Asteroth all women with magic must submit to the Maidens of the Aurum and serve through them while all men must return their magic to the Aurum

Nightbreaker – Aurum-forged sword of the Grandmaster of the Knights of the Aurum

Nox, the [Noks] – one of two powers formed from old magic in the cataclysm, the Nox represents darkness. It sits in opposition to the Aurum and is said to take many forms, but it is worshipped as a goddess by the people of Ilanthus

Old magic – primal magic torn into two opposing forces by a magical cataclysm long ago, now passed into legend

Othertongue – secret language of magic known primarily to witchkind

Pact, the – peace agreement between Asteroth and Ilanthus which ended the last war

Paladins – senior Knights of the Aurum, touched by its light and blessed, filled by the light when its power is invoked which makes them stronger, faster and lethal. Servants of the Aurum, and the queen of Asteroth, her protectors

Sacrum, the [Sak-RUM] – a stone circle now enclosed by the temple in the palace at Pelias which houses the flames of the Aurum, the most holy site of the Aurum

Sanctum, the [Sank-TUM] – secure compound in the royal palace in Pelias housing the Maidens of the Aurum
Seven Sisters, the – a stone circle near Knightsford
Shadow kin – creatures formed from shadows which can beguile, infect and overpower humans, turning them into monsters serving the Nox. They use music, illusion and brute force to hunt and trap their prey. When a bargain is made, shadow kin often claim the price
Shadow-wrought steel – metal forged with the power of the Nox with the intention of containing or harnessing magic. The sisterhood are skilled in this art, forging the weapons to fight and capture others
Sidonia [Sid-ON-ee-ah] (city) – capital of Ilanthus
Sisterhood of the Nox – society of Ilanthian witches dedicated to serving the Nox
Thirbridge [THUR-bridge] – village in the forest of Cellandre near the border with Ilanthus
Witchfire – a magical spell which conjures flames, used primarily as a weapon as very difficult to control
Witchkind – people able to wield magic, able to command or cajole the powers of light and dark, or attuned to old magic in some way

PROLOGUE

TWENTY YEARS EARLIER

The village of Thirbridge might well have been at the end of the earth.

It lay deep in the Forest of Cellandre, in the furthest corner of the kingdom, the loneliest and most isolated place in the world. Elodie had run as far as she could go. Any further and she would be in enemy territory in more ways than one. But no one would look for her here.

She dismounted and tied her horse to the solitary hitching post outside the inn. The child was still bundled against her side under her cloak. Asleep now, thank the light.

Every bone in Elodie's body ached. She just wanted to fall to the ground and sleep herself, right then and there. But she couldn't.

She had to keep going. To find somewhere safe.

She had been following the lines in the earth, those places of old magic, and they had brought her here. They only skirted the edge of the village and then swirled back into the depths of the forest. In the morning, she knew, she would follow them again.

But for tonight, just tonight, she would have a meal, and food, and maybe a bath. Oh, how she longed for a bath, steaming hot, with the luxurious handmade soaps and precious oils she had left far away in Asteroth. The thought strayed to what else she had left behind and she recoiled from memories.

The child stirred. A child already, not the tiny baby she had been when they left. She had his eyes, his hair... She was the image of him...

Elodie winced and hushed the girl, stroking her long black tresses until she settled again.

'Storm's coming,' said the innkeeper. 'I warrant you'll be staying longer than a night.'

Elodie nodded, staring at the darkening sky to the south through the open door. 'Maybe.'

'What's your business?'

'I'm... I'm a healer.' She needed to learn not to hesitate, she chided herself inwardly.

'You're young for a healer,' he commented, unaware, or uncaring, of how rude that sounded. 'And the babe's father?'

So he'd seen her there, snuggled in against Elodie's side, huge dark eyes blinking at this strange world. Well, how could he miss her? She was a beautiful child.

'He's dead.' That lie came far too easily. Well, it wasn't exactly a lie. There was no father to come after them now and anyone who did... well, she would just have to take care of that if and when it happened. 'I need somewhere to stay, somewhere to look after her.'

'In Thirbridge?' He sounded startled. She wasn't sure she blamed him. Clearly, no one came here willingly.

'Not... not right in the village. Nearby, maybe. But somewhere quiet, private. I can help your people—healing, midwifery and... and other things—but I need solitude and access to the forest for supplies.'

He raised an eyebrow. 'Oh aye, that kind of healer, are you?'

Witchkind. The word was left unspoken between them. Elodie met his gaze levelly, unwavering. Let him think what he wanted. Better that they were a little afraid of her than anything else.

'Do you know of a suitable place?' she asked.

The innkeeper nodded slowly. 'I know somewhere. Not far, but far enough. In the forest itself. But there's a darkwood.'

Elodie sighed. Of course there was. In a place as thoroughly riddled with veins of old magic as Cellandre, there was always a darkwood. She would take care of that.

This, then, was where she was meant to be.

The child stirred again, her bottom lip wobbling. Inwardly, Elodie cursed to herself. She was not a natural mother.

'She's hungry,' she told the innkeeper. 'I'll need warm milk for her.'

'Go to the parlour. I'll have something sent in for you too. Does your horse want stabling?'

Elodie almost laughed. Her horse. 'He wants selling,' she replied. 'I've no more use for him.'

The tower in the forest was desolate and lonely. From a distance it looked like it might topple over in a strong breeze, but it was solidly built and once cleaned it would serve.

After she had seen to a broken limb, checked up on a very pregnant baker's wife and two children with fevers, she had already won the trust of these people. Some of them even tried to play with the child while Elodie worked, although never for long. She was too strange, with her endless dark eyes and the way her hair seemed to move of its own volition sometimes, like smoke.

That very first night, once she had shooed them all safely away, the storm came. Just as she had known it would. She locked the doors, shuttered the windows and prepared herself.

And then she noticed the child was missing.

Cursing, she tore outside into the darkness. Wind lashed the rain against her face, soaking her in seconds, plastering her golden hair against her head. Overhead, the canopy of the forest raged like the ocean but she paid it no heed. All that mattered was the child, protecting her, keeping her away from the shadows.

Elodie conjured a ball of witchfire in her hand and ran through the trees. She could feel the darkness rising around her, trying to smother the light. She pushed on, pouring more and more of her energy into keeping the flames alive, pushing back the shadows.

'Wren?' she screamed. Panic tightened her chest, crushing her lungs. 'Wren!'

And then she saw her. Standing on the edge of a gully that seemed awash with shadow kin. A powerful place, which should have been shining with old magic but instead was a feeding ground for darkness. It had called them here, the magic, and the shadow kin had turned it into a darkwood. A place where they could thrive and live on magic stolen from the land.

By the Aurum, it was so close, like it had been waiting for them.

Wren stood on her thin little legs, too pale in the darkness, her arms stretched wide as if inviting the darkwood in. Her hair had grown long and wild, winding around her as if it was ink in water, moving with a will of its own.

'Wren!' Elodie shouted. 'No!'

Wren looked back at her, face pale, dark eyes wide. She looked afraid. So afraid. She didn't understand what was happening. How could she? Elodie hadn't explained because it had never occurred to her that Wren would understand. But she did. That much was clear.

The shadow kin were singing to her, their sibilant whispers brushing against Elodie's skin and making it shiver. How much more powerful must they be to Wren, weaving their dark magic around her, entangling her.

She was just a child.

Elodie drew the knife from her belt, Aurum-blessed steel, the finest in the kingdom.

She was just a child, a little girl. But one with magic inside her, so much magic. And if she ever succumbed to the call of the darkness, if the Nox ever claimed her...

The Nox was broken and shattered, but that didn't mean its remnants didn't still have power. And if it ever realised what Wren could offer...

There was only one way. Elodie knew that now. She should have done it straight away in the sight of the Aurum, back in the Sacrum right then and there when she broke the Nox's power and scattered it, before she ever had a chance to grow attached.

It was a kindness.

Gritting her teeth, Elodie advanced. The wind tried to drive her back, the rain tried to blind her. Thunder rolled overhead and moments later lightning lit up the sky.

Wren was watching her, terrified but not moving one way or the other. The creatures ensnared her, knotting themselves in her hair, teeth and claws and voices so sweet. She wasn't even trying to fight them.

'What did I say?' Elodie snarled at her, rage and betrayal and everything in between coursing through her. The little girl covered her face with her hands and sobbed, but Elodie couldn't let that sway her. 'What did I clearly say?'

She hurled the witchfire at the shadow kin, scattering them. At the same instant, she seized Wren's hair, wrapping it around her fist and dragging the girl to her knees. Wren screamed in terror and Elodie hated herself. But she didn't stop. Couldn't stop. The knife flashed with the burst of lightning overhead, severing the dark strands close to the scalp.

It was like dropping a sluice gate in a dam. The flow of power stopped. Wren sobbed loudly, audible now as the raging wind died away and the storm subsided to nothing.

In Elodie's hand, the lengths of black hair turned to smoke and drifted away.

And with that, the shadow kin were gone.

Carefully, Elodie gathered Wren in her arms, gently now, soothing her. The little girl shook as if she might fall to pieces, tears covering her face.

'Reach for the light,' Wren whimpered over and over again. She was answering, Elodie realised, the first words she had ever spoken.

Elodie cradled her close, rocking her to silence, sitting there in the moonlight, in the now silent but watchful forest. She stroked Wren's shorn head, the ragged bits of hair and bare scalp. By the light, she'd have to be more careful, keep her hair short, keep her power in check. It was the only way. Elodie could feel the darkwood, still there all around them, coiled, wary and hungry, full of resentment.

Waiting. Just waiting for Wren.

Let it try, she thought fiercely. Let it try to take her child away.

THE PALADINS' BOOK OF WISDOM

Listen well, for this is a warning.

Beware the places where the lines in the earth meet, where the stones are circled, and where the shadows whisper the sweetest promises. Once places of power, of old magic, they have become feeding grounds for shadow kin. These dark creatures cluster where once the light and dark met in perfect balance, preying on the unwary, luring travellers off the path and offering bargains to those desperate enough to seek them out. But a bargain made in the darkwood will never bring anything but misery and despair.

Wander not idly there.

We fight the Nox, now and always, with flame and sword.

CHAPTER 1

WREN

The fury of the storm raging outside couldn't smother the sound of the woman's suffering inside the simple cottage on the edge of the village. Her sobs and cries sent Elodie running up the stairs, her instincts as a healer always taking control in moments like this.

Wren followed in her wake with all the bags slung around her, like she was a pack animal rather than an apprentice. The stairs were steep and narrow, cutting right through the heart of the home, but that didn't matter to Elodie. It didn't even slow her down. The healer was a force of nature. Wren had known that all her life. It was unavoidable. Nothing got in her way, especially when someone was in need of help.

Lindie's cries of pain ratcheted up a notch and Elodie vanished behind the door to the bedroom. Wren was about to follow when Pol appeared. He'd been lurking at the other end of the landing and looked as if he was about to throw up or pass out. Wren's stomach dropped at the sight of him.

She'd loved him once, or had fancied she did. Dreamed of a life with him, rather than one banished to the forest with

Elodie. Handsome, funny, skilful Pol, who was a better hunter than anyone in the village. Who had chosen Lindie.

He looked haggard now. 'Can you—can you help her?'

The words felt like knives. Other words, words spoken in anger and fear not so long ago, rang around her head instead.

You're a freak. A monster. I don't even know what you are.

Wren shied back but he reached out and grabbed her arm in his fist. Her breath caught in her throat.

'I'm needed,' she whispered, her voice strangled. Afraid.

She'd never imagined she'd be afraid of Pol, back when the summer breeze had touched her skin alongside his hands, when they'd laughed and never had a care in the world.

But she wasn't the only one scared now.

'Please,' he said urgently. 'You have to help her. Please, Wren, anything. I'll do anything.'

He meant it too. Pol had never loved Wren. Not really. She'd been an idiot to think he did, that he might. That it was even possible.

But he adored Lindie.

Everyone did. She was beautiful, gentle, the perfect girl. A woman now. She was no more a girl than Wren was anymore. She was Pol's wife.

Wren still recalled the smile Lindie wore on her wedding day, when they had all stood in the village square to celebrate them. Elodie had turned away with a snort of disgust. But Lindie had caught Wren's eye just before she left with the healer, and she'd smiled that smile. That nasty, triumphant, petty smile.

'Wren,' Pol hissed and his hand tightened to a circle of iron, squeezing into her skin. 'Wren, you have to—'

Her whole body stiffened in disgust.

She didn't have to do anything. Lindie could die screaming for all she cared. Lindie could—

Wren caught the thought and pushed it down, turned it

aside. No, that wasn't right. No one deserved death, especially not for having the misfortune to marry an idiot like Pol. Childbirth was unforgiving and the complications Elodie suspected here were dangerous indeed. And unnatural.

'Let go of me Pol. And get out of my way.'

But he didn't. 'I know what you can do. Please, whatever it takes. We only wanted a son, and we thought the darkwood... but this... Not like this. Help her. Whatever the price, I'll pay it. Just do it.'

His touch was bruising and Wren felt the brush of the shadows coiling around her, stirring her hair against her shoulders. He had no idea what she could do. Not really. But what little he did know had been enough to make him cast her aside and choose Lindie instead.

'Wren!' Elodie shouted from inside and Lindie cried out again, the sound torn from her throat. Pol started, and then seemed to realise he was still holding Wren. He pulled back as if scalded. They stared at one another and Wren wondered if that was guilt she saw in his eyes. Elodie's voice sounded again. 'Where are those candles?'

Wren pushed by Pol like he was made of air and closed the door of the bedroom firmly behind her.

The scene inside was bad.

Lindie was red-faced and drenched in sweat. Her mother knelt beside her, muttering prayer after prayer to the Aurum, much good that would do her. Elodie was already moving with her usual ruthless efficiency, closing the shutters against the night and scattering the protective herbs all along the boundaries.

'Candles,' she snarled again, the harsh voice completely at odds with the beauty of her figure and face. This was even more serious than the message had let on. Something terrible was happening here. Not just the perils of childbirth. Something else. Wren could feel it crawling up the edges of her consciousness, like the shadows she'd already had to push aside.

Wren shook her head and dumped the bags on the ground at the foot of the bed. No time for hesitation now. The shadows still pressed so close. She could feel their power like a shroud and the meagre candles the family had lit burned low, their flames guttering. She'd brought a stack of fresh ones, ones that she and Elodie had made only yesterday, as if they had known what would be needed. Perhaps Elodie had. Wren moved as quickly as she could, jamming them into holders and placing them around the room in a circle, then a second one, inside that, surrounding the bed.

'I'm sorry,' Lindie wept as the contractions subsided. 'I'm sorry. I only wanted... I only wanted—'

Whatever she had wanted was lost in the next wave of agony that ripped through her.

We only wanted a son. That was what Pol had said. What had they done to ensure that? Where had they gone? He had mentioned the darkwood. Oh this was bad.

Wren knew that people from the village sometimes went into the darkwood for bargains. Some boons were greater than others. Some came to nothing. Elodie had warned them not to almost as often as she had warned Wren not to stray there. At least Wren had the sense not to ask anything of those places of power. Bargains made there were always double-edged. But they didn't really connect the darkwood with the Nox itself. The Nox was gone and the darkwood had been there forever and... well, it was only a superstition, wasn't it?

I'll pay it, Pol had said. Wren shuddered. What had they done?

Lindie screamed, this time full-throated and desperate, and Elodie pressed a pale cold hand to her brow, muttering words in the othertongue the villagers couldn't hope to understand. Wren could barely follow the secret language of magic herself.

Light blossomed there, a faint glow that slowly permeated the woman's body, illuminating the room in an eerie flickering gold.

The candles were ready. Wren took out a taper, ready to light them, but before she could something rattled the window, like a hand reaching out and trying to get in.

The night seemed to still, falling silent all around them. Not just quiet – something deep and endless, a complete absence of sound. Even Wren's own breath sounded too loud in her ears. Darkness swelled up outside, beyond the shutters, beyond the house. It came from the forest. It came from the land itself, and it was waiting. Wren was aware of Lindie still sobbing and crying, of her mother still praying, the same useless prayers over and over, but it was too late. The darkness had come to claim what it was owed.

'I only wanted to give him a son!' Lindie shrieked, the words twisting with her torment.

Wren reached for the shutters, to secure them again, and the wind tore them from her hand, flinging them open. Shadows flooded the room, coiling around the people within, climbing the walls, hanging over them like a vast tower of night about to drop on them and tear them limb from limb.

'Now Wren,' Elodie commanded.

But Wren's hand shook. The darkness was singing. She could clearly make out a voice. It was soft and enticing, like a memory of long ago, a lullaby. She didn't know the words, couldn't make them out, but the tune was—

She leaned into it, trying to listen closer, trying to hear.

The song of the Nox was an echo, murmured by the shadows. It sang to Wren, a special song, just for her. It was hungry. It wanted so much. More than anyone could ever give. More than she had in her. But the Nox was gone, defeated and scattered. Everyone knew that. Only fragments of it remained. And yet it stirred something, something she'd pressed down and hidden away for so long that she—

'*Wren*!' The alarm in Elodie's voice speared through her and Wren jerked back. Her hand was on the window itself, ready to throw it open, reaching for the mass of deeper darkness pressing against it on the other side. Her hair was wild around her face, almost blinding her. And the candle still in her hand was coated in frost.

'Now!' Elodie said, her teeth gritted. Was she holding it back all by herself? She was shielding all of them. But Elodie only had so much strength.

You have no place here, the voice whispered, the one that sang the lullaby, the one that whispered in the night. *Come away with me. Let me in.*

But Wren had heard its lies too many times. Elodie had warned her, time and again, and Elodie was always right. Always. She slammed the door of her mind against it and pushed the darkness back, driving it from the house, from the village, back into the deep woods. It took her breath with it, her heart thundering against her ribs.

Then there was nothing.

CHAPTER 2
WREN

Wren woke up on the floor, the candle still clenched in her hand. What remained of it.

Wax pooled on the ground and the pitiful malformed piece in her fist carried an impression of all the lines of her palm. A soft wail filled the air but Lindie wasn't screaming anymore.

Wren looked up to see Elodie standing over her, with such an expression of disappointment that she felt a cold rush of shame fill her aching body. Black strands of hair spilled around her face, unruly and wild, and far too long.

'The baby?' she asked, her voice harsh against her throat.

Elodie held out a hand to pull her to her feet. 'Safe now. Healthy. A girl.'

Wren brushed herself down and glanced to the bed where Lindie and her mother were fussing over the swaddled child. 'She said she wanted a boy.'

Elodie raised her eyebrows with a certain air of disdain. 'For that idiot husband of hers, no doubt.'

'That's what he said,' Wren replied softly. 'That they wanted a son and they...' She couldn't finish it. Telling Elodie felt like betraying a confidence even now. Even when she didn't owe Pol anything.

Elodie spun back to the bed on one foot.

'Did you go to the darkwood and make a bargain?' she snapped. Lindie looked up, face the colour of parchment, eyes wide and wet. Her mother gave a shocked gasp. 'What were you thinking? A bargain in the darkwood is never without cost and you could have paid with your life, you stupid girl. Besides, what use is a boy?'

'We... we just...' Lindie stammered.

'Just nothing. You won't be able to stay here. It will have marked you now, will have its eye on you. That's what happened here tonight. Had that baby been a boy, nothing would have stopped it coming for you, Lindie. You should move south. Away from here. Away from any area of old magic.'

Lindie's mother gathered the baby in her arms. She bustled around the bed. 'My sister lives in the east, near Farringdale. She'll take them in. Her husband needs help on his farm.'

'But Pol's not a farmer,' Lindie protested indignantly.

'Pol's lucky either of you are still breathing,' Elodie snapped. 'Enough. What were you thinking? We fight the Nox, not welcome it in.'

'But the Nox is gone. It was just a bargain... just the darkwoods.'

'There's no just about it,' said Elodie, and Lindie seemed to curl in on herself in fear as the hedge witch glared at them both and then, pointedly, turned her back on them.

She reached out, smoothing Wren's dark hair back from her face with a gentle hand. Elodie was sunlight and gold, everything about her. No more than twenty years Wren's senior, it sometimes seemed that she was so much older, or perhaps ageless.

Her voice, this time, was no more than a murmur. 'You should rest. That was close.'

'I'm sorry,' Wren began but Elodie just shook her head.

'Not your fault, love. We'll talk later. At home.' Where it was safe to say such things out loud. Her hand still caressed Wren's hair, her pale fingers sliding through the silken locks, taming them with a touch. 'Now, let's pack up and leave this young family to their new life.'

A young family that might never have been, that had begun with a foolish dark bargain. They'd gone into the woods together to get her with child, hadn't they? And asked the shadow kin of the darkwood for a boy, for Pol's pride. Oh he loved Lindie, but he was a selfish bastard through and through. Had the child been the promised boy, had the Nox found its way inside to take it or Lindie...

With her warnings Elodie had explained that there were places where its servants still performed rites to glorify it, every debauchery, every vice, all in its honour. A child imbued with its power would be a prize indeed to those who still served it, and the shadow kin knew that. They made bargains, they tricked the unwary. The fragments of the Nox were always waiting, those shadows with their seductive whispers.

Wren forced a smile onto her face and Elodie's bright blue eyes didn't miss the strain it took to do it.

Elodie wrapped the length of Wren's hair around her hand and gave it a gentle, teasing tug. 'We'll have to deal with this too, won't we?'

Of course they would. It was already getting out of control. Wren nodded grimly.

It didn't take long to pack up their paraphernalia. Elodie spoke to Lindie, blessed the child with rosemary and yarrow, and left a garland of wildflowers above the window for protection. Wren hung back, holding the bags again, averting her eyes. Pol burst into the room as soon as he was given leave and made straight for Lindie, greeting her with wonder and kisses. He didn't so much as glance at anyone else. Not even the child.

For the best, Wren told herself. Definitely for the best.

'Take more care, if you wander in the woods again,' Elodie warned them. Even the weight behind those words didn't sound as terrible coming from her. But Elodie had that way with people. Though the undercurrent of warning rippled along with her voice. 'The darkwood is not for us and any bargains made there are dangerous. Leave soon. Find a new life where it's safe for you both, and your daughter.'

Pol looked up, defiant, and Wren winced. He really was a prize idiot. 'There was no harm in it. Besides, it didn't hold, did it?'

Elodie straightened, and the dimly lit room suddenly grew brighter, the wave of warmth coming from her unmistakable. Lindie pulled back, shielding the child, and her mother's muttered prayers came a little faster.

'There could have been great harm. We live in the light of the Aurum and under its watchful eye by day and by night. But there are places it cannot see, and the traces of the Nox are always ready for the unwary. Old magic is not like anything you could understand. It feeds the shadow kin and they call the remnants of the Nox. They offer all kinds of things, but none of it ends well for the unwary. Stay out of dark places, Pol, or you may not be so lucky next time. Take care of your chosen wife and your light-given daughter. It's time to find a different home, a safer one. Wren, time to go.'

Wren followed Elodie down the stairs, aware all the time of Pol staring after her, his gaze furious.

Did Elodie really have to say that last part? His chosen wife?

The journey home was ripe with awkward silence. It was dark and the moon was only the thinnest sliver in the sky. It could have been worse, if the child had been born a few days later, without so much as the thin thumbnail of light available now.

Elodie strode along the narrow path and Wren followed, lost in her own thoughts. They skirted as widely as possible around the darkwood, that patch of tangled shadows and malevolence that clustered around the old nodes of power in the land here. It was only when they were home, the door of their tower in the forest's depths sealed and warded, the kettle on the fire and everything packed away, that Elodie took down the hairbrush and the scissors and pulled out the chair for Wren.

'Do you have to?' Wren asked. Her hair whispered against her skin, soft and beautiful. Part of her. Alive. Alive with magic.

Elodie pursed her lips. It might have been guilt. Or regret. It might have just been irritation. 'You know I do.'

Wren sat there, as still as a statue while Elodie began to cut, ignoring the tears that slid silently down her pale cheek. It had to be done. That was the rule. Once it got to a certain length, it had to be done. Otherwise... otherwise... it drew attention to her. And no one wanted that.

CHAPTER 3
WREN

The next few days passed uneventfully.

Wren spent the mornings gathering fresh herbs. Her head always felt strange after her hair was cut, especially when she was moving about doing her chores, as if it was too light, somehow. In the afternoons, she worked with Elodie in the kitchen, preparing the herbs to be dried, or steeping them, or any of the other procedures she could do with her eyes closed. Elodie watched every step, pausing once in a while to rub her shorn head affectionately or correct whatever she was doing wrong.

She was always doing something wrong. No matter how small that error might be.

Wren had known for years that she just was not cut out to be a hedge witch like Elodie. She had an innate magical spark, that was completely obvious given... well, everything. But she didn't have the patience, the ability to deal with people or any sort of real acumen for the work. Not the way Elodie did.

She could learn the othertongue, bits of it, but it came haltingly to her lips. Elodie's magic wasn't her magic.

In other places she would have a different teacher, another path to follow. She'd read about the city of Pelias or the far-off

College of Winter in Elodie's books, and heard travellers in the village talk about the Maidens of the Aurum or the rebel witchkind of Garios.

But Wren lived deep in the Forest of Cellandre, in the furthest corner of the kingdom. Half the forest was lost to the darkwood, and ofttimes only the great southern road offered safe passage. The village of Thirbridge was the nearest settlement and, after that, the distant border with Ilanthus was always a danger. Especially to witches.

And Wren didn't know what else to do. This was her whole life. She had never known anything else. Elodie had raised her, cared for her, loved her – in her way – for as long as Wren could remember. Her mother. Although that was never said.

They looked nothing alike. People speculated that she must take after her father. Where Elodie's hair was gold, Wren's was black as night. And while both were pale, Elodie's skin was touched with the sun, even on the greyest day, while Wren's might have been drenched in moonlight. Elodie had eyes like a cloudless summer sky and Wren's were dark, almost black and endless.

Unnerving, Pol had said once. Like they had no colour at all, just darkness.

'Don't crush them, little bird,' Elodie chided. 'Just cut them. What knife are you using?'

The wrong one. Clearly. Wren gazed at the mangled remains of the sweetbriar she'd been preparing. She'd have to throw that out and find some more tomorrow. It was too late in the day to gather it now. The buds would be closed. She scraped them off the board into the waste bin.

'I'm sorry,' she sighed.

'You didn't do anything wrong, you know? That boy is... he's not worthy of you.'

Was that it? Wren started to answer, to say no of course he isn't, but the words stuck in her throat.

Elodie seemed to understand. She was no stranger to regret and lost love herself. Though she never spoke of it, Wren had heard her cry out in the night, screaming in grief and pain, calling for Roland. Whoever he was. Wren hadn't asked in years, not since she was a child. She hadn't dared. Elodie never spoke of it. Just completely ignored any questions about that name, about her past, about Wren's father. About whether it was the same man or someone else.

Elodie sighed. 'Why don't you get some fresh air? Take a walk? I have some things I need from the village if you want to go that far?'

Which might mean checking in on Lindie and the baby, or seeing Pol? A shudder went through Wren's body at the thought.

'You don't have to,' Elodie added. 'It's just supplies from the trading station. But they can wait. There's nothing urgent.' She said it gently enough. Elodie was just trying to give her something to do, something to take her mind off everything. Like Wren was a child who needed to be distracted. She needed to grow up and face her mistakes.

'I'll fetch my cloak,' she murmured and tried to smile reassuringly. She ran her hand through her cropped hair nervously. It always took time to get used to it being this short. It wouldn't last of course. Hair always grew back, Elodie would say, as if that was a comfort. It really wasn't. 'Do you have a list?'

Of course she did. Elodie was always prepared. She made lists constantly. As she had said, there was nothing urgent on it, but it did give Wren something to do. And sometimes she just needed to walk through the forest, in its green-gold light. She was one of the few people who could do so without fear of harm. The forest looked after her, that was what Elodie always said.

Ever since she was a child, the song of the forest had been her lullaby. She had dreamed she had friends there, children like herself who danced with her. Sometimes she thought she still heard echoes of their laughter in the birdsong, their whispers among the leaves.

She'd be home long before it was full dark anyway. She always was. Her days were as predictable as the tides. And they always would be. One day, when Elodie was old and tired, Wren would take her place as hedge witch. She'd find an apprentice of her own, if anybody wanted to learn the little she had to offer, and Elodie would doze by the fire until...

'He would never have been good enough for you, little bird,' Elodie said as Wren opened the door, peeling back the wards so she could pass through with ease. 'You know that, don't you? But somewhere out there, there's someone.'

How would she ever find anyone living here in the middle of nowhere, in the darkest forest, on the edge of the kingdom? Wren froze, her shoulders tightening under the green of her cloak. Someone? Maybe in her dreams. Part of her wanted to say something cutting and vicious, to tell Elodie not to make promises she couldn't keep. She hadn't had her happily ever after, had she? Whoever Roland was, he had been gone for all of Wren's twenty years and Elodie had been entirely alone.

Men had tried. Rangers, villagers, passing soldiers... Elodie was having none of it. Sometimes forcefully. More than one had limped away from her, cursing her name. More than one had vanished in the forest.

Between the darkwood's magic, and Elodie's, they didn't stand a chance.

CHAPTER 4

WREN

The village wasn't far, if you knew the right path to take. Of course, if you didn't you might never be seen again. But Wren had grown up here. The darkwood had been her playground as soon as she could walk and it had never turned on her. Not once.

Which should have been a warning in and of itself.

It sang to her, called to her. But she remembered what Elodie had always said and tried to only ever reach for the light. She just wished it wasn't so hard.

The village was quiet when she arrived. There was nothing sleepier than Thirbridge on a late summer afternoon. Devin Carter gathered the supplies on the list quickly, his careful chatter running past her. Elodie kept a monthly account at the village trading station, which made everything easy. Half the time she never paid anyway. Those she helped or those who owed her would often just deal with payment for her. Hedge witches were like that. They served the community beside which they lived. And that community looked after them.

If they know what's good for them, Elodie would sometimes

mutter darkly. Wren was never entirely sure if she was joking. But they were not part of the village. They were always separate, always apart. If she hadn't known before, Pol had made that completely clear.

It was as if by thinking of him, no matter how briefly, she summoned him.

He lurched out of the door of the tavern as she passed, almost colliding with a taller, slender man, deep in discussion with the stableman about his horse.

'Wren?' Pol shouted, her name slurred by ale. He'd started early then. 'I want to talk to you.' She bent her head and hurried forward, holding back from running. Without Elodie here, with that much alcohol in him... The wind rose around her and the trees on the edge of the forest moved, beckoning her forward. If she could just get there before—

'Wren! Stop, curse you. You did this, didn't you? You did it on purpose. You cursed the child inside her. Admit it!'

The words brought her up short and she turned. Something was wrong with the baby? What did he mean? Pol bore down on her, tankard still clenched in his fist.

'What?'

'A girl,' he snarled, spittle flying from his mouth. 'What am I going to do with a girl? And now they're talking about sending us to Farringdale. What am I going to do all the way out there? Do I look like a farmer? Lindie's already packing. All set for it, she is.'

Wren sucked in a breath. She had to get away from him. Now. As far away as she could until someone could make him see sense. Lindie's family maybe, or his father. Someone. Elodie would have to talk to them.

People did what Elodie said. They always had done. Anything else was unthinkable. If Elodie said they ought to go to the rich and fertile farmlands around Farringdale then that was what they would do. They'd be much safer there in the east than back here, where the darkwood could tempt him again.

And when a witch, even a hedge witch, told you to go somewhere, you went. Whether you wanted to or not.

And Elodie was indeed a witch. So was Wren, for that matter, though she might wish she could forget it.

We are witchkind. We will live free or die. That was what Elodie always said. Wren tried to think of it as a mark of dignity.

The wind blew harder, pushing him away from her abruptly. Pol cursed and he tried to keep walking, but the dust blew up into his face, leaving him spluttering in rage. Wren pressed onwards, as fast as she dared, making for the edge of the village. The tankard hurtled past her head, missing her by only a fraction and clattering on the ground.

And then he was on her.

Grabbing her by the scruff of the neck, he hefted her off her feet and shook her like a dog with a rat. She opened her mouth to cry out and felt the shadows rise between the trees, along the edge of the buildings. Just early evening shadows, pale things, but that didn't mean they were useless.

She'd promised she wouldn't use them. She'd sworn it to Elodie. She would reach for the light. That was what she had said all her life. She would *always* reach for the light. But there wasn't enough here and the darkness answered more readily.

That's the problem, Elodie had told her. It always does.

Pol's hand closed on her throat and he snarled. Darkness flared in his eyes, and she thought, just for the second before he tightened his grip, she saw something else in him. Something shadowlike, flitting like smoke behind his eyes, lurking inside him. They'd gone into the darkwood. Maybe he hadn't come back alone...

He was going to kill her. This drunken, miserable, bully was going to—

Abruptly, Pol was jerked back from her. Wren dropped to the ground, down on her knees, gasping for breath, while a man like a shadow himself towered over them both. He grabbed Pol by one shoulder and punched him hard, just once, but with the full force of his body behind the blow.

Pol crumpled, but his cronies were already emerging from the tavern now, followed by others who wanted to see what the fuss was about. Others who wouldn't take kindly to a stranger flooring one of their own...

'Are you all right?' the man asked, the one who had been talking to the stableman. He bent over her and she had a sense of a delicately handsome face, dark-skinned from the sun, concern making his blue eyes seem even brighter. He clearly wasn't short of coin judging by the travelling clothes, and the cost of stabling a horse behind the tavern.

He reached out his hand to help her up and she was about to let him, when she saw three of the men from the tavern behind him.

'Look out!' she shouted.

He moved as if on instinct, even as she warned him, like he was made of water or wind, twisting aside and ducking to avoid attack, almost like a dancer. Wren watched in amazement as he effortlessly dodged the clumsy blows. Pol's friend Dale went down in a heap over her rescuer's feet and he whipped up his cloak to tangle around Owin's head, bringing him down too.

'Gentlemen,' he said, barely out of breath. 'There's no need for this. Why not go back to your drinks and leave the bullying to someone else.'

They scrambled to their feet again, but didn't look quite so sure of themselves now. Pol snarled at both Wren and the stranger but backed off, muttering darkly, 'You'd want to keep going, good sir,' he called back. 'No sense in getting into fights over a witch's bastard.'

Wren made her decision. She had to take the opening as it

offered itself even if it meant deserting the stranger. There wasn't going to be another chance, not when Pol had got half the village riled up against her. She'd have to warn Elodie. She grabbed the bag of provisions she'd dropped and sprinted for the forest as fast as she could. The shouts behind her told her they'd noticed and they'd changed their mind about retreating now she'd left the stranger's protection. They were coming after her.

Cursing, she plunged through the treeline, struggling through the dense undergrowth and praying they wouldn't follow. Knowing they would.

They were that stupid, and drunk enough for the sense they'd been born with to have taken a leave of absence. Or maybe the dark spirit she had glimpsed was not just in Pol now.

Which meant she had only one choice. She had to make for the darkwood and hope for the best.

The forest closed around her. Deep, verdant greens and all the colours of the natural world, all the things that soothed her senses. Her heart still thundering, her breath coming only in gasps, she slowed her pace. If she kept running blind she'd fall afoul of the forest in no time. She knew this path, knew her way.

Those pursuing her did not. They might think they did. They'd be wrong.

She'd get home, tell Elodie what had happened and she'd sort it out. The village headwoman would take Pol in hand, she knew that, if Elodie demanded it. And if they didn't, Wren couldn't ever set foot in the village again, which Elodie would not take well.

If they cross me, they'll know about it, Elodie had said on more than one occasion. Wren could only hope that was the case now, that Elodie was right.

Tears welled up in her eyes, making the forest around her blur and twist as she made her way around the valley's edge and turned towards home. It wasn't fair. She'd loved Pol. She'd thought he loved her. She had made the mistake of trusting him with the truth about her magic, about the things she learned from Elodie and the wonders she could perform.

And he had been horrified. Truly horrified. He'd rejected her, and told them all she was a monster. No one in Thirbridge had ever looked at her the same way again.

Heartbroken, she'd admitted it all to Elodie who had listened, sympathetically enough, and then offered, in all seriousness, to curse him. *His dick will never stir again*, she promised.

Why hadn't she taken the hedge witch up on that offer right then and there? It might have saved everyone a lot of trouble. Especially Lindie.

Wren sniffed loudly, and trudged down a rabbit run of a path into the valley below, the trees pressing close around her. The shadows here were deeper, darker, and somehow that was a comfort.

It shouldn't be. She knew that. The forest here had always been a safe place for her. Not for anyone else. But the darkness in this area was different, the darkness of a womb perhaps, a place of shelter from the storm, the one place where, as a child, she could always hide.

She was still hiding.

Behind her, she heard horse hooves, and she froze. Someone was still following her. The villagers wouldn't, not this deeply, but the stranger...

Regret made her stomach clench. It wasn't safe in here, not for the unwary. Skill at fighting wouldn't help. This magic was old and strong. It was hungry. She turned back, ready to step out and warn him.

But the dark horse had no rider. It stopped when it saw her, snorting warily, pawing at the ground. The reins hung down, abandoned. Bags were slung from the saddle, and various weapons, all signs of a traveller rather than a local. Not that anyone local had a horse like that. Huge, black, with a long rippling mane and tail, a thoroughbred warhorse.

It had to belong to the man who had saved her. The way he'd moved, the way he'd avoided the village men and made them look like clumsy dolts, he had to be a trained warrior. A knight perhaps.

He'd come after her, right into the darkwood.

ON DARKWOODS

BY PILAGIA OF SIDON

The Nox is gone, broken and banished years ago. The queen of Asteroth sacrificed herself to destroy that power, to break the earthly incarnation it had formed. She had defeated the powers of darkness, saving the Aurum, consigning the Nox to the dark beyond.

But parts of the dark power of the Nox remain, lingering in the darkness, in the shadows, calling to those who might still serve.

The fragments travel along the lines of old magic in the earth, clustering, pooling, growing in strength and creating shadow kin. Places like old stones and darkwoods.

If you would seek power, seek it there.

But be prepared to pay a price.

CHAPTER 5

FINN

The inn was rowdy for so early in the afternoon. Some kind of farewell. Though the man at the centre of the crowd clearly didn't relish the idea of starting a new life somewhere far away. Finn couldn't divine why.

So instead he had decided to keep to himself. He'd had a drink, eaten some bread and the local cheese, which wasn't bad at all, and then made his way outside. He had only intended to stop in the wretched little village to rest his horse. The road from Sidonia, Ilanthus's capital, was long and hard, especially this road, off the beaten track and through the forest. He'd hoped that if anyone was following him – which no doubt they were – they'd never expect him to go this way. No one came to Thirbridge and he could see why now. He was more concerned with reaching the stables and getting Dancer back, with making ready for the road to Knightsford, when all hell had broken loose.

The scrawny pale boy with huge eyes had looked absolutely terrified at the sight of the thug bearing down on him. And of Finn himself, to be honest, even when he'd beaten off the attackers. He had rabbited for the woods as soon as the opportunity presented itself.

Finn should have left it there. He should have just walked away. Anyone else would have.

Well, no. The Grandmaster wouldn't have. Paladins saw it as a duty to protect the innocent. The Knights of the Aurum did not walk away from someone in need. And so neither could he. That was the thing about vows, even the lowliest of them. You couldn't pick and choose when to uphold them.

The village men gave chase, full of drink and fury, turning on the easy target once Finn disengaged. He ran to the stable and mounted, reeling Dancer around, then plunged after them, ignoring the warnings shouted by those behind him.

He knew the forest around here had a dark reputation. But a forest was just a forest. There were worse things behind him, far worse could be following. He didn't warn the villagers of that. No need to cause more fear and panic here. They lived near the border with Ilanthus. They knew the risks. War was not so long ago as all that. Raiding parties still happened. Maybe not here from the looks of it, not for a long time, but they had to know. The road still ran north and south, even if it was a minor road. He'd been so careful, he had thought, picking this route so as not to draw attention to himself. As far as they were concerned, he was just a traveller passing through. And now he had already drawn far too much attention to himself. The Grandmaster would be furious.

But Finnian Ward had always caused trouble wherever he went. It was in his blood, his brothers-in-arms said. He couldn't help that. He was a lodestone for strife.

Dancer whinnied a warning as they entered the forest and it crowded around them. He slowed his pace, lest the horse take injury on the uneven path, and followed the sound of the men. No sign of the boy now. He couldn't have vanished more effectively if he'd been shadow kin. Finn hoped that boded well for him evading his pursuers, but somehow he doubted it. Presumably they knew the forest as well.

There was something about the woods here that made his skin crawl. The deeper they went the quieter it seemed, which was never good. It should be alive with birdsong, with animal life, but here... the shadows pressed closer than they should.

The sound of the men fell away as well. Perhaps they'd become bored and returned to the tavern. That was the best-case scenario. But the other possibility, that they had already found the boy and done him harm... well, that wouldn't do. Not when Finn had extended protection. True, they wouldn't know who he was or what his protection might mean but that didn't matter. In the blink of an eye it had become a matter of honour.

They reached the edge of a valley, where a stream cut through the forest and into the earth itself. Making their way down the slope, Dancer whickered softly, and hesitated to cross, but Finn urged him on.

The horse was normally fearless. This was not a good sign.

As he made to climb the other side of the valley, Dancer dug his hooves in entirely.

'What is it?' Finn asked, trying to urge him onwards, but to no avail.

That was when he heard it.

Music drifted from the depths of the valley, upstream, where the darkness of the forest was even deeper.

He couldn't see anything through the tight-pressed trees and undergrowth. The sunlight was barely penetrating the canopy here and came through green and gold, as if falling through stained glass.

Where on earth was he?

And that tune. That music. He knew it. Not that he could name it but there was something... something so familiar...

He dismounted and left the stallion where he was, intent only on following the music and investigating. Just for a moment. Just to see who would be here in the deepest part of the forest playing... a harp? Or maybe a lute...

It sounded like something from his earliest memories, something from the shadows of his childhood. Before they turned to nightmares.

Whitethorn rose in front of him, in full bloom, its sharp thorns like a barrier. But when he reached out his hands, the branches seemed to fold back. Beyond that he saw elder trees and they pressed close, their long branches sweeping against him. Willow trailed through his hair, tugging it loose from where he had tied it, tangling in it.

Come deeper, the voice sang. A voice unlike anything he'd ever heard. *Come deeper, beloved. We've been waiting such a long time for you.*

He followed the sound, the music, the voice. It sang to him, stealing his thoughts even as they tried to form.

This was wrong. He knew this couldn't be real. But the moment the thought came, it seemed to melt away, smothered in the strange music and the shadows that thronged underneath, tangling around his feet and legs, winding up around his body.

He fell back into the embrace of the darkness, and felt the caresses engulf him. There was only pleasure, only the music and the song, and that bewitching voice.

He was back in Sidonia, in the labyrinthine palace complex, his mother singing to him. He was safe. He'd never heard of Asteroth or the war the royal family had unleashed. There was no black blade at his throat, no laughter from his brothers, no feeling of ice creeping into his skin as he was laid out in the chamber of sacrifice and—

And the enemy had yet to arrive at their gates.

He struggled to free himself. This wasn't right. This was an enchantment. It had to be.

A soft laugh caused a ripple over his body, stilling him, stealing his wits again.

Are you trying to fight? Poor boy, why do that? It's over anyway. This is the end. Give up now. The Nox is coming. She's the one you've been waiting for, dreaming of. Give yourself to her. It's inevitable. No one can escape their fate.

Who? Who did it mean?

There she was, the dark goddess to whom he had been promised. Waiting for him. Meant for him. Just as he was meant for her. Helpless before her. Her creature, her chosen, made to live for her, and to die for her. He had no other choice.

She bent over him, her long midnight hair like a veil around her moonlight skin. Her eyes, so dark and endless, holes into the otherworld, into the darkness of Nox itself. His goddess smiled, smiled at him, and he found his mouth mirroring the expression. Because he knew her as well. She had haunted his dreams and his nightmares, always there, always waiting.

He'd thought he had cheated fate. But here she was.

In the darkest part of the darkest forest.

His body responded, even while his mind continued its futile struggle. He might as well embrace the inevitable.

His Lady carried with her the scent of night flowering jasmine. It wrapped itself around him and drugged his senses. Some distant part of him said this was wrong, that this was not real, some part that could feel the insidious touch of darkness winding its way around his helpless body, dragging him through the forest, through the undergrowth, locking him tighter and tighter in an enchantment even as it pulled him into its stronghold.

But the rest of him didn't care. How could he care? This was meant to be. This had always been meant to be.

Don't be afraid, the Nox incarnate whispered. But he wasn't.

There was no fear left in him now. Whatever his father had done to him, whatever his brothers had planned, whatever the threats and the sense of dread when he had first set foot in Asteroth a hostage and a prisoner from a lost war not of his making—

It was all past. It was all gone. There was only her. His dark queen. A goddess of shadows thought long lost. And he was hers.

Just as it was always meant to be.

CHAPTER 6

FINN

The shadows lifted him, carried him, stretched him out. They winnowed their way through his clothes to the skin beneath. Finn gasped at the touch, cold and insistent, determined, and so frighteningly gentle.

The touch of the Nox. She was the Nox embodied in flesh, and she had come for him at last. Claimed him as she always meant to. He was hers through and through, her creature, her fated sacrifice. Hers...

She bound him with tangled vines made of shadow and stretched him out before her. And soon there would be a blade and blood and it was all he wanted.

Pleasure built up inside him, unbearable, ungovernable. It surged with his blood, the blood that rushed along his veins and sang out for her blade as well as her kiss. She was everything.

He'd been a fool to think swearing himself to her enemy, to the Aurum, would make a difference. He'd never belonged in Asteroth. Every vow had been a lie, every promise, every hope. Just as every guarantee Grandmaster de Silvius had made to him – every time he'd assured a terrified boy of his safety and promised to make him strong, to make him a holy warrior of the light who would drive away any lingering shadows – had been nothing but falsehoods. Just lies crafted from the vain and foolish hopes of a child.

Finn knew himself, knew what he was. Here now, spread out, helpless before her, bound with shadows and held in darkness, awaiting the end and the wild pleasure of her touch as she slowly destroyed him. Shadow kin clustered around him, waiting, laughing, hungry.

And then, all at once, they fell quiet with a terrible expectancy.

The forest stirred, peeling back like curtains, allowing another form through. A black horse followed in her wake, docile and calm.

Her creature. Just as he was her creature.

And for a moment, he thought he recognised the horse. Her new form was strangely familiar too. She wasn't so fearsome now, smaller, less... less all-powerful. Just a girl, his mind seemed to murmur in relief. She was just a girl.

And yet, she wasn't. Power surged through her, dark and terrible, drawn from the land itself and tempered in the dark fires of the Nox.

He knew her. He worshipped her. He had been a fool to think he would ever escape.

'Let him go,' she said, her voice strangely loud in his ears. This wasn't the voice of a seductress, a dark goddess intent on making him her slave. This sounded... different... human...

He shuddered, trying to fix the world back on its axis, trying to grab hold of reality again before it was too late. She was no dark goddess incarnate, no shadow kin queen. She was human. He was sure of it. But even as he fumbled after understanding, it slipped through his fingers like smoke.

Around him the darkwood shivered, reluctant to obey the girl, distressed to be so commanded. Its grip on him tightened and pain sparked through him, amplifying his pleasure, making him gasp out loud, and lose that thread of sanity he had been grasping after. His struggles subsided again.

This was where he was meant to be. This was who he was supposed to obey. Why had he ever thought of fighting?

'I mean it,' the girl said, irritably, as if speaking to a misbehaving hound. Her dark hair seemed to move around her pale face as if she was underwater, like a living thing. She said something else, something in a musical language he didn't know, but which sounded strangely familiar.

Like the song he'd heard. In his dreams, in his nightmares. Her song, which had haunted him all his life.

The tendrils of shadow released him and he fell before her.

On his knees. That was right too, wasn't it? Where he should be? Yes, this was where he should be.

But she knelt as well, her dark eyes keen and focused, and her voice was no longer soft and seductive. She sounded worried. That couldn't be right. What did she have to be worried about here, in her place of power?

'Can you hear me? I'm going to get you out of here but you're going to have to help, understand? Can you get up?'

Her hand touched his face, flat against his forehead as if she was testing his temperature, but as he moved it slid down his cheek. He turned his face to it, pressed his lips to her palm. She started back, her eyes going even wider in sudden alarm. But she didn't pull away. She seemed frozen there, staring at him.

But this was what she wanted, wasn't it? Finn knew it in his heart of hearts, this was what she wanted from him. His submission. His obedience. And his life.

That had always been his fate.

He had to make her understand that he was hers, that he understood where he was and what was expected. He would do anything for her. Anything.

He would gladly die for her.

Slowly, Finn leaned towards her, seeking her out like a

plant reaching for sunlight. She didn't pull away, as if she too felt the magic surrounding them both. The kiss was everything. Desperate to please her, he brushed his lips against hers. Her mouth was warm and welcoming and Finn felt himself falling into her. She tasted like spring and summer, like every dream of desire he'd ever had. Deepening the kiss, he slid his arms around her, tracing his fingertips against her pale skin, through her midnight hair. It seemed to cling to him, as if every dark strand of it wanted to draw him closer and keep him there.

'Stop,' she whispered, breathless with desire, her body flush with his. 'We have to stop. This isn't real.'

Not real? No, it was everything. There was nothing more real than this kiss, than her, than the raging need inside him.

He felt her body answering him, her desire making her heart pound against his chest, her heated skin shiver beneath his fingers. And he wasn't alone. She was exploring him as well. He could feel her tremble on the edge of surrender. Her eyes closed as he cradled the back of her head, let his thumb stroke the sensitive line of her jaw. She arched against him with a moan, her body pressed against him now. His erection strained between them, pressed against her so there could be no doubt of his need for her.

Abruptly, she grabbed his shoulder, her fingers digging in almost to the bone, and she forced him back from her. Surprise made him freeze and she dragged one arm free.

Then she slapped him, hard. The sound of her hand on his cheek echoed through the trees. 'You have got to wake up.'

CHAPTER 7

WREN

The kiss robbed Wren of her senses.

That was the problem. And it was due to the darkness, the power of the Nox and the depths of the darkwood, the wildness that raced through her veins. She knew that need, that hunger, but never had it overwhelmed her with such ease.

Because with him, touching him, it was so much stronger, so much more than anything she had ever encountered.

She'd tried to drive the darkwood back with a few words of the othertongue and somehow that had just made everything worse, like she had stirred it up and it was determined to teach her a lesson for her temerity.

But that hadn't been the worst of it. He'd kissed her and she was lost in his arms. Helpless. Like a lovesick fool in an instant.

Pol had kissed her, but that had been an awful fumbling thing, all tongue and teeth and hot breath, all about him and his needs. But this...

Too much. That's what it was. Far too much.

She shoved the stranger back as best she could and then, when he surged towards her again, blind with desire, she hit him as hard as she could.

The sound of the slap was like a branch breaking underfoot. It seemed to set her free.

'You have got to wake up!'

The world around them went silent. Terribly, horribly silent and she felt the whole forest move.

Not the forest, but the darkness within this patch of darkwood. The thing that had always lurked there, waiting for her to give in.

Elodie had been right, all her warnings, all her dire predictions. *Don't spend too long in the depths of the darkwood, little bird. Don't lose yourself in there, don't give in to your passions, don't let it lead you astray.*

Always the warnings. Never an indication of what she should do if it all went wrong. Like this. No hints on how to get out of it.

The traveller from the village looked dazed, like he'd been struck on the head with a large rock, rather than slapped by a woman half his size.

The pupils of his eyes had gone wide, eating away the blue to a narrow rim and his mouth – that beautiful sensual mouth that had done such things so as to drive her to distraction – hung open. He tried to focus on her, frowning, and ran a shaking hand through his long chestnut hair. Then he reached out once more, as if drawn by an unseen force.

His fingers brushed against her face again, the sensation intoxicating. She felt herself bending towards him again, like a cat seeking his caress. He buried his hand in the depths of her hair...

Her hair! She could feel it against her neck. Not too long. Not yet. What had she done? How much magic had been flowing through the air around the two of them? She pushed him back again, hurriedly, and felt for her knife.

His eyes fixed on it as she drew it and survival instincts

finally kicked in. She hadn't meant to threaten him with it but... well, if it worked, that was good, wasn't it?

So why did she feel bereft?

'What—what have I done?' he murmured, blinking at her, dazed. He looked heartbroken, as if he had failed her somehow and that was the worst thing he could imagine. Wren got to her feet and he struggled to follow her.

There wasn't time for this. Wasn't time for anything. They were too deep in the darkwood and it was far too strong. It had already gathered strength from him. She could feel the fragments of the Nox drawing together, the sense of it like razors against her skin as it reinforced itself. The shadow kin would follow, and soon.

Grabbing the horse's reins in one hand and his arm in the other, she dragged them both to their feet and pitched forward, through the trees.

Briars snagged at their feet, brambles pulling at their clothes, but Wren didn't pause. She couldn't. They had to keep moving as quickly as possible. It was only when they fell into the clearing by the path back to Thirbridge that she let herself breathe again.

It was quiet here. They were clear of the darkwood. It was safe. Or as safe as it could be.

The remnants of the Nox that lingered in the darkwood pulled back. But they were still there, still watching, their hunger unabated.

She let go of the man as quickly as possible. Touching him, feeling his warmth and his strength, was a really bad idea. There was something about him, something like an addiction just waiting for her to fall prey to.

'Where are we?' he asked, his voice a little surer now. A good sign.

That had been close. For both of them.

'We're clear,' she said, bending forward to catch her breath. Her head was swimming.

'You're the boy from the village.'

The boy? He thought she was a boy? The short hair, she realised, and her clothes... Yes, that was probably better.

If he didn't realise what had happened, if he thought it was all part of a magical snare, all a dream or a nightmare, he'd be more likely to go. She needed him to get out of the forest and then she could head home in safety. Elodie would never forgive her if she turned up trailing a lovelorn stranger behind her.

'You saved me, I saved you. Fair exchange,' she replied, making her voice as gruff as possible. With her short hair and her practical clothes, she could pass for a boy. She had to.

If anything he turned even more pale. Some people, Elodie said, had a problem with two men. Perhaps he was one of them.

'I'm sorry. I saw... There was a woman. I thought... Was it a dream?'

More like a nightmare from the look of it, she thought. But he didn't recognise her now. Perhaps he didn't remember the details. If they were lucky.

'A hallucination,' she told him quickly. 'The darkwood can do that to the unwary.'

'Did I—' His hand touched his mouth, and then his cheek where she'd hit him and his face flushed. No, he remembered. In the way one remembered dreams perhaps, but he knew something had happened. A flicker of horror gave way to regret and contrition. 'I have offended you. I apologise. I was... I was not myself.'

Wren almost laughed, despite the urgency of their situation. The understatement of the century. In any other circumstances she might have, but it didn't seem so funny right at the moment. He gave a curt bow. 'I'm in your debt. My name is Finnian Ward... Finn. If you should ever need—'

Finnian Ward... she almost smiled. It was a good name, she decided. Finn.

What was she thinking? She didn't need his name, good or not. She was never going to see him again anyway.

'It doesn't matter. The forest is dangerous, filled with enchantments. You should go back to Thirbridge. It's that way.' She pointed down the road winding through the trees. 'Stay on the path this time.'

'You didn't use the path.'

No, she hadn't. But she at least was safe in this forest. He was not.

She'd been too intent on getting away from Pol and his loutish friends. She'd have to tell Elodie about that even if she kept her encounter with Finn to herself. And she didn't fancy that conversation either. Elodie had threatened to leave the area before this and there was every chance this would be the deciding factor. Pol and Lindie were meant to be leaving but the others had been involved and they wouldn't be so forgiving, would they? And there was every chance Pol would refuse to leave. Because he had always been an idiot.

Perhaps it was time for Elodie and Wren to move on. They had been here twenty years, but now it was feeling less safe by the hour. A hedge witch could find work anywhere, she'd say, so long as she stays out of the notice of the knights and witch-hunters. Which wasn't entirely true. Some places, sure, the more remote the better. In the cities, they tended to lock witches up, or coerce them into service.

Or enslave them.

Or murder them.

The forest was safe. The forest was home.

'I know this place. I live here.'

'Alone?'

Wren frowned. Suddenly he was asking a lot of questions.

Perhaps it was better when he was all addle-minded. At least then he seemed docile.

'With my... my mother.' Best not to get into the details of all that. The less he knew the better. 'Finn, listen to me, you really should be getting back to the village, or heading on your way south if that's what you'd prefer.' The village might not be too happy to see him right now either, and if he was in his right mind he'd realise that too. 'Knightsford lies the other way, but it's a couple of days' travelling. It's the nearest town, and there's a garrison there. The royal road runs south from there.'

'Knightsford,' he nodded, as if only just remembering something. 'That's where I was going before—those men in the village—'

Why wouldn't he just leave? 'They're just bullies with too much booze in them.'

'Yes of course, but they mentioned a name.' He paused, examining her more closely now. Could he see her hair edging towards her collar? Had he realised she wasn't actually a boy? 'Your name?'

She hadn't given him her name. How could she? He thought she was a boy but, if she confirmed her name, he'd know differently.

She was about to reply – although what she was going to say, she didn't know – when he held up his hand for silence. Before she knew what he was doing he dropped to the ground, his hand pressing to the earth, as if feeling for something. When he looked up again, his bewilderment had melted away. Instead, his eyes were cold steel and his mouth a hard line.

'We have to hide. Now. Someone's coming.'

CHAPTER 8

WREN

Wren cursed to herself. She thought she'd given Pol the slip.

'They won't come this far in. Not even on the road. They're scared of—'

'Not them.' Finn mounted fluidly, turning the horse around in a circle, and held out his hand to her. 'There are mounted soldiers coming. Lots of them. We don't want to be out in the open. You know this place. Come on.'

Something in his urgency infected her, and suddenly their positions were reversed. He knew what he was talking about and she did not. Wren could hear it now, distantly, the sound of horses' hooves, a great many of them, and with it the pounding of metal, armour, weapons. An armed force, travelling south at speed. That couldn't be good.

Soldiers never came through here. Thirbridge wasn't worth their while.

She grabbed his hand and swung up behind him, clinging to his broad back to hold on. Beneath them, the horse moved restlessly. It could sense danger too.

Elodie would understand, wouldn't she? The tower was the safest place Wren knew.

Wren also knew she would never hear the end of it if she turned up with this stranger in tow, with his weapons and his warhorse. He wore travelling clothes, but he was made of muscle, and she'd seen the weapons he carried, secured about the horse and on his person. The way he moved, the way he fought... he had to be a knight of some kind. Or at least trained by them.

Elodie had always had choice words to say about knights. Along with quite a long list of others.

But right now... right now there was an armoured host bearing down on them and he was all Wren had. Even if they'd been following him.

There had to be somewhere else, another option. Taking a breath to push back her first panicked instinct she looked around, and saw it.

'Back there, into the trees,' she said. 'There's an incline and a ridge. You can see the road ahead from there but stay concealed. It should be safe enough. They won't be able to see us up there.'

At least she hoped not.

He urged the black horse forward, slowing only when they entered the edge of the forest again, just enough so the horse could find his footing safely.

It was a good hiding place, one of her favourites. One where you could see without being seen. She used to watch the roads from up there, whenever she could sneak away from the tower. She'd imagine where the various travellers were going; Sidonia, perhaps, with its dark towers, or Pelias, perched on the edge of the great sea. But it didn't matter. Not now. They needed to hide and this was the best place. The only place available to them.

If these soldiers were coming from the north, they came from Ilanthus. And that was never good news.

She needed to warn Elodie. But going now would risk bringing the danger directly to their tower.

Indecision made her cling to Finn's back even more tightly, as the horse headed up the slope. As they reached the summit, Finn dismounted, leaving her perched up there. She let herself down carefully, aware of the horse's every movement, and went to his side, where he leaned over the top of the ridge, examining the road.

Smoke rose from the north road, beyond the trees, and Wren felt something catch in her throat, something hard and uncomfortable. There was only one thing in that direction. Thirbridge.

It had to be. There was nothing else for miles around except forest. The village was burning.

Had they put them all to sword?

'Look in Dancer's saddlebags,' Finn said. 'There's a—' His voice fell still when he glanced at her frozen expression. 'Never mind. I've got it.' He rummaged in the bags and then came back with a small case, and a flask. 'Drink some of that. It'll help.'

Wren watched as he opened the case and took out some kind of metal tube. Gone was the soft, bewildered man, dazed by enchantments. His eyes were sharp, every movement succinct and determined. He twisted the tube deftly and it expanded into an elegant telescope, smaller but not so different from the one Elodie kept mounted on a stand in one of the upper rooms of the tower. He lifted it to his eye and peered out over the forest. Capable, she thought, practised. She... she had to stop thinking about him. Wren brought the flask to her mouth and took a large mouthful.

It wasn't water. It burned down her throat. She could feel its heat in her chest and she coughed, spluttering as she pulled the flask back from her mouth.

Finn raised one eyebrow, even though he never looked away from the telescope and whatever it showed him.

'Never had spirits before? Maybe take it a bit easier. It's strong stuff. Comes all the way from Sidonia itself.'

'I suppose you go there all the time. Did they follow you here?'

He shrugged his shoulders, which wasn't an answer. 'They weren't meant to. They also come looking for witches. You wouldn't know anything about that, would you?'

Her stomach roiled. She could blame the alcohol, but she knew she'd be lying. 'No.'

'In the village, they called you the witch's bastard.'

'Well they say a lot...' She caught her own words. They weren't going to be saying a lot of anything in Thirbridge anymore... '*Said*... by the light...' Fighting the urge to throw up, she turned away from him. 'She's just a healer. That's all. Not a witch.' Except Elodie called herself a hedge witch all the time. And the things they did... it wasn't all herbs and tinctures, was it?

Elodie's skill with othertongue was different though. Special. And far beyond the remit of mere hedge witches. Light danced to Elodie's whim. It always had done. And for Wren, the shadows did the same. Sometimes. When she could keep hold of them.

And if a horde of soldiers and witchhunters from Ilanthus poured into Thirbridge, with fire and sword, the villagers were going to do and say whatever was necessary to make them go away. Even if it meant turning Elodie over. If they were given any time to speak at all.

Holy light, the baby and Lindie, her mother, Devin Carter...

Everyone Wren knew...

'There are far too many of them to be after just one witch,' Finn muttered.

Wren shoved his shoulder and, when he looked at her, she snatched the telescope from his hand. He seemed to find that amusing, though he didn't laugh. It wasn't a time for laughter. 'By all means, be my guest.'

Below them, a group of Ilanthian soldiers appeared through the trees, coming down the Knightsford road. They stopped where she and Finn had stopped, milling around. A man on a grey stallion removed his helmet, revealing white-blond hair. Wren focused on him, bringing him into view. Handsome. As handsome as the man beside her, but older, and harder, with an air of privilege that couldn't be ignored. He studied the trees, and then turned almost as if he was looking right at her. Grey eyes, like steel.

'Leander,' Finn growled. 'The crown prince himself. This is not good. We need to move. He'll find our tracks and—'

What was he doing on first-name terms with the Ilanthian crown prince?

'No, they're leaving,' Wren told him, as Prince Leander gave an elegant hand gesture to his troops and they thundered on down the road ahead.

'Don't bet on it. He doesn't give up that easily.'

'How do you know?'

But Finn didn't answer. He moved back towards his own horse, keeping low to avoid detection from below just in case.

'I need to get word to Knightsford. He won't dare go that far, I suspect, but they need to be informed. I don't know what he thinks he's after right now, but he's caught the scent of something. There should be a royal garrison at Knightsford at the ready to move north and intercept them at the first sign of an incursion. Or at the very least we can send a message further south.'

'But Thirbridge,' she said. 'We can't just... we have to help them.'

He shook his head. 'We can't. Leander doesn't travel with so small a force. The rest of them are back there, burning everything in sight, killing everyone they find, covering their tracks.

Or his tracks, anyway. Thirbridge is already gone. He's hunting. He won't stop.' The bitterness in his voice made Wren pause and she looked up at him in alarm.

'What's he hunting?'

A strange kind of wind rippled through the trees around them, making the leaves whisper and shake. Wren thought for a moment she heard Elodie's voice. It was like a warning, a cry of alarm. She couldn't make it out but she sounded... afraid? That wasn't possible. Nothing scared Elodie. But as soon as Wren thought she heard it, it was gone. She was about to ask Finn if he'd heard it too but he didn't so much as glance at her.

Finn kept his gaze locked on the retreating figure, even though he didn't have the telescope to see any details. Perhaps he didn't need it.

'Witches,' he said in a voice thick with loathing. 'Me. His two favourite quarries. Take your pick.'

'SONG OF THE WITCHKIND OF GARIOS'

Witchkind are older than time, and stranger than dreams. They wander and are free.

Those who would chain them should take heed. Though beaten and subdued, they will rise. Though chained, shackles will be broken. Though driven to exile, they will return. They will rise again and again until they can rise no more.

Witchkind wear nothing they do not choose to wear, bear nothing they do not choose to bear, submit to the will of no one they do not love.

We are Witchkind. We will live free or die.

CHAPTER 9

ELODIE

With Wren on the way to the village Elodie went to the upper floor to look out over the trees, to sit with the soft breeze coming through the open window carrying the distant scent of the sea from so far away. Light, she missed the sea...

It seemed like a lifetime ago since Elodie had last seen the light glinting off the waves. Since she'd arrived at the tower in the midst of the Cellandre Forest and had finally found peace and sanctuary.

She had made it her own. A home for her and the tiny child she brought with her.

She had gone so far as to make a bargain with the old magic in the forest.

She opened the chest she kept locked, hidden up here, and stared at the fragmentary remains of that old, forgotten life. And sank into her memories. Those things she kept shut away from everyday life. And from Wren.

It held almost all the things she had managed to take with her on that fateful night. All of her dearest treasures. All but one.

Elodie opened the chest only when she was certain Wren

would not appear. The girl had a way of moving in almost complete silence, even as an infant. She would appear from the shadows, her dark eyes always alert and watchful. There were so many things Elodie didn't want to have to tell her, not yet. Perhaps not ever.

She loved Wren so much, but the past... the past was dangerous. Secrets needed to be kept. And one would lead to another, and another. Letting one loose would bring all the lies tumbling down.

The locket nestled in the palm of her hand, a golden disc marked with the flames of the Aurum. It had been a gift, a cherished and special gift, and the day he gave it to her was supposed to be the happiest of her life. That was what everyone said anyway. But Roland... Roland had understood. He had always understood. There was no chance of joy in her marriage. There never had been a chance. No matter what she had hoped for.

Elodie bowed her head over it, stroked the surface with her fingertips and slowly, torturing herself with every movement, she opened it.

His face gazed back at her. The portrait was perfect, even in miniature. It captured everything about him, the light in his dark eyes, the strong line of his jaw, the curve of his mouth and his ever unruly hair. She'd painted it herself. So long ago. She'd poured her love into every brushstroke. The locket was just to hold it. The portrait was the treasure.

Her eyes burned with tears, and she closed the locket again. All the same she kept it clenched in her hand and tried to control her emotions. And failed.

It didn't matter. The pain never really faded. She'd spent more years away from him than she had with him. Her whole adult life. And the pain never faded.

But once upon a time he had been her every joy, her dearest friend, her secret love.

Until her actual life made that impossible. Because that was always going to happen. She'd been a fool to think otherwise. They had both been fools. But oh, it had been nice to dream, if just for a little while.

She'd only been a girl herself. And now... well, it wasn't like she was ancient. She wasn't even forty.

Elodie never willingly drew attention to herself. She knew better than that. The wrong word to the wrong person, the wrong connection... everything would fall apart.

She'd have to do something about Pol Turner. She had been telling herself that for some time but she'd hoped his marriage would sort him out. More fool her. It just made him even more vindictive. He wanted far more than he was ever going to get out of life, thought himself entitled by his strength, good looks and frankly only adequate skills. He thought he could have a wife and child on one hand, and... what? A hedge witch as a plaything. No, never. Especially not her Wren.

Farringdale wasn't far enough away for her, and the sooner they left the better.

Roland would have beaten him black and blue as a lesson. No, Roland would never have let the self-aggrandising little prick get anywhere near the girl. Elodie should have been more like him. If Roland had been here... One look was all it would take. Her Paladin, her champion, her knight-at-arms, her... her friend. And her lover. He'd know what to do.

She had been as smitten with Roland as Wren was with Pol, once upon a time.

Holy light, she'd been a fool.

Her tears felt hot against her skin and she carefully kissed the locket, ready to put it away again, to seal up her past and close it all back up in the chest. Hidden, safe, but never forgotten. Not by her.

A sudden sensation like a thin blade digging deep in her sternum jolted Elodie's attention to the here and now.

Something was wrong. Terribly wrong.

The wards she had long ago woven through the forest were a part of her and she knew the moment they were breached. The old magic warned her. Pushing back from the chest, she got to her feet and made for the window. All around her the trees were still. Nothing was within sight of the tower. She checked the other quadrants, a window at each side, but there was nothing at all. The forest stretched out around her in all directions and—

A thin line of smoke streaked the sky to the north. Cursing, she grabbed the telescope and swung it around to get a better view. Thirbridge, it had to be. There was nothing else in that direction until the border, which meant...

Elodie heaved in a breath and turned back to the table in the middle of the chamber. The old clay dish in the middle didn't look like anything, the kind of thing to serve a communal meal or fill with fruit, perhaps. She took the water jug and poured the contents into the bowl, filling it right up to the edge. Leaning on the table, her arms braced to support her, she stared into it and forced her mind to clear. To go elsewhere, to the wards, to the edge of the trees, to Wren...

Her heart slammed against the inside of her chest as the water swirled and her own face stared back, frustration marking lines on her brow.

'Show me!' she said, impatient and afraid.

For a moment the world resisted and she pushed harder. Magic was second nature to her and always had been. It wove around her, threaded through her life. It would do what she wanted. It had to.

She closed her eyes and pictured the great flames of the Aurum, tried to clear the image of the devastation the last time she had stood before them – the smears of blood on the marble floor and the great white stones of the circle, the viscera, the broken bodies – and see it once again in its purest form. It was a risk, reaching out to it like that, but the Aurum never denied her.

That was her sin. Denying the Aurum. Turning her back on it, and on her predestined life. Running away.

But it was always there, just beyond her waking mind, no matter how far she ran, no matter how many walls she raised in her mind. Even if she didn't want to admit it. Didn't want to let it in. But she had no choice. The Aurum stirred for her, blinked to wakefulness, just for a moment.

'Show me,' she said again in othertongue, a command, and it responded.

The water glowed with sudden light, golden and bright, rippling like molten metal. And in it she saw—

Fire leaped from house to house, doors barred from the outside, screams, desperate terrible wails, men cut down in the square, blood pooling, the flash of blades in the sunlight, warhorses trampling faces she knew until no one could hope to ever know them again...

No, this couldn't be happening. There should have been more warning. There should have been something.

Where was Wren? She had to find Wren.

The images in the bowl swept across the forest and she saw more horsemen. The one in the lead pulled off his helmet and white-blond hair fell free.

Elodie's heart jerked like a fish on a line. It couldn't be. Not here. Not now. She pushed herself back so sharply that she almost upturned the bowl. But that face was unmistakable. He'd grown, filled out. The boy she had known had become a man. Still beautiful, of course, all that line were. But also cruel, haughty and relentless. She knew them all too well. The line of Sidon.

'Light curse you, Leander,' she hissed, as if he could hear her. In the water, he looked up at the sky as if perhaps he could. He had a sense of magic, like a hunting dog sniffing out prey.

He lifted his head to the sun, as if searching for her. He'd been a child when she last saw him but he had grown into a man as handsome as his uncle. And from the glint in those cold eyes, just as heartless.

This was bad. Beyond bad.

Why was he here? It couldn't be her, she'd been too careful. She'd done everything she could to shield herself and Wren.

But their enemies were here anyway.

She had to find Wren first. One last chance then and she'd have to pray Leander didn't sense her. Or worse, sense Wren.

She'd have to be quick. And then... then she'd have to run. They both would. But only if she could find Wren first and warn her. They could regroup and she'd open a path through the light to somewhere else. Anywhere else. Somewhere safe.

She couldn't leave Asteroth, but it was a big country. There were many hidden places like this. She just needed to find the right one.

Once more she focused on the glowing water and bent her mind to the girl, to her little bird, to the exclusion of all else. To hell with caution. This was an emergency.

And this time she found her. On the Elenwye ridge, with a telescope to her eye, her mouth twisting in alarm as the poor girl realised that Thirbridge and everything she knew was gone, that her life here was over, that the thing Elodie had always warned of had come to pass and there was nothing she could do.

Elodie's heart ached for her, though she'd never show it. She knew that feeling, remembered its sting far too keenly. To feel it again, when she'd thought they were safe—

Curse it, they had been safe here for so long, close to the border, but not too close. Far from the Aurum and its knights but not too far. Certainly not within the range of the witch-hunters of Sidonia. Until now.

What could have brought them across the border? That was an act of war, a breach of the accords drawn up at the end of the war when the Pact was agreed. Heads would roll for it. Literally. She could name some of them. There had been hostages exchanged and guarantees made. What would make Leander risk this? And why would Alessander allow it?

Wren scrambled back in shock, perhaps feeling the touch of Elodie's consciousness or perhaps just in horror at what she was seeing, and someone caught her, taking the telescope from her shaking hands, speaking to her in a way that calmed her.

Elodie let out another string of curses as she saw the man with Wren and recognised him. Not him, not really, but his eyes.

Bluer than blue, bright as a cloudless summer sky. The kind that laughed and sang with joy, that could make a girl believe anything. Believe in love, believe in possibilities, in a future. The kind that lied as easily as blinking. The eyes of a traitor. The worst kind of traitor. Dear light, they were everywhere. Closing in on her.

'Don't listen to him, little bird,' she whispered, forcing power into the words, reaching out across the space between them to make them fly to Wren's mind on the wind. 'Don't trust him. Run, my love. You know what to do. You have to run. We both do.'

Wren frowned, her eyes narrowing. Elodie saw her mouth form a question and the man with her shook his head. Of course he did. He wouldn't want her to hear, to receive a warning at all. Shadows coiled around them, shadows that blocked her voice from reaching Wren.

Was it already too late? Was that which should never be awakened already stirring? Was her Wren already lost?

No, not after all these years. She wasn't having it. And if Wren couldn't hear, if the dark powers were stopping her, Elodie would just have to find another way to warn her.

At least Wren knew what to do. They had always discussed

this, what to do in the case of danger, or attack. What to do if they needed to run.

But first she had to buy Wren time. She needed to get Leander's attention. Because, of all people, the crown prince of Ilanthus could not be allowed to get anywhere near Wren.

Elodie slammed her hands down on the table and the bowl jumped, water and light spilling everywhere.

This time she reached out not with a breeze but with a hurricane, and her voice was a roar within it. The othertongue wasn't just a song. It was a scream.

'*All right, you bastard. It's me you're looking for and we have old scores to settle, you and I. After Evander, after everything. Come and get me.*'

CHAPTER 10

WREN

Wind tore across the treetops, not a breeze this time, but something focused and determined. It almost took Wren off her feet and she stumbled into Finn's arms. They huddled together as the wind abruptly subsided.

Below them, the horsemen reeled around and galloped off south. They didn't hesitate, just tore down the road.

Wren's heart thudded against her chest and she felt the knot of panic in her throat thicken.

Finn let her go as if reluctant to do so. 'That wasn't natural,' he said.

Of course it wasn't. Wren knew that. Her every nerve was tingling with alarm. That was a warning and she had a very good idea of where it was coming from. But there were no words. It tasted of Elodie's magic, but it was oddly dulled.

A warning though, it had to be.

She needed to get out of here. That was what it told her. Head into the forest, as deep as she could, hole up there and wait. Just as Elodie had always told her. If she stayed out of the patches of darkwood, she'd be safe enough.

'Give me the telescope again,' she said and Finn obeyed at

once. A man used to taking orders, she realised, and filed that away for later.

Wren swung the telescope around and caught a glimpse of more smoke, this time to the south. In the direction of the tower. Elodie's tower.

'No!'

She was running before she even knew what she was doing, scrambling down from the ridge, Finn's telescope still gripped in her hand like a talisman or a weapon, her knuckles white. She didn't know how or why, because the Ilanthians couldn't have been anywhere near it, not yet, but her home was burning. And the horsemen were heading right for it.

'Wait!' she heard Finn call after her. 'Holy light, wait!'

But she didn't. She couldn't. Elodie was in trouble and those men, Ilanthian soldiers, were heading straight for her. Were there already perhaps. Because the smoke meant fire. And the fire meant—

If they wanted to find a witch they wouldn't find one more powerful than Elodie. What would they do with her? Kill her? Torture? Worse?

She couldn't picture Elodie enslaved, broken, but she'd heard too many tales of what the Ilanthians did with witches.

If something like this ever happened, Elodie had been clear. *Run and hide. I will find you. Never put yourself in danger.*

But that presumed that Elodie herself would not be in danger. And Wren couldn't abandon her now.

Wren threw herself through the trees, relying on her own instincts to lead her. The forest itself seemed to respond, sensing her urgency, peeling back out of her way. She blessed it and thanked it as she ran, unable to waste breath on the words. But it knew, it had to know. The shadows beneath the leaves moved, surging around her, and it felt like the whole of the forest was an ocean, roaring around her, billowing in waves, tempest-tossed and wild.

By the time Wren stumbled out into the clearing on the edge of the lake, the tower was already in flames, a torch burning high into the sky. Smoke and soot swirled around her.

This couldn't be happening. It couldn't.

As she stumbled to a halt, she heard the panicked whinnies of horses, the shouts of the riders and she turned, ready for their attack.

Four of them fanned out ahead of her, emerging through the gap in the trees from the road south. So she had been right, they'd been coming here. For Elodie. For her.

And suddenly she remembered why she was meant to hide. Not come back here.

'Take her,' the leader shouted, his voice cut by the storm she had brought with her.

There wasn't time to think. All she could do was react.

Elodie had always warned her not to reach out to her power in anger or in fear. Control was key. Measure out what was needed, control the flow and by all the Light keep a handle on it once released. Use the othertongue sparingly. It had to be done that way because otherwise the magic that threaded through her body and the world around her could run out of control. And it had on more than one occasion. But Elodie had been there to help her, to counter it.

But not this time... this time...

Elodie was gone. Elodie could be dead. She could be lost. They might have already taken her or she could be up there, her body burning. What choice did Wren have?

Wren felt the magic locked deep in the earth underneath her and reached for it blindly. It surged in response to her touch, winding itself around her, draining shadows from the trees and the rocks, from the depth of the water, from the rising column of smoke. It rose like a wave around her and, as the horsemen charged towards her, she made ready to unleash it.

But the shadows weren't ready to release her. They clung to

her, smothering her, dragging her down. She pushed harder, tangling herself with them, trying to gain the upper hand. It wasn't working. Normally just a nudge or a request would do it, but this time...

Shadows ignited in her blood, rushed along her veins and she breathed it in. Something dark and powerful, dangerous, which threatened to sweep her away.

She wanted... she needed... she burned...

The weight of it crushed her, ground her to pieces. She had to break through whatever it was doing to her, to get hold of herself again and—

Her legs went weak and she heard her heart thundering inside her.

No... not just inside her. Everywhere, all through the forest, all around her. Old magic, dark magic, the touch of the Nox...

Something struck her middle, lifting her off her feet and carrying her away.

Too stunned to react, she struggled to keep hold of the threads of darkness, dragging them to her core, but they spilled loose regardless, as if they had a mind of their own.

Something tangled, snapped. And she felt it like a punch in her guts, driving all the air from her as her spell fell apart.

CHAPTER 11

WREN

Finn slung Wren up across the saddle in front of him. Dancer galloped across the open ground like a streak of shadow given solid form.

The knight bent low over her, urging the horse on, through the edge of the lake in a spray of water and back into the trees on the far side.

The sound of pursuit was unmistakable. The horsemen from Ilanthus crashed through the undergrowth, their mounts screaming in protest as they were driven on.

Wren tried to catch her breath but everything swirled around her, the shadows surging in her head made it all feel wrong. She couldn't focus, couldn't control any of it. Her body burned, ached and all she could think of – stupidly – was Finn's nearness, his body pressed to hers, keeping her on the horse. Behind them, the forest snarled and shivered like a wild beast and the shadows inside it awoke.

This was bad. Really bad. She remembered Elodie's warnings far too late now. *If you call to the fragments of the Nox in the darkwood, it will always answer, little bird, but it won't always do what you want. You could lose yourself, like so many have been lost. Never reach for the dark.*

But Elodie had never really understood. It wasn't so much reaching for the darkness. It was always there, always trying to get to her. She fought to keep it away. Sometimes she just let down those walls, just for an instant.

This time had been different though. This time she hadn't just allowed it in, she had demanded it come to her, serve her, help her...

And when she did... a spear of desire dug deep inside her, twisting, a pleasure cutting along the edge of agony. *Give in*, it seemed to tell her, singing to her in that voice that seemed like a lullaby. *Just give in and it would be everything.*

Wren struggled for reality. She had to get a grip on herself, on the world as it was. Not on this swirl of ungovernable emotion.

Dancer's muscles strained beneath her, and sweat stood out on his skin. The smell was raw in her nostrils. Behind her, Finn was a knot of tense muscles, entirely fixed on escape, guiding the horse through the trees. But one false move, one unseen obstacle or ditch, and it would be over.

Wren closed her eyes, fought for equilibrium and turned the shadows back, forcing up her barriers again, shutting herself off. It was agony. A conscious severing of something so intrinsically part of herself. Tears burned in her eyes.

Everything slowed. It wanted her to release her control, to give in to it. That was all it had ever wanted. For her to be part of it, to let it into her mind. She felt the darkwood still reaching for her, its voice soothing.

No, not the wood, not the forest. This was the darkness itself, the darkness that lurked beneath, the shadows she turned aside, the shades she heard whispering in the night. It was everywhere.

Those who gave themselves unconditionally to the Nox lived short lives, sunken in every depravity. And the joy of it was absolute, or so they said. If you went to it and made a deal it would give you anything. Or at least that was its promise. Those who had even once felt its touch on their minds, on their bodies, would never be the same. It left its mark, and a ghost of desire that never faded, for which nothing else would ever compensate. Elodie had refused to discuss it, but even in a tiny village like Thirbridge, people talked. Deals could be struck, like whatever arrangement Pol had struck to have a son. But those who gave themselves completely...

And it was calling her. Coming for her. She could feel its touch, like a single fingertip stroking the length of her spine. It sang, it murmured, it whispered.

All she had to do was stop pushing it away. All she had to do was let it in. It would give her everything, every pleasure, every delight. All the power she could imagine.

And as she was fighting, she felt his mind brush against hers. The man with the white hair.

He served the Nox. And he was powerful with its magic. Entwined with its power.

Her breath caught in her throat as she felt invisible fingers trace a line across her lips, as she felt his magic brush against hers. He knew where she was.

He was still behind, somewhere, the white-haired man with the fairest of faces. He had pulled back, the better to concentrate on reaching her through enchantment. His men pursued them, but he sat still and alone on the back of his white horse, in a shadow-dark glade, his eyes closed, his lips moving. She could picture him, reaching for her. He wanted her, needed her. His voice was a song of seduction as intimate as that of the shadows she had heard all her life.

No. He couldn't have her. He wouldn't have her.

She opened her eyes, trying to see over Finn's leg, jostled back and forth like a sack of vegetables. His voice still urged

Dancer on, a litany of encouragement, determined and desperate. Another kind of song.

And behind them, a wall of night was rising up through the forest.

Blacker than midnight, deeper than nightmares, consuming trees and horsemen alike. A great wave of shadows, ready to crest and crash down on them all, swallowing them whole.

No, she whispered, or tried to whisper, as she realised what this meant. But she didn't have the air to make a sound.

Had she done that? How could she have done that?

She couldn't drive it back on her own. She wasn't strong enough, not without Elodie. There was no way she could stop it. Not when it contained all the shadows she had pulled out of the darkwood...

Dancer gave a terrible whinny of alarm. Even with the greatest training in the world and the most valiant heart, the stallion couldn't fight its instincts. It reared up on its hind legs, tried to swing away while Finn fought for control. Something crashed into their backs, the darkness so solid that it flung them forward.

The ground dropped away as the force of magic pushed them over the edge of a ditch or a ravine, or the Aurum alone knew what. And, suddenly, they were all falling.

The forest floor slammed hard into her body and then Finn slammed into her as well.

Just as abruptly everything went still. Far too still.

Darkness rolled over them, silent and terrible, like a blanket above them, cutting them off from the rest of the world.

Dancer screamed, not in terror this time but in agony. The noise brought her to her senses so fast her stomach twisted in knots.

She knew that sound. Knew it, had nightmares about it, hated it. That was the sound of a creature dying, or so close to dying that there was no saving it.

Beside her, Finn moved, his body up and lurching towards the broken body of the stallion before she could do or say anything. She saw him lay his hand on the creature's shivering skin, try to mouth soothing words, but fail. The knife he carried at his belt was in his hand and it flashed once, twice.

Everything went still again. Too still. Too quiet.

She slumped down into the wet mulch at the base of the ravine and heard only the sound of Finn's ragged breath. It echoed around her. From the horse, there was no sound at all.

The fragments of the Nox all around her drank down the death. She felt it surround them both, absorbing Dancer's demise like wine, as she desperately tried to push it back from the two of them. Felt it laugh at her feeble efforts. Then slowly it faded, back into the darkwood, back into the shadows, sated for now.

'I'm sorry,' Finn whispered, brokenly. Not to her. Those words weren't meant for her ears. She felt like an interloper of the worst kind hearing them. 'I had to. I just—I had to. I'm so sorry.'

Then he went quiet again, except for that ragged breath.

Wren pulled herself up on shaking hands, and crawled across the forest floor to him.

He'd put the horse out of its misery, but he'd loved Dancer. Every nerve of her being told her that. She reached out to comfort him. This was her fault, all her fault, and she had to—

A sob broke from her lips when that sensation of hunger swept through her again.

She thought of the moment Finn had kissed her, his lips devouring hers, his mouth hot and ravenous, his hands on her skin. She wanted to tangle her hands in his hair and pull him to her and—

Not now. Not here. She shied back, horrified with the thoughts.

Not like this.

What kind of monster was the Nox trying to make of her? Revolted, she forced it away, trying to raise a shield of light as Elodie had taught her. All that she managed was a shaky barrier, barely a circle, but it was enough. The othertongue came thick and haltingly to her lips, but she forced herself to say the words, to drive back the darkness. Somehow she succeeded.

The desire the dark magic engendered in her slid away, making her feel broken and nauseous.

If he hadn't come back. If he hadn't tried to help her—

Wren gave a sob of despair and curled in on herself. The shadows swept by them and she clung to any fragile light she could muster. The witchhunters were still looking for her. For both of them. Finn had said as much.

She should have just run. Hiddén. Why hadn't she done what she had always been told?

'Are you hurt?' It was Finn's voice.

Everything hurt. Everything.

Shaking and clearly afraid, but somehow still strong, his hands closed under her shoulders, lifting her. He didn't even know her name and he was still trying to help. What sort of man did that? For no reason, trying to help because it was the right thing to do. What sort of man—

'Stay with me. Can you hear me? It's all going to be fine. We just have to—we just have to—'

It wasn't going to be fine. Nothing was. And she had no idea what he thought they just had to do...

Wren's strength, such as it was, gave out, and she slumped down into the darkness in her own unconscious mind. She welcomed it.

CHAPTER 12

WREN

The smell of woodsmoke and the crackle of a fire woke her.

Wren was lying on the forest floor, wrapped in Finn's cloak, her head resting on one of the saddlebags. Finn sat opposite her, gazing into the flames, as if his mind was a million miles away. She watched him, the light playing on his fine features, reflecting in his dark blue eyes.

She didn't know where they were. Some distance away she could hear a stream, and a night bird called out softly through the trees. It wasn't quiet. There was nothing of that deep empty silence of the darkwood. Just the forest at night, which was probably a good sign.

Her clothes felt loose around her body and she realised she was just wearing a shirt. Her tunic, leather jerkin and cloak were folded neatly on a rock nearby. Which meant someone had undressed her, presumably checking to see if she was wounded – not completely but enough, enough to realise...

Wren pushed herself up, and Finn started as if under attack, rising to a half crouch from sitting, a knife in his hand. That same knife. At least it wasn't the sword still strapped across his back. He froze, staring at her, and sank back down to the ground.

'You're awake.' His voice sounded rough.

She just nodded slowly. Her head was pounding and her body felt wrung out like an old rag. There was no sign of Dancer. Of Dancer's body. He had moved them both away from the scene. He must have carried her.

'I'm sorry,' she tried to say. Her own voice came out in a hoarse croak.

Her hair whispered around her face, coming almost to her shoulders. She froze as she tried to push it back, to hide it.

'You're a girl,' he said, and winced. 'A woman, I mean. A—'

'A witch,' she finished for him. 'An apprentice, anyway. Not a very good one.'

Might as well warn him that she'd be no help at all. Before he got his hopes up.

He just raised his eyebrows.

She felt the urge to explain, but even then, it all came out wrong. 'I didn't mean to—I was trying to stop them and I—I failed, didn't I? I'm sorry. I didn't mean to get your horse killed.'

He slumped down again, the knife still in his hands. It was covered in blood. So were his fingers.

'No, that was me. I should have... I don't know. I should have been better, kept more of an eye on the road ahead.' Except there hadn't been a road. Or any light to see it if there had been, not with a wave of pure darkness bearing down on them. Finn let out a small, bitter noise. 'These things happen, isn't that what they say? He was a good horse though. Saw me through a lot. The stablemaster is going to be so... so angry.'

His voice sounded bleak and broken and she didn't know what to do. It wasn't as simple as he said, clearly. He was trying to say the right thing, trying to be strong and hide his emotions. But he couldn't. He was grieving. He just didn't want to let her see that.

But she could see far too much.

'Who are you?' he asked at last, once he had gathered his thoughts again, or steeled himself for an answer.

'Wren,' she said.

'Wren what?'

'Just Wren. I live here.'

'In the darkwood?'

'In the forest,' she replied carefully. A witch from the darkwood... that was not a title to carry lightly.

'I see,' he said and prodded the fire with a stick, lost in thoughts.

'Who were those men?' she asked, eager to change the subject as quickly as possible. She didn't want him to think about what a witch from the darkwood might be capable of doing.

It was the wrong tack. He looked away, staring into the darkness beyond the trees now, his mouth hard. He bit out the answer. 'Ilanthians.'

'Witchhunters?' The words made her shiver. Elodie had told tales of terror about the Ilanthian witchhunters. They grabbed women from their homes and dragged them back to their fortress in Sidonia. They enslaved anyone with a scrap of power, bound them to the service of the Nox, or what remained of it, and used them in unspeakable ways to try to raise that dark power again, to gather the fragments together and make it whole. To control magic for themselves.

If they ever come for us, it's better to die first. Never let them take you. If they come, you run and hide. Understand? I'll take care of it.

Was that what she'd done? Wren wouldn't put it past Elodie to set fire to the tower rather than let them take her.

Was Elodie dead? No, she couldn't be. Not Elodie. She couldn't let herself think that.

Finn finally spoke again. 'Witchhunters. Among other things.'

'The man in charge of them, who is he? You knew him.'

'Everyone knows him. Leander of House Sidon, the crown prince of Ilanthus. We need to get word to Knightsford as soon as possible. If he's here...' He sighed, as if the weight of the world had settled on his shoulders. 'He's dangerous. And it means that he's not keeping to the Pact.'

'The Pact?' she asked.

'At the end of the last war, there was a treaty. It's known as the Pact. To the Ilanthians it was a humiliation. If it's broken that could lead to another war. And even if not... well, it's not good.'

That much was clear.

'You said he was hunting you.'

'You don't miss a thing, do you?' A bitter laugh came from his lips then and she didn't like it. He barely sounded like himself, the little she knew of him. Maybe that was part of the problem. She didn't know him, not really. 'He is. But now I fear he has another prey in mind.'

'Where did they go?'

'Why don't you tell me?' he said. 'I don't know what you did. I've never seen a power raised like that. It wasn't just Dancer that died back there.'

The other men then, the Ilanthians. The shadows had swallowed them up.

That wasn't her. It was the darkwood, or the forest itself.

She hadn't done anything. Except... except she had...

She had called the powers that lingered there. Oh, she might not have meant to, but... Ever since she was little they had come if she called them and in her panic, in her terror...

No, she couldn't have...

'I don't know what you mean.'

The look he gave her branded her a liar. 'I went back and

checked. Dead horses, dead men, torn apart, crushed and broken. Shadow kin. Nothing else does that.'

Oh. She chewed on her lower lip. There had always been shadow kin in the darkwood and they had always been attracted to Wren, dancing attendance on her if she let them. Wild creatures spun from the fragments of the Nox that lingered here, but usually they avoided anything that might fight back. Elodie had taught her how to drive them off as soon as she could learn the words to do so. But this time she had called them, the shadow kin.

That sentient, rage-filled darkness, those voices that had whispered to her, that hunger, that need...

She pushed the thoughts away. She couldn't face them right now.

'And the prince?'

He laughed. 'Oh no, not him. He retreated long before it got near him. But he'll be back with reinforcements. I know him. He will not give up, especially now that he knows what you can do.'

'But I—'

'Don't give me that. What else would have done that?'

She let out a shaky breath. She had to persuade him that it hadn't been her. Not directly, not intentionally. 'The darkwood. It answers sometimes. Never like that, not before. But it's dangerous. It... it has shadow kin and other things living there, gathering together... Elodie says—'

'Who is this Elodie? If she's teaching you she must be powerful indeed. Is she your mother?'

'She's... she's...' How did she explain? Her mother, although Elodie had never said it out loud. There hadn't been a need. And now she might not ever get a chance. Everyone else said it though. They were snide about it sometimes. A beautiful woman who arrived alone with a child in her arms. The witch's bastard... that's what they had called Wren. Now the words hung around her neck like a noose. 'She was in the tower. That's where we lived. And you saw it.'

The flames, so hot, consuming the whole building. Like it had been doused in oil and burned from the inside out. No one could have got out of that.

'You think she's dead?' he asked and his voice gentled again. He was trying to be kind. Even in the midst of all this, he was trying. That was the sort of man he was. She didn't deserve that, not if she really had called up that wall and the shadow kin within to tear their pursuers apart.

Wren shrugged. She didn't want to think it. But what other option was there? She just couldn't seem to force the words out, so she settled for staring at him defiantly, aware of the tears burning in her eyes. He read her face easily. 'You want to go back and look, don't you? It won't be safe. We should go to Knightsford. We can get help there.'

And on foot it would take days. But she needed to know if Elodie was there now. If she was still alive.

'I'll be careful,' she told Finn. 'What if she's hurt? Or captured? What if this Leander has her?'

She couldn't say the rest. All her other fears. But invoking the prince of Ilanthus's name seemed to do the trick.

'Fine,' he sighed. 'But we will go only in daylight. And you do exactly what I say, understand? No tricks, no adventures of your own. We stay away from the darkwood. And definitely no magic.'

She let him think it was his decision to make. It was the least she could do.

CHAPTER 13

WREN

The tower loomed over them, black and empty, the morning light playing through the smoke that still hung in the air around it. The windows were gone, as was the door. Everything inside on the lower floor had been destroyed.

Wren tried to force herself to keep breathing as they stepped inside. The heat must have been intense, which told her at once nothing natural had done this. No normal fire.

Elodie had spoken about conjuring witchfire on occasion. It was a weapon of last resort, she said. That amount of magic was only to be used in desperate need.

Wren had never seen it though, and certainly never managed to produce so much as a spark herself. Light was not her forte. She was better at driving the darkness away than drawing the light to her. Now she wished she had listened properly. At least she might understand better what had happened here.

Wren ran her hand down the soot-blackened wall. Her fingers came away coated in a thick sticky darkness, which she hurriedly wiped off on her jerkin. It felt like tar.

Glancing back, she saw Finn examining everything with a critical eye. He was as aware of what all this might mean as she was.

'Tell me about her,' he said at last.

Wren shook her head. 'What is there to tell? She raised me.' And now she was gone. No one could have survived this.

The kitchen and workrooms were destroyed, the distillery must have gone up in a fireball, and their living room and bedrooms were ash, but as they moved further up the winding staircase, it wasn't as bad.

The round room at the top of the tower looked like a whirlwind had gone through it, and everything stank of smoke, but the flames had not reached it. Elodie's treasures were strewn everywhere. Even the precious telescope lay broken on the floor.

So the Ilanthians had come here, before she made it back. They must have.

Had Elodie still been here? Had they taken her? Was she already on her way back to Sidonia in black metal chains enchanted to suppress her magic, destined for a lifetime of slavery?

They had certainly taken anything of actual value, not that there had been much. Even the chest that Elodie kept locked at all times had been smashed open, the contents rifled through and most of it gone.

Elodie thought Wren didn't know about her secret treasures, but Wren had always been a curious child and suspiciously good at sneaking around, poking her nose in where it didn't belong. That said, she had never examined the contents of the chest too closely. They had always been Elodie's secrets and they felt private, sacrosanct.

Wren knelt before it and a sob lodged in her throat. She couldn't breathe. Her heart felt like it would tear itself out of her, and her eyes burned as she tried to sort through the scattered remains of a life.

At the bottom of the chest she found a locket. How had they missed that? On the floor beside it she found a leather-bound notebook, the cover etched with the symbol of the Aurum, the wheel of flames. It was battered and well used, old. She opened the book to find Elodie's neat writing covering the pages. So much of it. Her eyesight blurred with tears as she tried to read it. A diary? She didn't remember Elodie ever keeping one but she could have, Wren supposed. It felt like an invasion, but what else did she have now? She flicked through the pages, brushing her filthy fingertips against the ink and wishing she could ask Elodie what to do.

The page shifted beneath her touch and she shied back with a cry.

'What is it?' Finn asked, instantly at her side. Had he been watching her? Waiting for her to pick something up? Or was he just as concerned about what they might find here as Wren was? 'What's wrong?'

The words on the page changed, the ink drawing together, moving like water until it formed other words. A warning.

Run, little bird, and don't look back. Make for the Seven Sisters and I'll find you there. Don't trust anyone, neither hunter or knight.

Elodie's writing, unmistakable and still moving, adding more as she read it.

They are looking for both of us and I will not let them take you.

'What's the Seven Sisters?' she asked.

'Standing stones, in a clearing in the southern end of the forest, not far from Knightsford,' he said, that touch of wariness back in his voice. 'They're old magic, the oldest. They stand at the conjunction of several lines of power, I believe. A dangerous place.'

She examined the locket again. It was beautiful, a delicate fancy, inscribed with the symbol of the Aurum as well. But why was Elodie warning her away from the knights while carrying treasures marked with their symbol?

'Elodie says to meet her there. In the book.'

She tried to show him but the words on the page faded again, leaving just a smear of water-stained ink.

Whatever enchantment Elodie had woven around it had done its job, it seemed.

'She's powerful, your Elodie,' Finn said, the wary tone never leaving his voice. 'And she escaped Leander. Probably used the fire as a distraction. Clever.' Was that a begrudging tone of respect?

She was about to say she had never met anyone more powerful, but Elodie was the only witch she knew and most of her practice lay in the mundane, in herbs and knowledge and healing. And in her link to the forest itself. All the other things Wren herself could never actually master. But that's when she heard it.

We are witchkind. We will live free or die.

It was like a whisper in the back of Wren's mind.

Now that sounded more like Elodie than the words in the book.

She swallowed hard. 'We have to go south,' she said at last. 'To Knightsford. You to warn them of the Ilanthians and me to the stones, to find her.'

'Can I see the locket?' he asked abruptly and she frowned. But there didn't seem to be a reason not to let him. As he took it his fingers brushed against her skin and he froze for a moment. Wren felt something like a shiver pass right through her before he pulled back.

Finn opened the locket carefully, as if afraid he'd damage it, and stared at the images inside.

On one side was a small child with dark hair and huge eyes.

Wren as she had been. She remembered Elodie painting it, remembered having to sit still, remembered fidgeting and squirming until Elodie gave up and released her back into the wild. Elodie had laughed at her, rather than been annoyed. Said she was a feral little thing and nothing would ever change that. But she'd said it with fondness.

On the other side the face of a man looked back at them. Handsome, strong, his hair and eyes as dark as Wren's, the lines of his face making him stern.

Finn snapped the locket shut. He shoved it back into Wren's hand and got to his feet, retreating to the far side of the room.

'What is it? What's wrong?' She rose unsteadily, as if the floor beneath her feet had suddenly become uneven.

'That's Roland de Silvius,' he said, his voice shaken. 'Made years ago, but there's no mistaking him. He's barely changed. Who is Elodie? Where did she come from?'

Wren shook her head, bewildered. How could he know the man in Elodie's locket? 'I don't know. We've always been here.'

'But she didn't come from here, did she?'

'No. We moved here when I was little...'

'And you never asked where from?'

Wren looked around the tower room that had been a sanctuary and a stronghold, right to the last. This had been Elodie's space. Wren herself had always preferred to be outside in the forest, in the greenwood, in the open air. Perhaps she should have paid more attention, but it was far too late now.

'She didn't like to talk about the past,' was all she could tell him, and he gave her a look like he'd worked out something devastating.

'I bet she didn't,' Finn muttered.

'Why don't you tell me what's wrong? And who this Roland is?'

But she remembered too many times Elodie crying out in

her dreams and nightmares, calling for Roland, weeping, his name on her lips like that of a lover or a lost soul. She screamed his name in the darkest moments of the darkest nights when the worst dreams tormented her. Whenever Wren had gone to her then, tried to help her or comfort her, Elodie had buried her face in her hands, refused to look at her.

Faced with the image before her, Wren began to suspect why. But she didn't want to think about it. She didn't dare.

Finn seemed to have gathered his wits now. He straightened, staring at her as if seeing her for the first time. 'You've never heard that name? Roland de Silvius, first Paladin of the Royal Court, Queen's champion, the Grandmaster of the Knights of the Aurum?'

All that? It sounded terribly grand, a list of a name. Too big for one man.

Roland... She might have heard that name. And Elodie had told her of the Knights of the Aurum of course. But none of the rest of it. Not Grandmaster, or champion or anything like that. Just Roland.

This didn't make any sense. Elodie was a hedge witch. A talented one no doubt, but nothing more, living in a benighted forest, miles from anywhere, on the edge of the civilised world. She had nothing to do with Grandmasters, or knights or Paladins. She scoffed if they were mentioned and warned Wren away from them. Even standing there now with Finn felt like some kind of betrayal.

'But why would Elodie have his picture in a locket?'

Finn took another step towards her and stopped, looming over her, suddenly a threat. She hadn't thought of him as one before. But the chance had always been there, hadn't it? He was tall, warrior-trained, and knew all about the Knights of the Aurum. Who had she brought into their home?

'A very good question, Wren of Darkwood. It's the type of gift one would give only to someone you loved, isn't it? And

Roland only ever loved one person. The one person he couldn't have of course, even if things had been different. We thought her killed in the battle for the Aurum twenty years ago. The love of Roland's life, so all the stories say—I never asked him, but I didn't have to. They are legendary. Roland de Silvius loved Queen Aeryn of Asteroth. The lost queen.'

FROM 'THE BALLAD OF THE PALADIN AND THE QUEEN'

Sing not of a heart so broken and lost,
Nor a queen with blood on her hands,
Sing not of a knight with a broken vow
Whose love lies in shadowed lands.

Never was there a love so true,
As the love that could not be,
Never was there a knight so bold
Nor a queen so brave as she.

CHAPTER 14

ROLAND

The locket in his hand was a tiny thing to contain so much loss.

In it, she was forever young, forever beautiful. And though she could never have really been his, Roland knew that their hearts had been one. Even if she had been married to someone else.

He had called her Elodie. Not her royal name. Her childhood one, almost forgotten by everyone else. It had become a private name, just for the two of them. The name of her heart, she had said.

How did he reconcile that with his honour and duty? Loving Elodie had been everything, all of it wrapped up in one. But that wouldn't have mattered. He had been helpless. From the first moment he'd seen her, he had been hers, heart and soul.

A girl wandering through the palace kitchens at night and a boy, who had been given the thankless task of tending a fire more as a joke than anything else. Because he wasn't the son of some great noble, or the scion of a great house. Because the Aurum had chosen him anyway, and many people thought it was a mistake.

Not her though. She'd stopped and stared at him, seeing

him for who he was in an instant. Because the Aurum was a part of her life, part of her. So infused in her blood, or so the seers said, that she might as well be its walking embodiment.

'He's no one,' the guard accompanying her had sneered. And Elodie had shot the tall man a scathing look. She had been beautiful even then, a tiny thing, spun from fire and gold.

'No he isn't,' she had replied. 'He's *mine*.'

And he had been. Right from that second, even if he didn't really know what it meant at the time. He would have done anything for her.

Someone cleared their throat behind him and Roland sighed inwardly, closing the locket and tucking it safely in the pouch at his belt before turning around. The tent was a billowing roof overhead, the breeze outside making it feel like a sail in a storm.

Waiting for his attention, Anselm stood in the doorway. His former squire, now a knight in his own right, and his most trusted aide.

'Reports in from the north, Grandmaster,' he said and approached the desk with a number of papers in his arms.

'Any news of Ward?' he asked, but Anselm shook his head.

'Just that he left Sidonia as planned. He's probably making his way here through the forest, avoiding the roads. You know how he is.'

Sneaky, the others would say. But Finnian Ward was so much more than that. He was the most promising among his knights, and would have joined the ranks of Paladins if only the Aurum was willing to acknowledge new vows. Or anything really. But since the queen had been lost, the Aurum was just a flame. Needing no fuel, it burned and never waned, its magic sustaining it. But it didn't react to anyone anymore. Not since that terrible night.

Blood on the marble, so much blood. Bodies strewn everywhere, broken like dolls, torn apart by the rising darkness... Elodie, illuminated by the flames, as if she was on fire within, while a wave of shadows bore down on her. She stood silhouetted with the Aurum behind her, and within her, the standing stones framing her, light in her veins glowing beneath her skin.

'Get back, Roland. Now!' The door slammed between them like the closing of a tomb.

Roland had always been loyal. He had always obeyed her command but it was the one time he shouldn't have. He'd been too slow. If he had only taken those few steps inside before it was too late...

It haunted him.

They had all known about the prophecy.

When shadows take the Aurum, the Nox will take the throne.

No one had believed in it, though. That was the problem.

King Alessander of Ilanthus and Elodie's father Prince Consort Jonquil had hoped to ease tensions with the ridiculous marriage – how they could have hoped to unite the two nations was beyond him. Roland knew as well as anyone the queen loathed her treacherous husband Evander from the first. She had tried to make it work despite that, to no avail. And then Evander had almost fulfilled the prophecy and doomed them all. He had come so close, and only Elodie had saved them with her sacrifice.

Roland didn't know how she did it. The Nox was a goddess, unstoppable and all-powerful. Brought into the heart of the Sacrum, it would have fed from the magic that filled the place, syphoning off everything that sustained the Aurum, destroying it. In battle the Nox would shift its shape, take on the form you feared the most and ultimately destroy you, but Elodie had found a way to destroy it. Because Elodie – clever, peerless, powerful Elodie – always found a way. He'd known that. He'd trusted in her.

That was the only reason he had left, rushing to raise the alarm. He knew she would hold, and he could come back to help her. Or die by her side.

The battle for the gate had been brief and brutal, Ilanthian spies falling on the guards to let in their troops. But the knights had turned back the tide and Roland had sprinted back to the Sacrum, desperate to save her. To rescue her.

He had been too late.

Elodie had slammed the door to the Sacrum on him, to protect him, and had faced the Nox alone. It had towered over her, vast and terrible, still taking form.

Afterwards the Maidens of the Aurum, those guardians of the sacred flame, said the Nox was shattered into pieces and driven back to the darkness from which it hailed. The chamber of the Aurum was bathed in blood, the flame burned on in silence. And there was no sign at all of Elodie.

And Evander's death had plunged them into the war they had been trying to prevent.

Only the fact that Elodie had already taken out the Nox, along with her husband, had saved Asteroth and given them victory.

While quiescent, the Aurum had still helped their knights and Paladins in the war that had consumed their kingdoms, whereas the Ilanthians had lost their dark goddess and their ranks had descended into chaos. Peace had been imposed by force of arms and a humiliating defeat, but the Pact had never truly been accepted. Even with the exchange...

Roland forced his mind back to the here and now, to Anselm and Finnian. 'I want to know as soon as there's any word of him.'

Losing Finnian would be too much. Not just for him personally – the boy was like the son he'd never had – but for the fragile peace, which hung on by a tattered thread. The Pact may not be fully accepted but it had saved countless lives. It meant peace with Ilanthus had to be preserved no matter what.

Elodie would have understood.

And there he was again, thinking about her.

CHAPTER 15

WREN

In the sunlight the forest seemed tranquil. Wren could almost believe that this was just a normal day.

Except that Elodie had gone, and that everything Wren owned was in a pack on her back. A few changes of clothes, the diary and the locket now safely secured around her neck, and that was it.

Finn insisted they leave as soon as possible, before the Ilanthians could come back. She didn't bother pointing out they had clearly already been there.

The ones who hadn't been killed in the darkwood.

She shuddered again. The sense of the Nox had been so strong, wrapping tendrils of shadow through her mind and body. She had lost all sense of herself in that moment, struggling to stay conscious, and she had felt... what? It was like a lingering nightmare, there on the edge of her consciousness. How many shadow kin had she summoned? What had she set loose on those men?

Finn set a punishing pace but she wouldn't let him think she couldn't keep up. She didn't need his pity. All she wanted was to get to the Sisters as soon as possible and find Elodie.

And get some answers.

The very idea that Elodie was a lost queen was simply absurd. It didn't matter that what little Wren knew about the woman seemed to confirm everything Finn said. When she had a moment she'd read the diary and see what clues it could offer.

But as they walked the forest grew strangely quiet. By evening the stillness was uncanny and she felt as if something was following them through the empty woodland. No birds sang, and there were no sounds of any other animals.

'This isn't right,' she said to Finn. 'It shouldn't be like this.'

He just nodded, scanning the treeline with wary eyes. She couldn't say he was nervous, but he was ready for anything, watching, alert, waiting. Not afraid.

But nothing happened.

That feeling of being followed persisted through the next day, the sense of eyes upon them as they made their way south. By the time they stopped for the night, they were both exhausted.

Finn lit a fire, a small and well-shielded one. It was the gift of the Aurum. They didn't want to draw unnecessary attention to themselves but fire was one of the few protections against shadow kin, not to mention the remaining fragments of power of the Nox.

They ate in silence, listening to the forest around them, not quite as still now. Wren heard night birds calling out and the rustling of things in the undergrowth. She didn't know what, but prayed whatever it was would keep its distance. Natural noises, though. That was the main thing.

Finn must have realised that too.

'Get some sleep,' he told her. 'I'll keep watch.'

Wren frowned. 'You need to rest as well.'

'I've trained for this,' he assured her, his rich voice confident and calming. Was it a particular tone he had learned or did it come naturally to him? 'I'll wake you later and you can give me a few hours before we head off with first light. I'll sleep when we're safe.'

There wasn't much she could say to argue with him. She was already exhausted, her eyes heavy and her body aching. And he could see it.

She bedded down on the soft earth wrapped in a blanket and tried not to let her mind spiral with thoughts, hard as that was. Between Thirbridge, the blazing tower, the dead horse, the man leading the witchhunters, and all of Elodie's secrets...

How had her life fallen apart so quickly?

She was aware all the time of Finn, of his eyes watching her in the night. But listening to him, his watchful stillness, the in and out of his breath, lulled her to rest. She matched her breathing with his and felt her heart slow, her mind quieten, and before she realised it sleep claimed her.

But so did her dreams.

Wren's footsteps echoed around her, a hollow sound that reverberated back through her. The ground beneath her feet was hard, like ice, but it was only when she stopped that she realised it was marble, highly polished so that she could see her own reflection beneath her.

Except it didn't look like her reflection, not really.

Her hair rolled in midnight waves down her back, longer than she or Elodie had ever allowed it to grow, and beneath it her skin was pale as moonlight. She wore a gown like gossamer that clung to her curves and glittered with a touch of frost at the edges, but she was barefoot against ice-cold stone. Everything felt brittle and dangerous in that liminal space, unreal and yet frighteningly real to her.

She tried telling herself it was a dream but it didn't work. Not this time. It was something else. Something more. Not a dream, nor yet a memory. She'd never been here, she'd never been like this.

The hall she wandered through was vast, with lines of pillars reaching high overhead and the far-off ceiling seemed to be painted to reflect the night's sky. But even as she raised her eyes to it, the clouds moved over the moon, and the stars swirled overhead. Not painted, but enchanted, an illusion, or... or transparent. Could it be made of glass?

Or maybe it was just a dream, she reminded herself again. It had to be. There was no place like this in the waking world.

But it felt so real. Far too real.

The breeze that stirred the air was cold. It brought up goosebumps on her bare arms and shoulders. She couldn't suppress the shiver than ran through her.

And somewhere else, someone laughed. A low, deep chuckle, masculine and knowing. It made her spin around, looking for the source, while at the same time heat rushed through her, replacing the cold. Not the warmth of fire or comfort. A rush of desire she couldn't control.

'Who are you?' she shouted, annoyed with her reaction. 'What do you want?'

He laughed again. Definitely a he.

'*Your heart flutters like a little bird*,' the voice murmured. '*But you are stronger than that.*'

Something touched the back of her neck, a gentle caress but with an undercurrent of something far darker. Wren gave a sob of alarm but her treacherous body reacted again, leaning into the sensation. This couldn't be right. It couldn't be real.

Ghostly hands slid up her arms, and Wren shivered at the touch, helpless.

'*Show me, beloved*,' the voice murmured, as if he leaned down over her shoulder to whisper in her ear, making her tremble. '*Show me what you can do.*'

All around them flames leaped into life, fire so bright and

blinding that she flinched back, covering her face. They rose like a barrier, reflecting in the marble, as if the white stone was covered in blood.

Fire rushed towards her, like a living thing, and Wren tried to retreat. But something caught her feet, her bare and vulnerable feet, and sent her slamming down onto the icy stone. She heard laughter, mocking terrible laughter.

'*Show me.*' The voice thundered with command and she felt her body react, the need to obey it terrifying in its intensity.

A wall of flames bore down on her and Wren cried out, her hands flung out before her, as if to repel it. The column of fire stopped in its tracks, as if frozen, and then slowly, so slowly, the flames turned black.

'*Oh yes. It's true. I knew you the moment I saw you, beloved.*'

'I... I'm not your beloved...'

'*But you will be. Oh you will be. My queen and my beloved, and everything in between. A goddess in waiting. I will give you this world and we will make it ours. I will show you such pleasures and you will give me such power. A fair exchange, I think you'll find.*'

The waves of need rippling through her increased and she fought against them. This wasn't right. It wasn't real. 'I don't want you.'

That laugh again, sultry and determined. The very sound seemed to call her a liar and part of her was afraid she was.

'*You will,*' he whispered, and his breath played along the side of her neck. '*Shall I show you what awaits?*'

She felt his lips on her neck, his teeth in her skin. Hands caressed her, pushed her back and a weight settled over her.

She could feel him in her mind as well, whispering, cajoling, commanding her to give in, to do as he wanted, to be his...

CHAPTER 16

WREN

Wren dragged in a desperate breath and screamed.

The world around her shattered and she opened her eyes to the night, to Finn standing over her, staring at her in horror. His sword was drawn, the blade turned scarlet by the blazing fire.

She scrambled back, tangled in the blanket and her cloak.

'Wren?' he said, but he sounded shaken. 'Are you all right? Talk to me.'

The sword didn't move. It didn't even tremble. It just pointed straight at her as if she was the threat.

'What is it?' she finally managed to gasp. 'What—what are you doing?'

'Don't move,' he told her curtly. 'Whatever you do—'

A growl rippled out of the night behind her. In spite of his command, she found herself turning.

Eyes like two blue flames stood out in the darkness between the trees. Eyes, but nothing natural had eyes like that.

Slowly, Wren pushed herself back towards Finn. He wasn't trying to hurt her, he was protecting her.

'What is it?' she asked. She'd never seen anything like it in her life, not even in the depths of the darkwood.

'Shadow kin,' he whispered, the word no more than a breath. As if in response to being named, the creature growled again, the tone more threatening. Wren felt it in the depths of her chest, like a reverberation that sent her heart skittering wildly.

'But it... it has eyes...'

Shadow kin were just shadows. They could hurt the unwary, and trick people off the path. They could lure you over cliffs or into deep water. They made bargains and cheated. And sometimes... sometimes...

She thought of the men back on the road, of the darkness she had called up and what Finn had said was left behind. There hadn't been shadow kin this strong in years. Not here. Elodie wouldn't allow it.

But Elodie wasn't here.

'They do have eyes,' he told her in a calm and patient whatever-you-do-don't-panic tone. 'And teeth, and claws too no doubt. It's strong to have taken a shape. Probably to hunt us. It fed well, if you recall? How fast can you run?'

She'd managed to creep back to his legs and she wrapped her arms around one. She needed to touch him. She needed something to hold on to. Something real. 'Not fast enough.'

'You're going to have to try harder than that,' he told her. 'I can't take them all on.'

'All?' Her voice cracked and she looked around wildly. At the edge of the clearing, where the shadows between the trees were darkest, more glowing blue eyes were appearing. Surrounding them. Even if she could have found the strength to run, there was nowhere left to go.

'We're going to back up to the fire,' Finn told her in a calm and reasonable voice. A voice she desperately wanted to believe. To trust. 'Slowly, carefully.'

She could barely move, but somehow she did. The aura of pure threat emanating from the creatures made her keenly aware of her position here. Prey. She was prey, through and through. Finn was all she had to protect her. He was the one thing she could rely on here, the one thing not consumed with panic and terror. He was a rock in this waking nightmare.

'How did they find us? They're drawn to magic. I didn't... I didn't do anything.' But she had been dreaming. And in her dreams... in the dream there had been the voice in the darkness. And part of her had welcomed it. No, she pushed the thought away. 'It wasn't real.'

Her voice shook and she hated the way it sounded. She hated the way these things made her feel. In a moment the fear bled away and something else took its place.

How dare they? How dare they come here, surround them, target them? How dare these insubstantial remnants of a broken power attack her? Attack Finn?

The rush of rage took her completely by surprise. It came with something else, something dark and endless that made her eyesight sharpen.

She could see them amid the trees now, great hulking things, made of muscle and teeth. They were fierce, and hungry, but that didn't matter. The one in front tensed, recognising that she could see it now and made ready to attack. It bared its maw at her. Wren looked into the blue fire of its eyes and she felt the anger surge through her limbs.

She moved without thought, throwing herself backwards, towards the fire, just as Finn had instructed. Finn didn't move, standing between her and the monster, blade waiting even as the creature burst from cover. It was huge, dwarfing him, even though he was not a small man.

His sword whistled through the air, an arc of silver, slicing into the shadow kin and bringing it down. For a moment, elation filled her. But then another burst from his left.

He swivelled to face it, his expression grim. Even as he ducked and danced back from the sweep of its claws, Wren knew how this was going to go. Another one came from behind him, bearing down on him, even as he registered its presence and whirled around to take on both at once.

Wren's hand closed on a piece of wood jutting out of the fire. It was barely burning, only ashes and glowing embers now, but it was enough. It had to be enough.

She yanked the stick free and snarled as the darkness recoiled from her and flames burst up all along the piece of wood. She charged at the creatures, wielding it like Finn used his sword. It crashed against the nearest one and the creature screamed, the sound echoing brokenly through the night.

Finn ran another through, and turned, ready for the next.

But he missed it, somehow.

The biggest one of all, twice the size of the others, slammed into him, knocking his sword away.

And its teeth sank deep into his side.

CHAPTER 17

FINN

The pain was incredible, blinding.

Shadow kin were meant to be spun from darkness, but this was real and solid. Too much so.

Finn thought of the remains he'd found in the forest and for a moment his heart faltered. They were going to kill him. They were going to kill them both. That knowledge froze him, and a wall of agony closed around him like the jaws of the beast itself. He couldn't help the scream that burst from him, but the answering cry was worse, torn from Wren's throat, raw and desperate.

Flames engulfed the thing above him. It shied back, shock making it release him and then rear up, towering over the two of them. Wren ran at it, only a burning branch in her hands, but flames seemed to billow out ahead of her and the darkness shrieked as she approached.

Witchfire? Was that witchfire?

'Get back from him!' she yelled. 'Get back!'

And to his eternal surprise, the shadow kin obeyed. All but the one that had bitten him. It hung there, as if caught in some kind of trap.

Wren hurled the burning stick at it, still screaming, the words incoherent now. It was a strange and twisted language that he almost knew. Pain made his consciousness wash in and out like the tide as he tried to place it.

The creature shook its head as if in pain or confusion, and then fixed its maddened eyes on her. Wren just stood there, unarmed, staring up at it as if mesmerised. Her hand dropped to her side, as if suddenly realising she didn't stand a chance now.

The shadow kin's maw plummeted towards her, like a wolf intent on a rabbit.

Finn's hand closed on the sword hilt and he moved without thought, surging up in front of her, bracing himself, the blade aloft.

And the creature struck it.

Steel, hand-forged by the Maidens of the Aurum in the old days, blessed by its flames. A holy weapon created to combat shadow kin and all creatures of the Nox. A sword once blessed by the queen and still carrying that holy light inside it.

He staggered beneath the sudden weight as the beast impaled itself and then sank to his knees beneath it. It thrashed, almost taking him to the ground again, and then went still as it slid down to the hilt.

Just when he thought it would crush him, it was gone, like a twist of smoke in a breeze, drifting away.

Finn's body went out from underneath him and he hit the ground harder than he would have imagined possible. It felt more like an unseen force had slammed into his back and laid him out, swatted him like a fly for defying whatever it had planned here.

The next thing he knew, Wren was beside him, turning him onto his back, her hands frantic at his torn and bloody clothes.

'Talk to me,' she whispered. 'Please Finn, talk to me. I need to see the wound. Do you understand? Please, say something.'

He blinked back the darkness crowding in at the edges of his sight.

She was terrified and lost, and he suspected she'd just worked some kind of miracle to save the two of them. But she really was astonishingly beautiful. Long dark hair spilled about her pale face. When had it got so long? It seemed to move like it had a mind of its own.

He reached up and caught some in his hand, tangling his fingers in it, feeling the silken slide of the strands against his skin. It had been short as a boy's when he first met her. That was why he'd mistaken her for one. And now it was long and wild, beautiful. How did it grow so quickly? Was everything about her magic?

Cold air against his skin told him she'd managed to open the jerkin and had exposed his side where the shadow kin had bitten him. It felt like ice, which was a bad sign. The pain was ebbing and that was not good either. It could be shock, and that was trouble enough, but it could be poison too.

Shadow kin killed in so many ways.

'Shit,' she said, in the most unladylike manner possible. But that was Wren, he realised. She wasn't like the women of Pelias, all restraint and composure. She was passionate and determined, a half-wild thing of the forest. She spoke her mind, but surely without him she was going to get captured, or lost, or...

Mind you, he told himself, you're not doing the greatest job of protecting her, are you? And considering all he had learned, or thought he had learned, about the woman she called Elodie, the woman who was probably her mother...

But all he had ever wanted to do was protect the weak, serve the Aurum and the crown.

Him? Serving the Aurum and the crown? That was a joke. He was a fool. He would have made a terrible Paladin, even if the Aurum had ever actually awoken to receive his vow. If it had done more than lift an eyelid like a sleeping cat and then ignore him. He was clearly cursed. It had to be his bloodline. He couldn't do anything right. All he'd done so far was lead Wren even further into danger. If she hadn't stopped to help him in the first place, she would have been home with Elodie when her mother decided to burn the tower and flee. She'd be safe now.

Whereas instead…

This was all his fault.

Her hand touched the wound, and he bit back a curse at the flare of pain that engulfed his body.

'So you are still with me?' she said, trying levity to mask her fear.

'Still here.' Barely. His head swam. Was it poison? Was he shadow touched? He'd heard stories but he thought bites like this would take longer to infect the pure of heart. Or maybe he wasn't so pure. How could he be, given who he was? He was already half a shadow thing to begin with. His family had seen to that. Would it take him now? He would have thought his body could have put up a bit more of a fight. The corruption took days to claim most. Another way he had failed. It figured.

'Wren, get the knife.' He touched his throat, to one side, where the pulse was pounding erratically beneath the skin. 'Just here. One cut, and make it deep. Quickly.'

She frowned at him as if he'd lost his mind. Perhaps he had. But it was better this way. He could feel the sluggish cold running through his veins. It wouldn't take long.

'Wren,' he tried again, fixing her with his gaze so she'd know he was serious. 'Please. Before it's too late.'

She frowned, the skin around her endlessly dark eyes tightening. Something like disgust moved her mouth into a hard line. He wanted to kiss that mouth. Even now.

Light, how he wanted to kiss her. Just once for real. One last time.

'Don't you dare,' she told him. 'Don't suggest such a thing.'

For a moment he thought she meant the kiss, but he hadn't said that out loud. She meant killing him. He almost laughed.

'You're just putting me out of my misery. Like I did with the horse. You must know what it will do to me... what I could do to you...'

He didn't want to be shadow touched, to lose what tattered remains there were of his soul, to become a monster consumed from within by shadow kin. He'd turn on her, on everyone.

Finn had struggled all his life to keep as far away from the remnants of the Nox as possible. It couldn't end like this. He wouldn't let it. If she wouldn't do it, he'd find a way himself. He scrabbled at his belt, seeking his knife himself, but before he could grab it, she knocked his hand aside. The next thing he knew, she'd pinned both his arms above his head, her legs trapping his. She hung over him, a veil of black hair masking everything but her face.

'Look at me, Finn Ward. I'm not letting you kill yourself. Not for this.' She looked so fierce. That yearning filled him again, wild and irrational. He wanted her. More, he wanted her to want him. He wanted to belong to someone who looked on him the way she did.

No. That wasn't his fate. And neither was this. It couldn't be.

'Don't make me become one of them,' he snarled, trying to throw her off, but she clung to him. Either she had gained some kind of supernatural strength all of a sudden or the poison was already stealing his. He'd fade and with that his sanity would drain away. He'd be lost.

She studied his face and then gave a strangled noise of pure frustration. 'Ugh, you stupid man. Hold still.'

Before he could argue again, she pressed her free hand to his side, so warm against his skin, against the ice creeping through his blood, and she whispered something in that strange language he didn't know. But he recognised it now, so close to him, whispering against his senses. Only the Maidens of the Aurum spoke those words. But they were words of power.

Wren threw her head back as the light ripped through her, her face a mask of pain.

It shouldn't hurt, that's what they'd all been taught in Pelias. The women who channelled the magic of the Aurum in the heart of the Sacrum, its blessed maidens, claimed its touch was only pleasure. That it was like a lover, leaving them never in need of a man. That was what everyone said. The touch of such light was bliss, and those who could touch it in return were blessed.

But in Wren's face he saw only agony.

And then the light flooded him as well.

CHAPTER 18

FINN

Light seared its way through him, igniting every vein, blasting any trace of corruption from him. And it was pleasure, just as he had been told, more pleasure than he had ever experienced.

Finn gasped out Wren's name, and when he opened his eyes to see her – because he had to see her – Wren kissed him, her mouth ravenous with need. Her lips burned against his, her mouth opening to him, and he was helpless. She branded him with that kiss, claimed him. Not just his body. His mind. His soul.

She was all he could ever have wanted, or needed, all he had dreamed of. She was everything.

The pain in her face faded, leaving only need. Desire. And a wild relief. He felt it too, and it spiralled out all around them, threading through the forest.

Her mouth moved against his, her tongue caressing his, her hands still holding him down as she explored every nuance of his kiss. A soft moan escaped her, hungry and desperate, and he hardened beneath her, desperate for release. She had to feel his need, pressed so close against him, body to body. Just the sound she made went straight through him and he was hers, body and soul. He knew that much, knew it with every beat of his heart, with every stolen breath.

Finally she pulled back, leaving him lying there looking up at her, dazed, helpless and still needing. Wanting her, all she could give him, eternally.

Shame filled her face. 'I'm sorry,' she stammered. 'I had to.'

Confused and still desperate he could only manage one word. 'What?'

But before she could explain she wilted against him, slumping down. The woman who had pinned him there, as if he had no strength left at all, suddenly could have been made of shadows herself. His strength surged back through him, the light of the Aurum coursing through his veins as if he glowed from within.

He had only ever felt a brief hint of this glory, standing before the Aurum itself.

As he'd tried to give his vows the Aurum had stirred for a moment, just a brief moment of wild hope before settling back into its long sleep. The Paladins had tried to encourage him, saying it hadn't reacted to anyone else, but that really did not help. The flame still slept and the light hadn't claimed him.

Until now.

Finn pushed himself up, gathering her limp form in his arms. Her eyes fluttered open, the long lashes matted together with tears. She gazed into his face, and those same tears spilled from the corners of her eyes.

'What did you do?' he asked, but she just curled in against him, hiding her face.

He sat there, cradling her in the darkness. Her chest rose and fell, and she shuddered in his arms.

He couldn't stay here like this. He just couldn't. No matter how much he wanted to. It was madness.

Finally, she stilled. Not sleep, not exactly. Exhaustion. The effects of such magic. He didn't know. Finn settled her as close to the scattered remains of the fire as he could and bundled her up in the blankets. He couldn't keep his eyes off her, even though he should be watching the forest around him.

But all around him the natural sounds of the forest had returned, night birds and the furtive movement of nocturnal animals, everything he would expect. It told him they were safe. For now, anyway. As safe as they could be. Nothing would dare come near them again tonight. The light Wren had called into him, channelling it through herself, had burned all the darkness away. From the forest in their immediate vicinity. From him.

What had happened back there?

He checked his side as best he could in the firelight, but there was no sign of any bitemark, let alone the insidious infection he would have expected. He was whole and unharmed, his skin as smooth as it had ever been.

Shadow kin bites were at best fatal. In the worst case they could infect their victim and turn them into monsters like themselves. Servants to the ghostly presence of the Nox, which lingered on in the world, with no real will of their own.

That would have been him, if not for Wren.

But the pain he'd seen written clearly in every line of her body wasn't right either. She knew the secret words, the other-tongue that the maidens who tended the Aurum learned. He remembered hearing it in the heart of the Sacrum, when they gathered together. The statues of the chosen stood around, silent and unmoving, their faces like masks. Those magical songlike words used tried to wake the Aurum. And someone must have taught her.

The queen. It had to be the queen. Queen Aeryn of Asteroth. The one who Wren knew only as Elodie. Who else could it be to know such things?

How was he going to explain that to Roland? Come to that, how was he going to explain Wren to him? Because even an idiot like him could see it. Even if she hadn't had the locket with

Roland's likeness in it next to her own. Even if he hadn't heard the rumours about the Paladin and the lost queen.

He knew Wren had hidden the diary in her bags. He should find it and read it, discover as much as he could, so he could present a complete report when they finally reached Knightsford.

But he couldn't bring himself to do that to her.

It wasn't that he had qualms about breaking a confidence, not when the security of the kingdom was at stake. He'd been in his native Sidonia to gather information, as one of the few able to travel between the two kingdoms with any ease. While the crown prince would kill him on sight, and take every pleasure in it, not everyone felt the same way. Until Leander took the throne, Finn still operated under a measure of protection. So long as he always returned to Asteroth. So long as he never dreamed of betraying those who had raised him. Or of ever going home for good.

But he didn't even know where home was. Not really. Finn was lost between two worlds, trying to make the best of it and find his own path forward.

So why did the idea of searching for the diary in Wren's bag and reading it feel like it would be the worst kind of treachery? He didn't owe Elodie anything. He didn't owe Wren—

Except he did. Especially now. He owed her his life, his humanity, everything.

The pulse of light still ran through him, a steady beat in time with his own heart, the liquid pleasure still not entirely abated. When he looked at her exhausted face, with the long black hair coiling about it, at the delicate contours of her features and the sensual mouth he longed to kiss again, he knew he was in trouble. Deep trouble.

Finn had fancied himself in love before. There had been lovers at the court, various daughters and sons of the nobility who liked to slum it with the ward of the Grandmaster, to risk fraternising with a son of Ilanthus for whatever thrill it gave them. He'd enjoyed his time with all of them, knowing all along the reaches of the relationship and parting without much regret. But he had never felt the fierce rush of need he felt whenever Wren was near. There had never been a moment like that second when her lips met his.

Finn didn't know what to do with it. It couldn't be natural. It couldn't be right.

In Ilanthus, where his people gave themselves over willingly to hedonism in honour of their dark goddess, such feelings were celebrated. But he had not been raised in Ilanthus, and Asteroth frowned on such things. Feared them. With good reason. What would Roland say if he confessed it to him?

A spear of shame ran through him. If he confessed his feelings about Wren to the Grandmaster, he'd have more problems than that. Especially if she was who he feared she was.

He couldn't keep thinking about it, about her. Whatever this was, he needed to push it down, force it from his mind and take charge of his own body. He could never act on it again and no one could ever know.

Not Roland, and especially not Wren.

Never.

From somewhere far away, on a breeze perhaps, he thought he heard laughter.

CHAPTER 19
ROLAND

Everything brought him back to Elodie. On the long ride north from Pelias, there wasn't much else to do but ponder the past.

How could it not, when everything he did was in her service? Even now.

The regents' council still existed in the vain hope that some day some trace of their lost queen might be found, that *she* might be found. That somehow the Aurum had saved her.

Sometimes Roland wondered if she had really destroyed the Nox, or if she had been devoured by it, and felt like the worst kind of traitor for thinking those thoughts. He had seen her there, framed by shadows, bathed in firelight. His last glimpse of her…

But there were still fragments of the Nox in the world, and its cursed shadow kin were still at large. Why would they survive when she did not? Elodie had been indomitable.

Rumours sometimes circulated that she had been found. A number of pretenders had come to the royal court over the years, but they had all failed the test.

Roland had known they would the moment he set eyes on

them. He would always know Elodie. *He's mine*, she had said. And the words were prophetic. He still was. Even now.

The regents' council had not been forgiving of such pretenders.

So, Queen Aeryn of Asteroth lived on as a saint in the minds of her people. She had battled the Nox to keep it from the Aurum, turned back the darkness from the holy light, and paid with her existence. That was what he had to believe too. The alternative – that she had left him, run away to live out a life without him – was too terrible. She had never been a coward. She knew her duty better than anyone, and time and again she had met it head on, no matter what the consequences. She'd even agreed to marry Evander, even though she knew what he was and all he stood for. For the sake of the kingdom. For the vain hope of peace.

The night of the wedding still haunted him. Roland had stood guard outside the chamber, torturing himself with the knowledge that, inside the room, she gave herself to another man. Until she cried out and he couldn't stand it any longer. He'd burst through the doors like a charging bull.

The thoughts of that bastard Evander still made his stomach knot with rage. His hands around her throat, pushing her down onto her knees in front of him. The audacity of the man. She was the queen. She was... she was Roland's everything.

'*We know how to deal with witches where I'm from*,' the Ilanthian prince said. '*I know where you belong. Now do what you're good for, woman.*'

How she hadn't already killed him with all the powers at her fingertip, Roland would never know. He had wanted to snap the bastard's neck that instant. It was like he'd bound her with some kind of power, curtailed the magic flowing through her veins, leaving her helpless.

Perhaps she was just stunned, too shocked to believe what was happening until it was too late.

'*Kill me and you invite war*,' Evander had the nerve to say. Rather than face Roland like a man. He'd fallen back on his position and the very real threat his people posed to Asteroth.

Elodie had stopped him killing the prince. Only Elodie would have that power.

'*He's not worth the destruction war could bring.*'

She'd hidden the bruises the next day, but she'd never spent another night with her husband.

Evander had never forgiven either of them. The rumours had spiralled. Roland didn't care. Couldn't care. He'd vowed to keep her safe from all harm.

Roland only hoped that when his precious Nox had devoured Evander it had hurt. He hoped it still hurt. He hoped it was eternal agony.

But it didn't change the fact that Elodie was gone and the fragile peace she had tried to build with that cursed marriage, and the thing the regents' council had scraped back together in the aftermath of the war, through hostages and reparations, was already falling apart. It had brought Finnian to them. That was the only good thing.

'Grandmaster?' Anselm's voice brought Roland back to the present once more. This was no good. A terrible habit to indulge himself in at the best of times. He had crushed whatever report he was trying to read in his fist, something about troop movements in the east and a new training ground.

They had set up camp on the side of the road, his pavilion in the centre, where he was at the heart of everything.

'I brought the file on the area,' Anselm said, with his usual efficiency, opening it on Roland's field desk beside the maps he'd requested. There were new and disturbing reports from the north, witchhunters on the move on the Ilanthian side and a stirring in the Forest of Cellandre, very close to the border. It did not bode well.

'Cellandre's been still for years,' Roland said, before glancing at the papers. He unrolled the map. Much of the Forest of Cellandre was uncharted, especially in the far north where it crossed the border with Ilanthus. The roads that ran through it were known to be dangerous, but not particularly cursed. 'There's a darkwood there, an ancient one, but it's small and settled ages ago. The people in that region reported nothing out of the ordinary in the last census, did they?'

Anselm shook his head. Of course, he already knew. The boy held facts and figures in his mind like a keeper of annals. Perhaps that would be what they would make of him one day, in service of the Aurum. Their history, their memory.

'Not a thing. They're a superstitious bunch, relying on hedge witches to care for them and guide them. Paladin Dane wrote a report on the area some years ago, which I've included in the file for you.' Anselm pulled the yellowing piece of paper out, finding it unerringly in the papers. 'But, unless the Ilanthians are going after hedge witches on our side of the border now... I don't know. They never seemed that desperate. There are enough people born with access to the shadows in their own lands. Do you want to investigate it?'

The forest was the most likely route Finn would take on his way back. A less used path, away from the main trade routes. They could head up that way and wait for him. Knightsford wasn't far and Roland knew he could manage things as easily from there as anywhere else. The role of the Grandmaster of the Knights of the Aurum had never been fixed to a single location. The ability to be constantly on the move was one thing that his masters had drummed into him. They brought him with them, training him to succeed them.

Now it seemed like he would be the last Grandmaster of the order.

'Why not?' he sighed. 'We were heading for Knightsford anyway. We can strike out north from there. Give the order.' Anselm bowed and left.

Roland sorted through the papers Anselm had left, reading through the regional reports, but everything seemed to be drawing his attention back to the northern border. Ilanthus. It was always Ilanthus. Even in times of peace their most belligerent neighbour – which invariably positioned itself against everything Asteroth stood for – was a thorn in his side.

It had stolen Elodie from him, long before the Nox had finished the job.

And when his father died, Leander would take the throne of Ilanthus. He would not want peace. Not for a second. He'd loved his uncle, or as near to love as any of that line could manage. He served the Nox still, even though it was lost to them. As lost as the Aurum was to Asteroth if Roland was honest about it. Oh fragments of the Nox's power still lingered in the world, in places of shadow and darkness, like the deepest caves, the wildest forests and moonless nights. The witchkind could detect it. The crown prince had long gathered witchkind under his banner and enslaved those who would not serve willingly. Rumour had it he was already performing the sacrifices necessary to raise the Nox, seeking out anyone who could aid him.

That was what Finn had gone north to determine. He'd been adamant he could find out, and well aware of the dangers it presented to him personally. But his blood should protect him, or at least that was what he had believed.

Roland could only pray he was right.

Even so, Asteroth needed to be ready for a new war.

Roland was building up the army but, while he could train soldiers up to the standard, and create knights, they weren't yet

Paladins, nor would they ever be. Paladins needed that divine spark that only the Aurum could bestow. They needed its light flowing in their veins. And the Aurum slept on. The women who tended the flame in the Sacrum in Pelias still spoke of the moments where it seemed ready to come alive again. More out of a desperate hope, he suspected, than any real evidence. Even Finnian's vow had barely stirred it.

He was beginning to fear it would never awaken.

The road ahead looked bleak and terrible.

The last page of Dane's report caught his eye and he stared at it for a long time.

The village of Thirbridge is a tiny outpost, home mainly to loggers, hunters and a few souls scraping out a living from the soil in the shadow of the forest. The darkwood presses close and its people have been known to wander there for favours. Sightings of shadow kin in the night and suspicion of witchkind blood in the locale. Rumours of a hedge witch of great power nearby, although the precise location of her home is unclear. The inhabitants are fiercely protective of her, and will not discuss her with outsiders. She tends them, healer and midwife both, keeping the villagers safe and stopping them from straying. The woman has a child. Further investigation advised.

It was an old report. Dane had written it but Roland hadn't seen it before. Dane had died two years ago in a random skirmish near Rookwood, when his knights had stumbled on a knot of shadow kin far larger than expected.

North then. He'd intercept Finn and get his report on Ilanthus. And maybe he would carry out the investigation of the darkwood and its hedge witch that Dane had suggested after all. If his old friend had thought it worth reporting, there was always a chance.

It would lead to nothing though. It always did.

FLAVIAN'S DREAMS OF THE AURUM

In the Sacrum, they say the Aurum sleeps. Its light flickers on the white stone of the walls, and on the sentinel stones encircling it. The Aurum was born when the Old Magic was broken, twin to the Nox, eternally in opposition to that dark chaos, the embodiment of order. The eternal flame. Sleeping, silent and still. Just a flame that never goes out.

But some suspect that the Aurum still dreams. Who knows of what it dreams but the sisterhood of Maidens of the Aurum speculate.

Some say it dreams of freedom. Some say it dreams of wholeness. Some say it dreams of a child lost so long ago, or the lost part of itself. Some say it dreams of the day when the Nox is no more, or the day when its sibling power returns.

And in the cool chamber beneath the palace, some say the Aurum plots.

It is light and order. It is careful and patient.

It has been waiting for so very long.

CHAPTER 20
WREN

They rose with the dawn and set out again. Finn said nothing of the night before. It was almost like he didn't remember. Which was probably best, Wren thought, as she washed herself in the nearby stream and then set about plaiting her hair to keep it back from her face.

She ought to cut it. She knew that. But she wasn't sure what was best. When her hair was wild, she could tap into the magic around them far more easily. After last night, she needed access to that power. If the shadow kin attacked again, she would have to fight them somehow. It was a risk. She knew that. What else could she do?

She almost lost him last night.

It shouldn't matter as much as it did. But he was all that she had right now. He'd stood up to help her, to defend her and rescue her. And it had already cost him so much.

With all the mysteries surrounding her past, surrounding Elodie, and with all his suspicion regarding that, she wouldn't blame him if he had just walked away. But she realised he couldn't. He needed to know the truth of it as much as she did.

Last night she had kissed him. She'd wanted to do so much more. Every nerve in her body had screamed at her to do more.

The fires of the Aurum blazing inside her, devouring her from within, had been an agony she couldn't have described. Elodie had never prepared her for anything like that. The shadows were soft and gentle, enticing, and of course a trap. The light, however... it hurt. It burned along her veins and, the moment she released it, that relief had made her delirious with need for him.

And he'd responded. She couldn't mistake that. He'd wanted her too.

But it wasn't natural. It wasn't normal. And she knew not to trust it.

If she reached for the light, the light burned her. The pain that had come with it had been the very reason Elodie had always warned her never to use any magic lightly. Because it was too easy to be lost in it and the agony of withstanding that need was almost too much for her. But the light of the Aurum didn't hurt Elodie, did it?

Wren wanted to weep with the injustice of it. She had promised so many times to only reach for the light, but every time, every single time, it was like pouring lightning through her veins. But if she reached for the shadows... well, that was another of Elodie's rules. *Never do that. They'll devour you whole.*

How did they do it, the witches of Pelias? They channelled the power of the Aurum, used it to perform miracles, even if the Aurum itself was silent. Elodie said all they felt was pleasure. Oh they didn't call themselves witches, the servants of the Aurum, the maidens, but Elodie had always said that all the fancy titles in the world didn't hide what they were. Witchkind were witchkind. They were meant to be free. But those women gave up their freedom for the kingdom, while the men either surrendered their magic entirely, or went into exile. Elodie had been scathing of their restraint and control, as if she didn't believe for a second that they really exercised anything of the kind. Wren had always thought she was being unkind, or maybe bitter that she wasn't part of such an illustrious company. She had clearly chosen exile herself.

Now she feared it was something else entirely.

Wren bit at her lower lip until the flash of pain brought her to ground again. No more magic. Not unless absolutely necessary. No light, no shadows. Nothing.

She had to stay in control.

But they were being hunted through the forest. By the Ilanthians, by the shadow kin, by who knew what else. She needed a way to defend them both, and last night had proved that more keenly than she could have guessed.

She could have lost him.

It shouldn't matter. Finn wasn't hers. He was sworn to the Knights of the Aurum. Elodie would order her as far away from him as possible.

Don't trust anyone.

But she did trust him. And she had a clawing feeling that she couldn't help herself when it came to him. Like they were somehow tied together. And whatever she had done last night to save him had only made it worse.

She longed to reach out and touch him, to entwine her fingers with his. To pull him close, body to body. To drag his mouth down to hers and kiss him until neither of them had breath left in them.

Elodie had always been clear. Magic – of any kind – was not to be conjured lightly. It had a cost, a price, and it took payment without warning or compunction. It changed things, people, emotions, needs. It was dangerous. The words of othertongue were only to be used when all else failed. They reached out to the powers beneath the surface of the world, the powers that resolved ultimately into the Aurum and the

Nox. Both might be dormant now, as conscious things, but their echoes and memories lingered in the world. Fragments of the Nox still wandered the world, working ill. And in Pelias, the Aurum slept on. Magic had a way of making its own will known, dark or light. People thought witches manipulated magic either way, but it was often the other way around. And if a witch lost herself in such power... terrible things could happen.

Elodie had never elaborated on what those terrible things might be, but after last night Wren could guess. If Finn had not been there...

That power had filled her almost to breaking point. She'd felt herself teetering on the edge. Anything she wanted could be hers, if she listened to the song in the darkest places of the shadows, if she let it in. She could be strong, safe, loved... if she just gave in.

He could be hers.

Just like the voice in her dreams had promised.

And she almost had, she realised. For Finn. To save him. To make him hers. She couldn't say what had stopped her. Perhaps just Finn, the way he had looked at her.

She couldn't do that to him.

As they continued to walk in silence, Wren turned the events over and over, tried to examine the feelings running riot inside her. But she kept coming back to the feeling of his body against hers, his kiss, the blind and all-consuming need she had felt. And still felt.

It was not as strong, but each time she so much as glanced his way, she felt it. A hunger. A want.

It wasn't right. She shouldn't be feeling this. He'd been hurt and in danger, and she had taken advantage of that. But she'd felt him respond.

They ought to talk about it, but she was not brave enough to bring it up.

Sometime after midday Finnian called a stop. They ate meagre rations in silence.

'I'll check out the path ahead,' he said abruptly. 'We must be nearly at the southern road. I want to make sure there are no surprises awaiting us.'

Surprises, like witchhunters, Wren supposed.

Part of her wanted to argue that it was too dangerous to split up, that they ought to stay together, but she no longer had the energy. Everything hurt and the constant guilt inside her made her miserable. So she just nodded.

'Stay here and stay hidden,' he told her. 'I'll be back as soon as I can.' He made to leave but glanced back at her, his eyes filled with something she couldn't define. Like he didn't want to leave her here. Like it might be the last time he looked on her. The thought sent a pang of alarm through her.

'Finnian,' she said. 'Please, Finn... take care.'

He hesitated, and his lips parted in surprise. Perhaps he meant to say something in reply but then thought better of it. Instead, he offered her a bow and then he was gone.

Sitting alone in the clearing, Wren closed her eyes, listening to the forest around her. All was good. The birds sang, and the leaves whispered their own songs. No danger then. No threats. She was deep in the greenwood and nothing could harm her here. It would warn her, if danger threatened. She just had to wait.

But the moment she let her mind relax, she could feel the insidious touch of the man from her dreams. His voice whispered in her ear, the voice of the darkness, promising such things. Ghostly lips trailed down the side of her throat, teasing the sensitive skin there.

Let go, little one...

Wren's eyes shot open, but there was no one near her. The world around was still undisturbed. Shadow kin couldn't come at her in daylight, and the fragments tangled in the shadows beneath the trees were too weak to do any harm.

What had she just heard?

She had to do something, something to keep her mind occupied and her magic-hungry body under control. Then she remembered the diary. She dug it out of her pack and held it in her shaking hands. Were there answers in here? There had to be. Or could Elodie use it to make contact with her again? That was a hope, albeit a desperate one. She didn't want to share it with Finn, as the words inside belonged to Elodie and he had enough suspicions about her already. A queen. Really.

And yet, she could half believe it. Elodie had often acted as if everyone needed to jump at her command. Wren knew that better than anyone.

The lost queen of Asteroth was a legend. Queen Aeryn had died fighting the Nox and it suited the regents' council to pretend she still lived in order to maintain power. A romantic story that didn't hold up to reality.

Elodie didn't like to talk about history, but the story was well known. Wren had heard it many times in Thirbridge. They'd never linked it to the hedge witch, but that was hardly surprising.

Here, in her hands, there might be some answers. If not about the fate of the lost queen, then about where Elodie herself had come from. It felt like an invasion of privacy, but Wren didn't know what else to do. It wasn't like she could ask permission.

Opening the soft leather cover, she began to read.

Elodie's writing looped gently over the paper, and Wren

was put in mind of her voice, of the way she told stories, especially when Wren had been small. When storms had raged outside and rain slammed against the shutters, when Elodie had snuggled her close and told her there was nothing to fear.

She could almost imagine she could feel Elodie's arms around her now.

Music came through the trees, the lullaby she had been hearing in the quiet moments, deep in the woods and their dark shadows. Such a soft and gentle sound. It lulled her to the edge of sleep. It seemed like so long since she had actually rested. If she just closed her eyes, and listened to that song, and let it take her—

A branch broke in the thick undergrowth behind her. She stood to her feet, scanning the treeline, looking desperately for Finn, hoping it was just him. But Finn moved noiselessly, and whoever this was did not. They tried, but they were not as stealthy as he was. She could hear them, coming closer.

Heart thundering, she waited, trying to ascertain the threat. Then, in one horrible instant, she saw them through the trees. And they saw her.

With a shout, men in the garb of Ilanthian soldiers burst from the trees, coming towards her. Wren bolted in the other direction, heedless of where it might lead. She only had the book and the locket, all the packs abandoned at their makeshift camp. She only had an idea of which way Finn had headed, but she knew she was running in the opposite direction now. But all she could do was run, scrambling over fallen trees and moss-covered rocks, stumbling through a shallow stream then up into a gully. It angled down the hillside, sheer rock hemming her in on either side.

This was a disaster. What had she been thinking? She didn't even know where she was going and the sound of pursuit was close behind. She could hear men shouting to each other, as well as horses and dogs. They were close, too close, and she had no way out.

At the end of the gully, a sheer rock face rose before her.

She turned around, hoping, praying for the time to dart back out into the forest itself. But the way was blocked already by the Ilanthians. They advanced slowly, lazily, eyeing her like a pack of dogs with a fox at bay, and she backed up until the rock pressed hard against her back.

There had to be a way out. There had to be.

The insidious whisper that ran through the back of her mind was hardly a surprise. She reached out to it and it answered, the touch of magic dark and enticing. It wound its way through her and this time she welcomed it, clung to it like a lifeline in a storm. A song, a murmur, a promise. The music of the shadows called to her. This kind of magic didn't hurt her, would never hurt her...

She had no choice. She had to keep her wits about her. She wasn't trying to drive away shadow kin this time, or heal their poison. Her enemies now were just men. And she could use the shadows to deal with men.

The othertongue danced on the tip of her tongue and instead of light she found the deepest shadows of the gully and called to them. They stirred lazily at first, and then awakened, coiling up around her like serpents ready to strike.

The men stilled, their eagerness draining away to rising fear. She could smell it on them, putrid with sweat. Good, this was good. They wanted her to be small and afraid. And now their situations were reversed. Her hair rippled around her as if moved by a breeze and her strength grew like a wave.

All she had to do was reach out, seize the shades uncoiled and ready, and the shadow kin would come when she called them. They would tear this sorry pack of hunters to pieces and she would watch. She would revel in it. She would make them sorry. Every last one of them.

And when she was done… when she was…

She closed her eyes.

There was a voice behind the darkness calling to her. Endless and dark and pulling her in like a vortex, swallowing her down. She struggled against it, this new horror suddenly making her aware of how close to the edge she stood.

'Don't fight it,' said a familiar voice. It shouldn't be familiar. She had heard it only in her dreams and it chilled her as much as it set a fire in her veins. But she knew it. Her whole body reacted to it instantly and her eyes snapped open, vision returning in a blinding flash of light. He stepped through the gap made by his men, tall and slender, dressed in a long surcoat of the finest leather tooled with patterns of silver. Beneath it, his mail shimmered like water in sunlight. His long, white-blond hair caught the last glimmering of sunlight in this dark place, illuminating him. And his face…

His face was beautiful. Not just handsome. So much more than that. It could have been carved from marble by the finest craftsman, high cheekbones, eyes the shape of almonds, a strong jaw and a mouth that twisted in a triumphant smile. His silvery grey gaze seemed to laugh at her and Wren felt the power in the shadows all around her purr at his approach. She released her hold, her rage draining out of her with the sight of him, leaving behind only the bitter aftertaste of fear.

Crown Prince Leander of Ilanthus – that was what Finn had called him. But she knew him. The scent of him, the feeling of his touch, his breath against her skin.

The man from her nightmares smiled wolfishly. 'Well, little bird, that was quite the chase, wasn't it?'

CHAPTER 21

WREN

Leander approached slowly, as if Wren was no more than a frightened animal to be tamed and won over. All around her the shadows seemed to bend back, slipping her grasp and letting him close in on her. The song went silent, escaping out of her grasp with a laugh. The traitor.

'What—what have you done?' she gasped, still trying to form some kind of rudimentary defence. There wasn't enough light here, not for her purposes, and by reaching for its antithesis, she'd lost the chance to use what there was. Elodie could have worked a wonder, she knew that, but Elodie wasn't here. All she had was a feeble excuse for magic that was failing her when she needed it most.

'Nothing, my little bird. But we are not enemies, you and I. You know who I am.'

She shook her head, even though it was a lie. She knew. She just didn't want it to be true. She didn't want them to take her back to Ilanthus to whatever dark fate awaited her there. But she couldn't seem to move and there was nowhere to go anyway, no escape possible.

He drew closer, his hand extended to her. 'Wren?' he asked. 'That's your name, isn't it?'

'How do you know that?' she snarled at him, and behind her some of the shades made a vain attempt to stir again. Her hair rippled with a breeze in the otherwise still air, its dark length moving like a living thing.

For a moment his pale gaze flickered to it in interest, studying its movement. And his smile grew a little softer.

'I know you from my dreams, my sweet little bird. Let us start afresh. I will not harm you. I will not touch you unless you wish it. But we have a place for you, a throne, if you will have it. We've been waiting for you for so long. And we have searched for so many years for you. You are a wonder to us, a treasure. You are everything we have been waiting for.'

She stared at him, unable to detect anything in his face that was a threat. And yet somehow everything was. It had to be. Her hand still gripped convulsively on the diary. There could be answers in there. She would never know.

'You searched for me?'

'You were stolen from us.' He sighed and shook his head so gracefully. 'There's so much I need to explain. Please, come with me. Let us talk. If you still wish to leave after I answer your many questions, that is your decision. I promise.'

She frowned, trying to work out whether she could trust him. Elodie would have said no, she knew that. So would Finn. But Elodie had told her not to trust the knights either, and there was no doubt that Finn was allied to them. She wrapped her arms around her chest, lifting her gaze to Leander's face again.

'I promise,' he said again. 'On my life. You are free to go, on my word. But please—you're tired, you're hungry, and we know the terrors you've been through, the dangers, the harsh treatment. I can help, Wren. Come with me now and let me help you.'

There was no way out of this. It was either agree and leave

with him peaceably, or be dragged off kicking and screaming. She wasn't under any illusions there. But no one had rushed her yet. Not one grabbed her or carried her off. Yet.

'You'll let me go.'

He nodded and his eyes carried traces of amusement. 'Of course.' His voice was the gentlest breeze against her senses, soothing and calming. It still felt like a trap.

What choice did she have really? She was already trapped. But he was offering her a modicum of dignity and there was, at least, that. One final thing to cling to. Let him have his way now and find her escape later if needs be. It was a logical decision.

Wren nodded and reached out to take his hand.

His touch was surprisingly gentle, not what she had expected at all. His fingers curled around hers, the touch careful and delicate, and he gave a small sigh, a sound that speared its way inside her, reawakening that blossoming pleasure she had felt with Finn. She almost snatched her arm back, but something stopped her.

Wren had expected to be seized and bound. But he wasn't doing that. What was he planning?

His soldiers parted as they walked through their ranks, and beyond the gully she saw horses awaiting. She could hear the music again, drifting through the trees, just a whisper now, trying to reassure her. Her throat tightened. He could carry her off here and now and no one would ever know. If she mounted up behind him, who would stop him if he decided to ride all the way back to the border?

Where was Finn? He ought to have been back by now. Had they found him in the forest and killed him? Or would he return to find her gone and think she'd left willingly?

And wasn't that what she was doing?

She imagined Elodie's face, the horror and rage, the disappointment. Oh that would be the worst. Not Elodie angry – a terrible enough prospect – but the sense that Wren was letting her down.

Trembling, Wren hesitated and Leander stopped, waiting so patiently.

'There's nothing to fear, I swear on my honour and my life, my lady.'

'I'm not... not a lady...' And definitely not his.

His laugh was musical. 'Of course you are. Or should be. Who has failed to treat you as you deserve?' As he approached his mount she pulled back again and Leander paused. 'If you would rather walk, we can do that? It isn't far to our camp.'

Good. That was better. She could trust her own two feet, couldn't she? And if she had to make a break for it, she would be in control. If Finn came back, they would stand more of a chance if she wasn't on horseback with the prince. She doubted he'd hand her a mount of her own. Besides, she didn't know what to do except hang on, which wasn't going to be helpful.

The camp wasn't far, which meant Finn might still find her.

Keep walking, she told herself. Keep your wits about you.

But... Leander promised answers. And she had so many questions. Questions Finn had been intent on avoiding, questions Elodie had never allowed her to ask...

'I would prefer to walk,' she told him as calmly as she could, amazed at how firm her voice sounded.

'Then we shall walk, my lady,' he replied and smiled that unnerving smile again. He still held her hand, but now he folded it over his arm and they made their way through the forest as if he was escorting her to a ball.

CHAPTER 22

WREN

The camp was pitched in the middle of a wide clearing. Some of the tents were utilitarian and a dark mottled green in colour, but in the centre was a tall pavilion of silks and leather, decorated with gold trimmings.

Leander threw back the door and led her inside. It was like stepping into a palatial chamber, with rugs underfoot and tapestries decorating the walls. It was as large as any of the rooms in the tower and had a luxurious air, which made Wren instantly on edge.

It was beautiful in the way he was beautiful. There was something otherworldly about it, which made her uncomfortable. It was too beautiful and she feared if she looked beneath the surface there would be a reason for that. A dark and terrible reason.

'First things first,' he said with cheerful confidence. 'Some food? Or would you rather bathe? We can replace your clothes, something more befitting your position, if you like?'

'My clothes?' True, they were caked in dirt and blood. She'd been wearing them for days since they fled Thirbridge. What must she look like to him? He was a prince.

Finn hadn't cared, a stray thought reminded her. Finn hadn't said a word. He'd been there with her, every step of the way.

Where was he? She didn't want to ask if they'd found him, captured him or, worse, killed him. She also didn't want to alert them to his presence in the forest, though she doubted they were unaware of it. To bring him up now felt like a betrayal and she couldn't do that.

'My dear Wren, I only want you to be comfortable. Come, a bath first and then food, and we'll talk, you and I, about everything.'

A bath meant undressing, meant making herself vulnerable. She couldn't do that. He must have read her doubt on her features. Lifting his hands, he took a step back, the picture of a man who wouldn't think of doing her harm.

'I'll leave the pavilion. No one will disturb you. You have my word, my lady. Let me do this one thing for your comfort.'

She wasn't sure why she agreed but the words came out anyway. 'All—all right...'

The moment she said it, he turned away, making his way back to the door and barking out a string of commands. The pavilion was alive with people carrying water, oils, perfumes and soaps, preparing a corner where a large copper bath was filled and made ready for her. Leander stood beside her, watching every detail, occasionally correcting something or suggesting an alternative. He did so gently, politely and with respect to those who were his servants.

Again, not what she expected from a prince of Ilanthus.

When everything was ready he dismissed them all and turned to her. 'Take your time. No one will disturb you. I'll have their heads if they dare.' Was he joking? He said it with a smile, but there was a hint of something else beneath the words, a threat, made of the sharpest steel. 'When you're ready, I will be outside, waiting for you. Just call.'

But before he left, he lifted her hand to his lips and kissed her fingers.

As if she was a lady indeed. It made her skin tingle unexpectedly and all the same she fought not to snatch her hand back. Part of her didn't want to.

And then she was alone.

Trying to calm her breath, Wren hugged the book to her chest and looked around her again. It was clearly his pavilion. Who else could command such luxury? There was a divan strewn with silks, throws and furs. Heavy curtains hung in front of the bath on one side, and a huge bed on the other. She stared at that for longer than she should have and the image of him sprawled loose-limbed in those sheets sprang to her mind, far too clearly. She retreated hastily.

The edges of the pavilion were pinned down but she could see gaps. Outside people moved back and forth. She could hear voices rising and falling, no sense of excitement or panic. Just conversation, like they were wandering down a village street. But too many people to just sneak out that way.

Wren tried to weigh up her options. Exhaustion made her mind dull and her body ache. And oh, the temptation to just be clean again was strong. She didn't have to take a long time.

It seemed such a shame to waste such an indulgence. Elodie had always abhorred waste, hadn't she?

Elodie was going to kill her. So was Finn.

But she could either sit here in misery or she could take what was offered.

Wren stripped off, piling her clothes and the book carefully within reach of the bath, and sank into the warm and fragrant waters.

The effect was intoxicating. She knew this was stupid, and probably naïve, but suddenly she couldn't bring herself to care. Everything had been awful for days and she was covered in filth. Her hair was matted and overlong, coming down to the small of her back. She worked it clean as quickly as she could, ignoring the dirt in the water. The soap was rich and lathered beautifully. Once she'd ducked herself under the surface a few times she couldn't remember a time she felt so clean.

She surfaced the last time, blinking water from her eyes, pushing her black hair away from her face. It was like magic, the bath easing all her aching muscles.

'Well you aren't exactly in mortal peril, are you?' Finn's voice sounded almost amused, except for the bitter defeat that permeated it. He stood almost at the foot of the bath, his hands folded behind his back. Behind him the half-drawn curtain hung at an odd angle, as if hooked back, framing him there. He gazed out over her head, a stoic expression on his handsome face, as if he couldn't bear to make eye contact. 'Do you want me to come back for you after you've finished?'

'Finn? What are you—what are you doing here?' she spluttered, went to reach for her clothes but then realised how much of herself she'd expose and shrank back down. Her heart surged in her chest. He had come back for her, come to rescue her. The towels were closer. She scrabbled for one of them, trying to make her arm stretch further than it would. 'How did you get in here?'

He gave a snort of bitter laughter and she winced. She didn't know him. She didn't know anything about him. This might have all been some kind of elaborate ruse and she was being unbearably stupid while they laughed at her behind her back.

But before Finn could give an actual answer, something slammed into the small of his back, sending him to his knees before her. Wren surged up, splashing water everywhere, and grabbed one of the large towels left beside the tub. She wrapped herself in it as she quickly stepped out onto the rug, dripping wet.

Leander stood there, sword in hand. Finn's sword, she

realised. And Finn's hands weren't just folded behind his back, they were securely tied. He caught himself jerkily as he went down, so he didn't land on his face, and looked up at her. Blood was matting the hair on one side of his head, and his mouth looked swollen and raw, as if the whole side of his face would blossom into bruises soon.

Wren looked from him to the prince, panic making her heart pound so hard she was sure they could hear it even from there. 'Please, don't hurt him.'

Leander kicked Finn between the shoulders and he went down, face first, onto the floor at the prince's feet. Air burst from his lungs in a soft grunt and he closed his eyes, defeated.

'Hurt him? Oh my dear, you have no idea what I'm going to do with this traitor. I've been waiting for years to deal with my little half-blood brother.'

CHAPTER 23

FINN

His brother was waiting for him. Because of course he was. Leander was no fool. That was Finn's role in all of this, wasn't it? It always had been.

Finn could handle the beating, and the humiliation. He expected it. Like he expected Leander to gloat, because that was one of the things he was best at. That had always been true as well.

What he hadn't expected was to find Wren naked in a bath. Perhaps he should have. Leander wasn't one to wait around but he'd want her clean and calm, a little bit pampered and compliant. The scent in the water would probably relax her, perhaps naturally, perhaps by design. He wasn't above using drugs.

Finn didn't expect her to rush to his aid when Leander kicked him to the floor and held his own sword on him. But she did. Vulnerable, naked save for the towel. But defiant.

'Please,' she gasped. And then, as if she only now realised the severity of the situation, she added: ' Don't hurt him.'

Leander of course was all threat and snide superiority but Finn barely heard him. Until he said the word brother. Her eyes went wide and fixed on his.

So much to explain. She'd never understand.

But she straightened up like a queen, her head held high despite the towel and her long wet hair. She might have been a sculpture of the chosen of the Aurum, forever watching in the circle of the Sacrum, bathed in its flames. Or perhaps one of the white standing stones surrounding it. Unbreakable.

'If you want me to hear you out as you said, you leave him alone. If you hurt him, I'm not going to listen to a word you say.'

As threats went, it was pretty terrible, but the way she delivered it went a long way to making it believable. To Finn's surprise, Leander gave a regretful laugh, and shook his head, but his voice gentled.

'If you knew what you were asking, Wren...'

Then he stepped back, and, as Finn rolled over onto his back, he saw Leander toss the sword onto the bed like it was some kind of child's toy. He turned away to issue orders to his people, like Finn was no threat at all.

Which given he was bound and on the ground, beaten half to death, he wasn't.

'Finn?' she whispered. 'Are you... are you all right?'

'You might want to put some clothes on,' he told her, aware of the harshness in his voice. He couldn't help it. He was here because of her and she'd been happily wallowing in fragrant waters.

But, by the light, he had never been so relieved as when he had seen she was unharmed.

Wren cast him a frustrated look, but it was Leander who spoke, his voice smooth and practised. He addressed Wren as if they were old friends. 'Here, Wren, take this. Ignore him. He has no manners.'

He held out a long silken robe, a swirling pattern of blues decorating the fabric. There was fur trim on the neck and around the hems. It must have cost a fortune. Leander walked past Finn as if he was part of the rug on which he lay and brought the garment to her, holding it out so she could turn her back to him, let the towel fall and slip into it while maintaining something like her privacy. It was a shockingly intimate moment and Finn felt his eyes burn with unexpected rage at the thought.

While she secured the robe, his brother cast a glance down at him and smirked again. He knew exactly what he was doing. Charming her. Being the prince, the suitor, the nobleman, while Finn... Finn was the soldier, the traitor, the thing lying in the dirt.

She didn't see it. Didn't notice. How could she? She'd been raised in a bloody forest with only her mother for company.

And now a prince showered her with luxuries, spoke to her like an equal and a treasured companion, and no doubt made her feel like a queen.

Finn's stomach twisted. All he'd done was shout at her, more or less. Ordered her about. She'd saved his life and he'd left her to be snared in Leander's trap. The fact he'd joined her only a little later was not much of a consolation.

He should have just gone to Knightsford and raised the alarm. She would have been fine. She was fine. She was...

Wren crouched down beside him and helped him sit. Her hands were unbearably gentle as she untied his. She gingerly inspected the blow to the head, which had taken him so very much by surprise. He flinched back, then rubbed his wrists.

'Don't—' he began.

'Shut up and let me examine you.' It was a tone not to be argued with. He'd bet she learned that one from Elodie. It was all hedge witch and healer. Comply, it said, or else. The finest drill sergeant in the land could not do better. She fetched a cloth dampened with warm water and carefully cleaned his face, her eyes never leaving his. He watched her chew on her lower lip as she worked. So he sat there, submitting to it, because what choice did he have?

It was almost a torture. He wanted nothing more than to lean into her touch, but Leander would see, and he would know, and what fresh tortures would come from that?

He couldn't find the strength to tell her that it didn't matter what she did to help him now. Leander would kill him anyway. That had been his brother's plan in following him. Their father was growing old and infirm. It was only a matter of time before Leander became king and he wanted no other sons of Sidon left when he did. It was their way, succession by fratricide.

They could dump his body in the forest and deny all knowledge. Even to her.

He had the feeling she'd refuse to believe him.

Or maybe... maybe she wouldn't. She didn't look so very sure of anything right now. And Wren wasn't an idiot.

All the time he was aware of Leander watching them, making his many calculations, scheming, looking for anything he could use.

Wren leaned in closer, her lips inadvertently brushing his ear, sending a shiver through him in spite of the situation. Her breath played on the sensitive skin of his neck and he closed his eyes, trying to block it out. This was not the time. There never would be a time, not now.

'Trust me,' she whispered. And he wanted to. Dear light, he wanted to.

Wren looked up, over his head, and fixed her gaze unerringly on his brother. 'What do you plan to do with us?' she asked.

Leander sprawled on the divan and someone had poured him a glass of wine. There was always a servant somewhere, or a spy. Someone in the background, protecting him, serving him, fulfilling his every whim. They were very good at not being seen. He drank half of his goblet's contents in one go and smiled, wine making his lips red as blood.

Holy light, Finn hated that smile. Though he had been

raised in Asteroth, his father King Alessander had wanted assurances of his health and education. Every so often he had been brought back to Sidonia to join the court full of vipers like Leander. There had never been word of his mother, whoever she was. The king found it amusing to set them all against each other. Even ancient as he was Alessander was cruel. Finn had learned that early on. And Leander took after him in every way.

Each time he could not have got back to Pelias quickly enough. Roland had always said it was his duty, but that didn't help. Being able to bring back information to the knights had been a comfort though. He hated Sidonia, and Ilanthus.

'What do I plan to do with you?' Leander repeated in a lazy drawl, almost as if he was mocking her. Perhaps he was. He just wouldn't want Wren to know that yet. But Finn knew. 'That's an excellent question. It all depends.'

'On what?'

The smile widened like the mouth of a shark. 'On you, my lady.'

CHAPTER 24
FINN

A slight tremor passed through Wren's hand where it still pressed to Finn's face. She pulled it away, clearly trying to hide her fear from him. But he knew. And understood. Wren knew how serious this was and that should not have been the comfort it was.

'What does that mean?'

She was going to make Leander say it? And why not? Make the bastard admit to what he wanted from her. Make him say it out loud. Finn just didn't want to be there to hear it. He didn't want to see her face when she realised she had no choice but to give in to him. Leander was a prince of the blood royal of Sidon. He took what he wanted.

Finn wanted to throw up at the thought.

'Come here,' said the crown prince. And it was definitely the real prince now, with that tone of voice. No doubting that. The charm was gone. 'And you,' he snapped, the command undoubtedly directed at Finn. 'You can stay right there. On your knees. If you move, you die.'

'Wren,' Finn whispered. 'Don't. You don't have to. Not for me.'

'Then for herself,' Leander interrupted. 'Or don't you want her to know the truth about who she is and what she may be capable of? Determined to keep that secret to yourself until you hand her over to your precious Grandmaster, no doubt. Now shut up or I'll gag you myself.'

Wren's eyes flashed with anger and she squeezed Finn's shoulder. It shouldn't have been comforting, not here, not now, but it sent a ripple of something through him. Something like resolve. Or encouragement.

'If I cooperate with you, you let him go.'

Leander shook his head. 'Impossible. He's family. And a traitor. He's been feeding information back to his precious Grandmaster for years. My father should have let me cut his throat when he first came back. There are laws to deal with spies.'

The set of her jaw changed subtly and Finn realised Leander had made a mistake, even if his brother didn't. 'Your laws don't work here, do they? You aren't in Ilanthus.'

Like that mattered to Leander. But she was right. He had no place on Asterothian soil. If the knights found him here, he'd be in deep shit. If he was captured, held for ransom, their father would do anything to protect him. Or at least that was what Leander believed. Finn wasn't so sure.

Alessander didn't bend until forced to break.

There was so much Finn was going to have to explain to her about his family. His brother. He should have done it already. Now Leander would twist everything and he'd never be able to untangle it for her.

Finn lowered his gaze to the floor and desperately tried to figure out a way to get the two of them out of this without dying, or causing an international incident that could plunge both kingdoms into a war again.

Maybe Wren realised it too. A subtle change seemed to

shimmer over her. Not magic. Not exactly. Something else. All he could do was stare.

Slowly Wren rose and crossed the pavilion floor, barefoot, the silken robe whispering about her body. Scent from the costly oils in the bathwater trailed behind her, lingering around him, reminding him of exactly what was walking away right now, of what he might lose forever.

The ache in his body was almost a physical pain. He had to watch her. He had to look up and see. He couldn't take his eyes off her. Everything about her was magical. If he had any lingering doubts about her, they vanished now. She didn't just have control of magic. She was magic. She lived and breathed it.

'Your hands,' said Leander and she held them out, palms up. He took them in his, long fingers wrapping around hers. 'Close your eyes and let me into your mind.'

'No,' Finn said, before he could think better of it, and his brother glared at him.

And just like that his game was over. The prince was bored. He'd had enough and Finn was breaking his stupid rules.

'Guards,' he barked. Wren jerked back, but he didn't let her go. He held her in a grip like iron as two of his guards entered the pavilion. He nodded at Finn. 'If he so much as sighs, cut his tongue out.' Leander's men surrounded him in an instant.

'No! Don't you dare hurt him!' Wren tried to yank herself free but Leander just laughed and pulled her down on top of him. She struggled in his arms and Finn found himself rising before he knew what he was doing. The need to protect her took over.

The blow to his stomach took the wind right out of him. They didn't hold back. Why would they? The more damage they did to him the better Leander would like it. They all knew that.

Then Wren opened her mouth and screamed, a high and

piercing sound that made him lose his mind. There was no other word for the sea of rage that crashed down on him.

Something seized him, inside and out, a light so bright it blinded him, burning through him like a firestorm. The same power as the night before, that blazing light of the Aurum she had poured into him to save him. And now it reacted to save her.

His body moved without thought, without reason. He tasted blood, felt his hands tearing through meat and howled with the need to kill. The two guards didn't stand a chance and he didn't care. He'd never hesitated to do whatever was necessary if the need presented itself, but he had always felt a sense of regret that it had been necessary. Human life was not to be wasted, or discarded. But this was different. This was a primal drive coming from deep in the back of his brain, rising from the pit of his stomach. It could not be ignored.

Wren needed him, and he had to protect her.

Light pumped through his body with his blood, fired with every breath. There were more guards coming, more than he could normally hope to defeat, but he didn't care. He hurled himself at them and took them down.

'Finn!' Wren cried out. The horror in her voice was the only thing that could have stopped him.

He was hers. He knew it better than he knew his own name. Hers. Her creature. Now and forever.

Leander was on his feet, holding her like a shield against his body, a knife pressed to her throat, so close the tip already drew blood. His brother was pale and the trembling in his hand might have been rage. But Finn doubted it.

'What have you done?' the prince hissed at her. 'What have you done to him?'

'Don't hurt him,' she whispered and her voice sounded broken, afraid of what he had become.

Hurt him? As if that was possible. Nothing could hurt him right now.

He was the wild animal, the hunter, and the forest itself. He was death waiting in the darkness. He was a firestorm.

Leander had given up pretending. 'Then tell him to stand down, bitch. Or this will end here and now. I'd hate to have to hurt you, but rein him in or things will get very unpleasant very fast.'

If he hurt her, Finn would tear him to shreds.

He felt the growl inside him building, rising, felt a desperate hunger, the need to kill anything that threatened her.

'Finn,' she whispered and her eyes were heartbreak itself. 'I-I'm sorry.'

She had done this to him, made him strong, made him wild, and he didn't regret it for an instant.

He burned for her. Only for her.

Finn hesitated. Why was she sorry?

A wall of Ilanthian guards slammed into him from behind, bringing him to the floor and into oblivion.

CHAPTER 25

WREN

Leander's body pressed hard against hers and the knife was a burning line against her skin. The trickle of blood crept lower and she trembled, hating herself.

Whatever Wren had done to Finn transformed him into a wild thing triggered by her scream, killing and maiming with an unholy speed, his eyes burning with blue fire, leaving her sick and shaking. She didn't know what she'd done or how, only that it must have come from her.

Just like the light that had healed him last night. Maybe part of that. She had changed him. Made him hers.

What kind of beast had she made of him?

The guards finally secured him and dragged him outside. Leander shoved her forward with his whole body, still holding the knife at her throat. His other arm encircled her chest, pinning her arms to her side as they stepped out into the encampment.

'Don't get any ideas,' he told her, in a voice that wasn't as firm as he tried to make it sound. She could smell his fear and, despite her predicament, it sent a thrill of vengeance through her.

His charm was gone now, that thin veneer of civility. It had all been an act. She'd been a fool to be taken in but there was nothing she could do about that now.

'What are you going to do?'

'I'm going to kill him. Like I should have done the moment I saw his sorry face. I thought to help you, show you the truth, to teach you. But it's going to have to be a different lesson, isn't it?'

She wanted to threaten him, to find some way out, but there was nothing. He knew Finn was her weakness now.

'I'll do what you want. Please, just... just leave him alone. I'll make him behave. I'll find a way.' She didn't know how she'd do that, but she had to try. She couldn't let him kill Finn.

'Too late, princess. There's nothing left of him there to control. Don't you see that?'

Manacles snapped closed around Finn's wrists and suddenly the strength seemed to go out of him. The metal glowed with an unearthly nimbus, as if she'd been staring into the sun and looked away, a sort of half-light glow. It was black and blue, and it burned. Finn bit back a scream, but the pain on his face was self-evident.

'That'll hold him long enough,' Leander said and released Wren. She staggered forward and fell to her knees in the dirt, staring at Finn, unable to tear her gaze away.

'Never seen that before, have you? Shadow-wrought, blessed by the Nox herself ages past. It negates the power you put in him. Now do as you're told or I'll put them on you as well. I'm told it's like ice, so cold it burns. Leave it on too long and it'll kill you. But you'd lose your mind first. Probably best you don't find out just yet.' Leander stalked towards Finn. Though never getting too near, she noticed.

Finn snarled at him, his body shaking with agony, his eyes narrowed to slits.

'Give me a sword. I want to do this myself.' The weapon handed to Leander was huge, the type of thing to be wielded with both hands. He lifted it with ease, swirling it before him without any apparent effort. His confidence oozed back through him and he grinned at her. 'I'll deal with this and then I'll be back to you. Don't go anywhere, little one. We're just getting started with your lessons.'

This couldn't be happening.

She fixed her gaze on Finn's face, his features taut with agony, his blazing eyes blind with it. He bared his teeth at the crown prince of Ilanthus. He knew what was happening. He knew he was going to die and there was nothing he could do. Somewhere within the feral creature she had made of him, he was still there. And he knew. His gaze latched back on to hers.

The force of the look struck her like a physical blow. Need, desperation, hunger, everything all wrapped up in one. It was as if a wild animal gazed at her from his eyes, but one who would do anything for her, who needed her more than he needed life itself.

Leander raised the sword. It glinted in the light of the setting sun, casting a long black shadow on the ground between them.

Wren's breath caught in her throat.

The shadow was stretching out towards her, darkening, and somewhere she heard the singing that haunted her nightmares. And the whispering dare that came with it.

You could destroy him if you wanted to. There are different words of othertongue. Words that can do more than you could ever imagine.

She could almost hear them, in the song behind the voice. Words that would solve everything, that would make her strong.

All you have to do is reach out. Claim them.

So she did.

Wren reached effortlessly through the veil of power that had seemed so solid. Through it and then beyond it… into a pure endless void where a thing made entirely of darkness waited.

She felt it gather itself together, turning its eyes on her. But it was cracked, like shattered glass, so many tiny fragments missing from its wholeness. And a single vital gap right in its heart, if heart was a word that could be used about something so hollow and empty. It was like a puzzle missing half its pieces but still trying to hold itself together.

She stared into the endless night, at the collapsed stars swirling through its eyes.

There was no light there and never would be. It hungered but was eternally empty.

And it looked back at her, standing there, helpless and so very small. Lost in its gaze, something touched her, probing. And then drove itself through her body and soul. It felt like lightning spearing through her to the ground, the earth itself making her a conduit.

When she opened her eyes again, it was like looking through the same fragmented glass. The encampment around her came alive with swirling lines of power. Wren tilted her head to one side, studying the way they moved. Light and dark ran like rivers through the ground, spiralling to a vortex around the two brothers.

Leander pulsed with the channels of shadow, standing over Finnian, the golden light threaded through from his blood. The shadow-wrought chains binding him suppressed it, but it still writhed beneath his skin, desperate to get out. To join the blazing flow surrounding him.

As she watched, hypnotised, the sun was setting, the night drawing in. The shadows, so many shadows, responded by stretching out around her. The balance between the powers was shifting. Light was not the answer. Not here and now.

Wren drew on those shadows now. And they answered as they never had before, racing across the ground towards her.

'What are you doing?' Leander growled at her. 'Stop it or I kill him.'

'You're going to kill him anyway,' she said, and the voice hardly sounded like her own. Calm, distant, determined. In such contrast to his, filled with the passion of his hatred and insatiable need for vengeance. Not even for anything in particular. Finn's existence alone was the insult.

Her eyes locked on Finn's, and he gazed up at her in fierce adoration. Trusting, faithful, ready to do anything for her. Even die, if she asked it. It was a different kind of power, his trust in her, her responsibility for him, one she had never expected and the strength of it shook her to the core.

More shadows raced towards her and she welcomed them, felt them inside her, crawling under her skin. Where she had always turned them away before she called them to her now, and oh, it felt good. The air shimmered, and the other Ilanthian guards edged backwards, fear making their loyalty to their crown prince waver.

And Leander knew it.

'You can't channel the Aurum, Wren. It will burn right through you.'

Wren laughed, a bright sound in all the darkness rushing in around her. He thought she was touching the Aurum? She may not know exactly what she was doing, but it was not light she was gathering to herself.

Light might be flooding into the places from which she pulled the shadows, but the darkness that filled her had nothing to do with the Aurum. There was only one thing it could be and she didn't dare to name it.

At the sound of her sudden amusement, Leander went even more pale and she saw the hands holding the sword tighten. Fear, she could smell it on him. She let a slow smile spread over her mouth, let him see it, and darker laughter rippled through the back of her mind.

The voice from far away seemed to sing to her. The one that had sung to her as a child. The one Elodie had always driven away.

Show him. Show him how wrong he is. They have grown arrogant these kings, without my hand at their throat. Make him bow and beg.

And she could. She knew she could. She could reduce Prince Leander of Ilanthus to a quivering wreck if she wanted to. She could turn him from a prince to a slave with a thought.

She only had to look at his brother. She thought she had burned all the poison of the shadow kin out of him. Maybe she had. But seeing how the powers flowed together with her new sight, how each filled in the space when the other was drawn... had she left something else behind? Something bright and terrible. Then, when she had been in danger, could he have pulled on that power to protect her? Just as she did now for him.

And, from the deepest darkness, something else was reaching out to fill her. She didn't even know herself. Perhaps she wasn't herself. But, delirious with power and righteous vengeance, she welcomed it.

'Take her!' Leander yelled at his troops, who stood as if spellbound around her, staring. His voice was a howl of panic. 'Take her down now!'

They couldn't. They wouldn't. She would kill them all if they tried. More and more shadows filled her and she wound them together, ready to lash out in a wave of nightmare and darkness.

'Wren,' another voice said, soft and tired. So very tired. 'Wren, don't. This isn't you.'

Finn? But how was it Finn? She'd turned him into a monster. She hadn't thought there was anything of Finn left in there.

'Wren, please...'

She stared at him, still on his knees, still staring at her, still at Leander's mercy.

No, that was not acceptable. He was a beacon in the shadows she wrought, bright and beautiful, blazing with light now, and she would not allow anyone to snuff it out.

'Finn?' she whispered, her voice surprisingly frail for the amount of power she could feel racing through her veins. She couldn't control it. It was slipping through her fingers even now, taking more of her than she wanted to give. It was flooding her. Drowning her. 'Finn, there's so much... I don't know what to... I can't...'

Leander chose that moment to strike, but Wren got there first, throwing herself forward, between the two of them. It shouldn't have been possible. She shouldn't have been able to move that fast, but the shadows twisted and the world blurred and suddenly she was there.

The sword plunged through her as if she was made of smoke herself, as if there was nothing there for it to strike. She flung her arms out and Leander flew back. The ground trembled and a roaring in her mind made her shake with it. All she knew was rage, unbridled and terrible. The shadows filled her now, every shadow in the place, every scrap of darkness, expect perhaps for that within Leander's heart.

Wren! Stop!

The voice shook through her, rattled through her mind and sent her to her knees. Elodie. It was Elodie. There was no one else it could be. She would know that if she no longer knew anything else.

You don't understand, she wanted to say. I have to. I need to.

No, my love. This isn't you, little bird. Please, stop. Don't give in to the shadows. Let go of it, Wren. Just let go. Help is coming.

Overhead the sky burst with waves of light.

CHAPTER 26

WREN

The ground trembled, and all around Wren people were running, shouting, raising the alarm.

The thunder was coming nearer and she saw light glimmering through the trees as well as the sky now, flooding the clearing. Finn gathered her in his arms, the chains so cold they burned against her skin, just as Leander had promised, but she didn't care. He was alive. He was holding her, shielding her as she had tried to shield him.

'It's a beacon. An Aurum-sent beacon!' someone shouted. 'Defend the crown prince.'

Elodie was coming. She had to be. She would always come when Wren needed her, dead or alive – and Wren still wasn't sure which – but it had to be her. The forest shook with her rage. Elodie was coming in light and fury. The sky lit up with waves of coloured light.

But it wasn't Elodie who arrived.

They came through the trees in every direction.

Knights flooded the clearing, their armour shining in the dying light. Their horses' hooves turning the earth to mud, as their blades tore through their enemies.

Wren tasted the blood in the air, and drank in the cries of death and destruction as they fell on the Ilanthians. Or perhaps it was the thing inside her, the mass of darkness and shadows she had linked to on the other side of reality. It relished every drop of blood, every death. It drank down every moment of despair and defeat and it laughed. Everywhere she looked, battle surged around her and all she could do was cling to Finn, to hold him against her and try to fight the fierce joy.

Leander vaulted onto a mount, his bodyguards surrounding him. They all fled, leaving his pavilion and his luxuries behind him trampled into the mud. Those of his men who didn't follow him immediately died, right there, ensuring his escape.

And, suddenly, everything went strangely still.

The Knights of the Aurum encircled her and there was nothing she could do now, no way to escape them. She couldn't let them take her either. Elodie had always been adamant. She had to make them go away, and leave her alone. She had to...

The darkness in her rose again, ready to fight them all, ready to strike them down or be extinguished doing so. She sobbed as she felt the thing in the beyond revel in the prospect and surge forward to fill her again.

'Wren.' The voice was a breath against her skin. Not Elodie. Or the voice of power. Not this time. Real and right there, with her.

Strong arms held her close, strong but gentle, the only real thing in her unreal world. She turned her head to look at him, only a fraction of an inch away from her. He blazed like a fire, all the glory of the Aurum in a human shape.

'Wren,' Finn whispered, his breath harsh against her ears, his voice strained beyond endurance. But his words... he sounded like Elodie, the words he said an echo of her words.

'Let go. Just let go. We're safe. We're going to be okay. Don't give in to it.'

She took a breath. Then another. She felt the shadows in her start to recede, that dreadful consciousness retreating, satisfied. For now.

It left her feeling wrung out and sick. Empty.

The world was righting itself but all it left behind was a terrible feeling of abject horror. It was part of her, she was part of it. But what...

You know what it is.

She had felt the touch of the Nox from its exile. The parts of it the lost queen had cast into the furthest darkness when she tore it apart and scattered it. So different from the diluted power found in the darkwood. And, through Wren, it had a way home. She wasn't even sure how she knew it, but she had opened some kind of doorway, and that worked both ways.

Another breath, and another, and the reality of it slammed into her mind like a fist. What had she done?

Even as the world shifted around her, lines of power melting away, she could make out the leading knight dismounting and coming towards them, a man tall and broad.

He removed his helmet to reveal his midnight hair and eyes as endlessly dark as her own. He strode across the space between them, his expression all concern, but not for her. He didn't know her. How could he?

'Finnian? What happened?' asked Roland de Silvius.

Wren felt Finn's arms tighten around her, as if he could somehow protect her from what was coming. He couldn't. She knew that. They had all seen her. They all knew what she'd done. Her world was about to change and there was nothing either of them could do about it. Not now.

ON THE ILANTHIAN-ASTEROTH WARS

In the days following the defeat of the Ilanthian army, chaos reigned in the royal household.

Besieged in the fortress of Sidonia, the royal family made supplication to the Nox, but the dark incarnation of the power was no more. Their goddess was broken and as defeated as their force of arms. No sacrifice was enough. Witchkind blood covered the black stones, to no avail.

In desperation, King Alessander brought his youngest son to the secret chamber, intent on using his royal blood to summon the lost goddess and attempt to make her whole once more. This had been the promise of the House of Sidon, that if they shed blood royal, the Nox would always answer.

Before the blade could fall, the Knights of the Aurum arrived, seizing the child and others of the royal line as captives, carrying them off as trophy and hostage.

So Alessander the Defeated gave up his youngest son to his enemies, and waited for his time to come again.

CHAPTER 27

ROLAND

The sky lit up in a way Roland hadn't seen in more than twenty years. An Aurum-sent beacon.

Every instinct took control, driving him and the other Paladins beyond reason and logic. The knights followed, trusting their leaders and their training as ever, investigating reports of Ilanthian witchhunters in the forest near Knightsford forgotten in an instant. They had ridden at that light, as if driven from behind by holy fire, as if drawn to it like moths, as if nothing else had mattered in the world. The world had thundered and burned and he had felt it inside him, beating in time with his heart, the song he knew so well. All Roland knew was that the Aurum was blazing through him, the light unleashed. He had heard her voice. He was sure he had heard Elodie's voice, calling them, rallying them to arms. And he had no choice but to answer.

Only one person had ever been able to send up a beacon like that, and she did it only in the direst of needs. His heart soared inside him, every nerve alight, as he looked for her.

The Aurum-sent beacon vanished as they attacked, but for those few moments it had been glorious. It had surged through his veins, strengthening him, filling his heart with endless courage. He had known it of old, the light of the Aurum as it had been wielded in battle in the past, bright and terrible. The way Elodie had wielded it...

For a moment his fractured heart had hoped... prayed...

But Elodie wasn't there. Of course she wasn't. Why would she be? Elodie was gone.

Stupid. So stupid.

But what did it matter?

If this girl could wield the light of the Aurum, if they had truly been blessed in such a way, he would pay any price. It was as if all his dreams had come true.

No. Not all of them. Not quite.

The girl wasn't Elodie.

He didn't know who she was. She'd passed out with the effort, even as the battle was done and Finn, beaten and exhausted, still bound in shadow-wrought chains, just held her, whispering her name over and over again. Begging her to stay with him.

Wren.

The routing of the Ilanthian incursion force took a lot less time than Roland had anticipated. They fell back through the trees and, though he sent a significant number of his men in pursuit, Roland himself stayed behind. Let the younger men have the glory of mopping up the rest. He had Finnian to think about and anything of use that might be garnered by way of intelligence from what had been left behind.

Leander had slipped through his fingers, but that was probably just as well. The peace was fragile enough and the crown prince desperate to disrupt it. He was too like his bastard uncle, Evander. Capturing the king's favourite son on the wrong side of the border was never going to work out well for anyone. His bodyguards had spirited him away as soon as the knights came within sight.

Just as well, or Roland had no doubt Finn would be dead now. It had been too close. Thank the Aurum for the girl who had saved the man he loved as a son. Whoever she was Roland knew he owed her a debt of gratitude.

The girl was pretty, though very pale and weakened from the magic she had channelled. She hid behind a mass of wild black hair, and curled in against Finn's body, clasping a small leather book in her hand, crushed against her chest. When anyone tried to come near, even for a second, Finn snarled at them with a ferocity Roland hadn't seen in him since he was a child, newly arrived from Sidonia.

No one had been able to make Finn leave her, not for a second, not even to see the healers.

The journey back to Knightsford was slow, Roland leading the way, Finn carrying the girl with him on a borrowed mount. What had happened to his beloved horse, Roland didn't know. There would be time for a debriefing soon, but at the moment there was no point. The first thing he needed to do was get them both to safety.

Later he could find out everything. Finn would tell him, once he'd rested and was sure the girl was safe. Roland knew him better than anyone.

Once he had dreamed of having children. A son to carry on his name, of course. Everyone wanted that. A host of strong boys, to train and raise in the knightly way. But a daughter too, as beautiful as her mother and as wise.

None of it had been possible. Roland's fault, really, for falling in love with a queen. And not just any queen. She had claimed his heart with just a look and that had been that. Even if he had wanted to love another it would never have worked out.

So raising the royal hostage in the aftermath of the devastation of the war had been not only an expression of duty to his country and the crown, but had become a pleasure. The wild little creature who had been deposited with him had grown into a fine young man, one anyone would be proud to call son. Brave, resilient, skilled, clever.

Roland would never be able to express his pride in Finnian. But he felt it keenly nonetheless.

Any time duty took the boy over the border and back into Ilanthus, however, Roland worried. With good reason, as the situation now demonstrated. Alessander might demand to know his youngest son was still alive and healthy, and Finnian might obey the summons, but they were all aware of the threat he posed to Leander and how much the crown prince loathed him. That Finn used those visits as opportunities to gather intelligence for Roland had always deeply unsettled the Grandmaster. It was too great a risk. But then, Finnian occupied a precarious position between the two hostile powers. Either of them would take any harm to him as a grave insult.

Not that Leander cared about that either. It was the worst thing that could have happened, the crown prince following him, capturing him. It could have ended in disaster for them all.

Roland watched Finn now, while the healer tried to coax him to cooperate, and knew it had been far too close. Leander must be very sure of himself to come here after Finn.

Assassins and witchhunters on Asterothian soil... it was not to be endured. Roland would see them hounded to the ends of the earth if anything happened to the boy. And as for the security here... He'd fortify the garrison of course. And increase patrols on the border. Those invaders already dead would send a powerful message to the Sidonian court, one he was sure

Alessander would heed. But what would it matter in time? Leander would want vengeance.

Roland suddenly felt old. Every one of his forty years weighed on him as if they were doubled.

Knightsford was a bustling town on the river, protected by high walls and fortifications. It was the last defence on the road to Ilanthus. The place to which people like the villagers of Thirbridge were meant to retreat. Roland had sent a scouting party there, to see if there had been any survivors. But he doubted it.

Anselm was waiting for him in the garrison office, and from his expression the news about Thirbridge was grimmer than expected. He listened to the expected report without comment, and then examined the list of those invaders captured or the dead who had been identified. Precious few of either and no word on Leander himself. Nothing to prove he'd been there but their own word, and Roland knew from bitter experience that the Ilanthians would die rather than identify their prince as having led them here.

'Is Finn... is he hurt?' Anselm asked tentatively. Their friendship had always been strong. Roland had found himself relying on that to protect his ward as much as anything else. He trusted Anselm.

'I'm going to see him now. They didn't treat him kindly. We got there in time, however, and that's something to be thankful for.'

'And the girl?'

Rumours were already flying then. 'That remains to be seen. She was exhausted. The use of magic seems to have drained her completely. She's lucky to have survived. You can accompany me, if you wish. I'm sure Finn would appreciate a friendly face.'

'He hasn't done anything wrong, has he?'

Trust Anselm to come to Finn's defence. Roland smiled.

'That remains to be seen, but there are many questions to be answered right now. Not least, what happened back there?'

The young knight's eyes narrowed. Well, he was always the clever one. 'And who is the girl?'

CHAPTER 28

ROLAND

Their footsteps echoed along the stone floors of the corridors leading to the infirmary and Roland was glad of the company. While he valued Anselm's opinion, he knew he would need to debrief Finn and couldn't immediately offer the comfort the boy might need. Having his friend there would be a boon to both of them.

The healer, in her long white robes and cowl, met them outside, her expression stern.

'You're going to have to speak to him, Grandmaster. We can't get him to cooperate in the slightest. He won't leave her side. Not even now she's sleeping.'

Finn, being stubborn. Not exactly a surprise. But this strange devotion was a worry.

Roland let the healer lead him to the small room in which the girl lay on a bed and Finn sat beside her, studying her face as if trying to commit it to memory.

'Report, Ward,' Roland said, though he didn't raise his voice. He didn't need to.

Old instincts overtook whatever had robbed him of his

senses at the Ilanthian camp. Finn was on his feet at attention before he knew what he was doing.

'Grandmaster?' he began and then faltered. He glanced at the girl and concern ghosted over his face. Concern for her. Interesting. She slept on.

'Your report. We can go outside so as not to disturb her, if you want.'

Finn chewed on his lower lip and swayed slightly on his feet. He looked wretched. The beating was only half of it. He looked like everything he was had been scooped out of him and only partially restored. Had the shadow-wrought manacles done something to him? But their effect tended to be on witchkind, and to Roland's knowledge Finn was nothing of the sort.

But something was different about him. Something Roland couldn't quite define, and Finn was not willing to share. Not yet.

'Ilanthian troops led by Leander followed me from Sidonia, and ambushed me in the woods. Wren... this woman... helped me.' His voice trailed off. 'We were captured. He was going to execute me.'

'And the light? Was it her work?'

Finn glanced at her before he could stop himself. So it had been. Finn didn't even have to give an answer. Roland let out the breath trapped in his chest, and saw the realisation of what Finn had just given away fill his eyes with shame. His panic was evident as the words spilled out.

'I don't think she knew what she was doing. I don't think...'

That hardly mattered. If she hadn't been properly trained in magic, training could be given. The innate ability was the thing. But Roland had never seen anyone untrained raise a beacon so bright, or make the sense of the Aurum's fire rise in his chest the way it had. Not since Elodie. This aftermath was because of the lack of training, not from any deficiency. Once she had rested and regained her strength, she would recover. 'Where did you find her? Who is she?'

Finn just stared at him as if he was stupid. Roland frowned, which he knew was the expression most of his men dreaded seeing on his face. His ward was no different. He forced his voice to gentleness, which belied the urgency he felt now.

'Finn? What aren't you telling me?'

Roland hadn't thought it possible to see Finn still squirm like a boy caught breaking all the rules after so long. But he did.

Meanwhile, Anselm had wandered to the bedside table where the girl's few belongings were stacked up neatly in a pile. He picked up a small leather-bound book and opened it. Leafing through the pages, he too frowned.

'Grandmaster?' He held out the book. The leather was marked with the symbol of the Aurum. Roland took it, suddenly unsure.

'I don't think it's her fault,' Finn blurted out. 'I don't think she knows. I don't think she knows anything.'

The pages were blank, all of them. Some kind of notebook but one with nothing written in it. Roland studied it briefly and handed it back to Anselm to return. Curious. As he let it go he felt the tingle of an enchantment around it.

'What else?' he asked the knight.

Anselm held out a locket dangling on a simple chain, also bearing the symbol. For a moment Roland thought that his heart might stop beating. It wasn't possible. Couldn't be...

Identical to his own.

'Roland, please,' Finn whispered, frantic to dissuade him. 'Don't.'

But it was too late. He didn't have to open it. He already knew what it was, what it would contain. His picture, his portrait, the one Elodie had painted, the match to one of her in his locket that he still carried with him after all these years.

How did this child have Elodie's locket?

'Where did you find her?' he growled, closing his hand around the metal as if to crush it in his grasp.

Finn sank back onto the chair and looked at the unconscious girl again. Pity filled his face. Not for Roland, but clearly directed at the girl. 'In the forest, near Thirbridge. Near the darkwood. There's a tower. She burned it.'

'This girl burned it?'

The boy shook his head dumbly. 'It was on fire when we got there. We went back later, Wren insisted. To look for *her*.' There was a subtle emphasis on the final word, and Roland knew that Finn believed what he suspected. That they had found her. That she'd survived that terrible night.

'Did you?' he asked hesitantly. He hated how tentative his question sounded. 'Find her?'

'Wren said... she said the book told her to meet her at the Seven Sisters, near here. That she'd... that Elodie... I mean...'

Elodie.

Roland uncurled his hand and looked at the locket finally. The catch was small and delicate. The two pieces had been identical so he knew the trick to opening it. When her engagement to Evander had been announced he had bought them out of some sense of fatalism. Not the kind of thing she would normally wear. Too simple for a queen. But he wanted something to remember her by, wanted her to remember him. She had painted the miniatures.

'*One for you. One for me. Just so we never forget. At least we had this.*'

Even after all this time, Roland realised, he had clung to that.

He'd thought she was dead, prayed she wasn't. Why had she never sent word? Why had she never returned? He would have gone to her, protected her. He would have done anything. And all this time she'd been hiding in the forest, near Thirbridge.

Why had no one ever looked there?

Except Dane had. Warrants investigation, his old friend had said. But he'd never done it, had he? Roland had missed that one vital clue and now...

His finger moved almost by itself and he flicked open the locket. Finn let out something between a sigh and a groan while Anselm, unable to resist, craned in to look.

It didn't just hold one picture. His own face stared back at him from one side, as he had been twenty years ago. Or at least, as she had seen him, because he didn't remember ever being the idealised face painted there. But that didn't matter. That was how she had seen him and that was how he had been for her. And he loved her for it.

But there was another picture on the other side, another portrait.

A girl with his black hair and deep brown eyes, with his mother's nose and a jawline like his father's but softer. A girl who looked like him.

A younger version of the same girl now sleeping on the bed.

'Oh,' Anselm said, coming to the same conclusion in an instant. 'She's your—'

And he shut up before he could say it out loud. Always the survivor.

Elodie had run away from Asteroth. She had never come back. Now, finally, Roland knew why.

Carefully, deliberately, he closed off every emotion that surged to the fore. Every last one. He had to.

'Finn,' he said. 'With me. Now.'

Roland snapped the locket shut and left the room without uttering another word. The legs of Finn's chair scraped on the tiled floor, and there was a hushed exchange with Anselm before he hurried in Roland's wake.

But what Roland was going to say to the boy when he

finally managed to make himself stop walking, the Grandmaster had no idea at all.

CHAPTER 29

WREN

The bed felt strange and the air too still. There was no breeze coming in through the window and no sound of birdsong. She scrunched up her face against the light. Why was she in bed in daylight? Her body ached everywhere and she felt… strange. Different.

'Wren?' said a voice she didn't know. 'It is Wren, isn't it?'

She opened her eyes to see a man she didn't recognise standing at the far side of the room. Not Finn. His blond hair caught the light behind him like a halo. He was wearing some kind of uniform but his face had a gentleness that made her initial panic subside.

'Who are you? Where am I?'

'I'm Anselm Tarryn. I'm a friend of Finn's. He's just… he had to see the healer or he would have been here. And then he had to report. I offered to stay with you. We didn't really expect you to wake up… Please, don't be scared.'

Wren pushed herself up on her elbows even though every muscle in her body protested. 'Was Finn hurt?'

'No. He says you saved him.'

Had she? Or doomed him? What had she done? Even she

didn't know. It had been like a fever dream of light and darkness.

She let herself slump back down again. Anselm had answered only one of her first questions, she realised. 'And where are we?'

Anselm smiled what was clearly meant to be a reassuring smile. 'Knightsford. At the garrison. We arrived to the encampment just in time. They would have killed him. I saw what you did.'

She closed her eyes. He'd seen. Which meant they'd all seen. Seen her embrace the darkness and reach out to whatever place the Nox still lurked. Connect with it, begin to draw it back from exile... At least that was what she thought had happened. But why wasn't she locked in a cage if that was the case? Why wasn't she in the same horrible chains that had bound Finn?

'What I did?' she echoed hollowly.

'You sent up the beacon to call us. You threw yourself between Finn and the blade. You set the world ablaze with the light of the Aurum. The Paladins felt it. The knights too. I've never experienced anything like it. Even the Grandmaster—'

The Grandmaster. Roland de Silvius. Her breath caught in her throat and she stared at Anselm, who gazed back unerringly, his green eyes very sharp. Oh, he missed nothing, did he? He knew. They all knew.

Just not exactly what she had feared.

She forced herself to breathe. They hadn't seen the darkness in her. Not yet. They had only seen the light when she had drawn the darkness away, into her. Because if you took away darkness light got in. That was one of Elodie's first lessons, when she was small.

But the very first was to never reach for the darkness in the first place.

Oh, she had made such a mess of this. She had done everything wrong. And they were going to find out eventually.

'He would like to talk to you,' Anselm said at last. 'I'm to escort you there, when you're ready. If you want to.'

'Finn?' she asked, distractedly.

A smile tugged at his lips. 'No. Grandmaster de Silvius.'

Oh. Of course.

What else could she do? It didn't sound like turning it down was actually an option, no matter what Anselm said. What could she say? She was too weak? She didn't want to? She just wanted to leave and run back to the safety of the forest? She still needed to go to the Seven Sisters and find Elodie.

If she didn't go to see the Grandmaster, eventually, he'd just come here instead. And that would be so much worse somehow, that she'd dragged him away from whatever he was meant to be doing because she, like a child, refused to move from her bed.

'I need...' She looked around and had to push the length of her hair back from her face. It was everywhere, spilling around her, half out of the braid someone had attempted to make of it some time ago. Her clothes... were probably back in the Ilanthian encampment. The robe Leander had given her was nowhere to be seen and she was wearing a simple white shift.

Someone had undressed her. She folded her arms around her chest as the thought of it made her whole body go cold. What else had happened?

Anselm seemed to recognise her distress. 'The healers looked after you. They are honour-bound to care for the sick and those in need, and to do no harm. Finn stood guard all the time. He refused to budge, the stubborn fool.'

Finn had been there. At least there was that. He had stayed with her. Even though he too had to know what she'd done. They'd been entwined together in that maelstrom of light and darkness. He had to know. He'd begged her to stop.

'Where is he? Is he in trouble?'

'Finn?' Anselm laughed. 'No. The Aurum bless you, no, of course not. But he refused to let them heal him until you were sleeping peacefully and even then... You can wait for him if you prefer. But the Grandmaster's time is precious.'

Would she prefer to have Finn with her when she faced the man who might be her father? Yes, of course she would. But she couldn't put it off forever either. And she suspected this was a conversation she wanted to have alone with Roland, even if she dreaded the thought. And her parentage, whatever it might be, was the least of her concerns.

'I'll... I'll need something to wear.' She wished her voice didn't shake quite so much.

'It shall be done, my lady,' Anselm said, with a bow, and left the room for a moment to issue some orders to someone outside.

My lady. This was not good. Not good at all.

Her eyes fell on the book lying on the bedside table. No sign of the locket. It wasn't around her neck nor anywhere in sight. She prayed she hadn't lost it. Apart from the diary, it was the only thing she really had of Elodie. Maybe Finn had it? Maybe he was looking after it for her? But she only had Anselm's word that he was safe and well, that he wasn't dead, or still in chains, or...

She grabbed the book and opened it. Elodie's writing spilled over the pages, Elodie's hopes and dreams, all the things she'd wanted to do, an Elodie who wasn't much older than she was now.

'Where are you?' she whispered.

The writing slid away again as the enchanted book revealed new words, the words of Elodie now. It had to be Elodie.

Come to the Seven Sisters. Now. You are not safe there.

Easier said than done. 'How do I get out of here? I don't even know where I am.'

But the words remained there, stubborn and insistent, just

like Elodie. As Wren watched, three more words formed from the swirling ink.

Don't trust them.

Anselm coughed discreetly as he entered the room again and Wren snapped the book closed. 'Someone will be along with clothes and will help you shortly. If there's anything else you need, don't hesitate to ask. I'm here to help.'

Don't trust them.

'I'd like to see Finn.'

He smiled again. 'As soon as the healers are happy to release him, I'm sure he will be here. We could barely tear him away from you to begin with. Are you hungry? Thirsty?' Wren shook her head, watching him carefully. She saw his eyes flick down to the book in her hand and back up to her face. Had he read it? Had it worked for him the way it did for her?

'My other belongings...' she said and then paused. Most of her things were lost in the forest somewhere when she'd first fled Leander.

'The Grandmaster will explain everything, I'm sure, my lady. And we will provide whatever you need.'

So that was that. No more answers were forthcoming until she saw Roland de Silvius. 'I'm not a lady,' she whispered, more to herself than him. 'I'm just Wren.'

For a moment she saw pity in his eyes, she was sure of it. If not pity then at least understanding of a kind. 'I'm afraid many things are about to change, Wren,' he said. 'You know that, don't you? Being who you are?'

Who she was? At least it was a who and not a what...

She shook her head, and then sighed when her hair fell over her face again, a veil of black silk that seemed to whisper around her. How she longed for a knife to hack it away and leave her free again. Maybe she should ask him for that?

But no. She doubted they'd give her a knife right now. And

she doubted that any lady was meant to cut off her hair as short as possible. Certainly not Roland de Silvius's daughter.

That was who they all thought she was, wasn't it? That was what she thought, even though the idea terrified her.

And Elodie's only advice was not to trust him, which did not bode well. How could it? Elodie had been hiding from him for all of Wren's life. And hiding Wren from him as well.

Why? What had Roland de Silvius done to her all those years ago?

CHAPTER 30
WREN

Once the healer declared that Wren could leave her room, there was an unexpected flurry of activity around her.

Anselm was effectively banished outside by a very efficient young woman as golden-haired as he was, who took one look at Wren and pursed her lips in a perplexed expression.

'I suppose we'd better get started as soon as possible,' she said. 'I'm Lady Lynette of Goalais, wife of Paladin Knight Yvain of Goalais, who heads the garrison here. Anselm has asked me to make you presentable. The Grandmaster is a busy man so his making this time for you is a great honour.'

And from that moment on, Wren was chivvied along to wash, dress in far too many layers of fabric and her hair was carefully brushed and braided. When she looked at herself in the mirror Lynette had ordered dragged into the infirmary room, she hardly knew the woman standing there.

'If I had more time and if this little town had more facilities, I could make you worthy of any royal court in the world,' Lynette said, as she examined Wren with a far more critical eye. 'It will be better when you finally get back to Pelias. But this is not bad at all. You have good bones.'

And she nodded as if that was the greatest compliment she could give.

'And your hair, my dear girl...' She sighed, and reached out to brush her fingertips along the length of Wren's braid. 'I know people who would kill for your hair. Right, come along. We cannot keep the Grandmaster waiting.'

Someone opened the door for them and Lynette swept outside. Wren hurried after her, almost too terrified to do anything else. Anselm's eyes widened as she appeared, but he said nothing and fell into step behind them.

'Don't be afraid of him,' Lynette went on. 'He's a good man. But he's used to leading men, not women. He just looks a bit grim, but he's really very kind. He has always been our most respected warrior. Yvain tells me that when he was a young knight there were those who made fun of him, because he was shy and could be tongue-tied, but they never did it once they'd seen him fight, I can tell you. Nor when the queen was in earshot. And look at him now. This kingdom would have fallen apart without him. That's what my husband says. Fallen apart.'

Wren didn't think she was actually expected to take part in this conversation so she just nodded and hurried along in the unfamiliar skirts. The gown was beautiful, far finer than anything she had ever worn before. Her own clothes had been made for the forest and for hard work. These clothes, soft and delicate, glimmering with bright threads and made of sleek silks, were like nothing she had ever seen.

They stopped in front of a simple door at the end of the corridor. There was nothing unusual about it, and nothing particularly grand. Just a door.

Elodie said not to trust any of them. And given Wren had somehow connected herself with the Nox back in the Ilanthian encampment, that was advice to heed. She wasn't safe here. She couldn't be. The Knights of the Aurum existed to combat the Nox. Everyone knew that.

They didn't know what she had done, had entirely misinterpreted what they had seen. Just as Leander had. But Finn knew the truth. She was certain of that.

And what might he have said to the man who raised him?

The door closed behind her with the finality of a tomb being sealed.

Wren stood there, without any of the guards or Lynette and Anselm to hide behind, looking at the broad back of a man bred for and honed by war. There was no other way to describe him. He was taller than anyone she had ever seen, with wide shoulders and long legs. He wore a light mail over his leather tunic, topped with a surcoat of a brilliant blue. In the centre of the cloak, which fell down his back, the flame of the Aurum symbol was picked out in gold. When he turned, she saw the face from the locket, although years had reshaped it. There was a new hardness there, a chill in his eyes, and strands of silver at his temples, a stark contrast to the jet black of his hair.

Wren straightened her back, held her head high and tried to make herself look him right in the eye. For a moment they regarded each other warily.

Was he really as nervous as she was? The thought was impossible. And yet, that was the feeling she had.

'Wren,' he said at last, his voice a deep rumble, but surprisingly soft, like distant thunder. Not a threat.

At least there was that.

But what should she call him? 'Grandmaster de Silvius,' she said, falling back on formality.

He leaned on the desk between them, both arms straight, and stared at her for another long moment. 'Where is Elodie?' he asked.

'I don't know.' Which was true. At least she didn't have to

start this with an outright lie. 'I was hoping she'd be here.' Or near here. But she didn't want to tell him exactly where. Elodie said not to trust him.

'She didn't tell you her plans?' He was still studying her and Wren shifted uneasily from one foot to the other. 'No, I suppose not. She always could keep a secret.'

'A secret like me?'

'So it would seem.' He held out her locket and Wren took it gratefully, hanging it back around her neck. He sighed then and gestured to the seat opposite his desk. Wren sank into it and he took his own. Neither of them spoke for a moment. Finally, he broke the painful silence. 'You must have questions.'

Of course she did. She'd be a fool not to have questions. 'Many.'

'And she never answered them either? She never spoke of the past? Of... of who she was?'

Had he been about to say 'of me?' or 'of us?' Wren winced, and looked to the floor. What could she tell him? Elodie had hidden him completely from her, as completely as she had hidden Wren from him. It was only in her nightmares she mentioned his name. No man would want to hear that, would they?

'No,' she said. And the narrowing of his eyes told her he knew that for the half-truth it was.

'She is Queen Aeryn of Asteroth, and she never mentioned it? Never spoke of marrying a prince of Ilanthus? Never mentioned fighting the Nox?'

Wren's mouth hung open. She closed it as quickly as she could. She knew none of that. Of course Elodie had never mentioned any of it. She'd clearly been trying to hide from it all. Why would she turn around and tell Wren when it was the last thing she wanted anyone to know? Especially not Wren.

She'd never even said she was Wren's mother. Not out loud. Not to anyone. Not once.

It was too much. It was all too much.

'We fight the Nox, now and always,' she told him, trying to push all the rest of it aside. That was what Elodie had always said and so Wren repeated it now. Like a comfort.

She gripped the seat of her chair until her knuckles turned white. It felt too much like the lie she was trying to avoid. She hadn't fought the Nox, had she? She'd opened the door and invited it in. She would have done anything to save Finn.

'With flame and sword,' Roland replied, intoning the words. 'The vow of the Knights of the Aurum.' A smile flickered over his lips. 'At least she taught you that much.'

Something bristled in the back of her mind.

'She taught me everything,' Wren countered, not willing to hear all Elodie had done for her dismissed in such a way. 'Everything I needed anyway.'

'In the forest, perhaps. But it's a whole new world now. Princess Wren of Asteroth...' He let out a long sigh, as if there was something profoundly disappointing about saying those words. 'This is going to take a lot of explaining. The regents' council alone are going to—'

Princess?

'Wait. I'm not a princess. I'm no one.'

'You're Elodie's daughter.'

No, she wasn't. She couldn't be. She didn't even look like her.

'She never said that. She just... she raised me but I don't... I'm not...'

He help up a hand to silence her and she was horrified to find herself obeying. The words died away in her throat. 'It's undeniable. Just looking at you... You are the daughter of the lost queen and, unless we find her, you will take the throne.'

The pronouncement stole her breath. She didn't look anything like Elodie. She knew that. But she did look like him and...

Oh. Wren closed her eyes. He wanted her on the throne. Of course he did.

'I can't do that.'

'You don't have a choice in the matter. It is your duty.'

No choice?

The shock inside her boiled away. And turned to anger.

There was always a choice. Elodie had taught her that too. No one else got to decide for her. 'If I am her daughter, and your daughter, and she was married to Prince Evander of Sidon, I'm not even legitimate.'

He looked up sharply and she knew she'd made a dreadful miscalculation. Elodie had always been so calm and kind. Wren knew she must have gotten her temper from somewhere and now she could be seeing where. Anger filled his eyes, making them black as midnight. And far too like those in her own reflection. She shrank back in her seat as he rose slowly, every movement filled with threat.

'Your blood by your mother is the only thing of consequence here. Whoever sired you is of no consequence. The queen was lawfully married but better that you don't carry the Ilanthian taint.'

The Ilanthian taint? Oh Finn must have had an exemplary upbringing hearing phrases like that from his guardian's mouth. Wren ground her teeth together while the world seemed to plummet away beneath her.

'No one will dare question your birthright anyway. Once the regents' council makes the proclamation that will be that. All the same, it's no good handing people weapons against you. Never say it again, do you understand?'

She swallowed hard on the lump in her throat. Why couldn't he have been kind? Loving? Why couldn't he have swept her up in his arms and told her she was the child he had always wanted? That was what happened in stories, wasn't it?

Tears burned in her eyes and she blinked them back. She wouldn't show him. She wouldn't let him see.

'You just want me on the throne, no matter what. For your own ends.' Her voice shook but she forced the words out. 'If you think to have a queen you can control—'

For a moment the anger in him cracked and she saw a flicker of shock, surprise that she could even think such a thing. He almost laughed, but the bitter twist of his mouth wouldn't allow it.

'No one has ever been able to control a queen of Asteroth. I am not about to start on that fool's errand. The council will decide but I can already tell you that you might as well get used to a crown, young lady. You are dismissed.'

CHAPTER 31

WREN

Wren couldn't get out of the room fast enough.

One minute Roland was calling her a queen, and the next he was dismissing her like a servant. How dare he?

Lynette was still waiting outside and Anselm was a little further down the corridor, but she pushed by them both and ran before the threatened tears spilled from her eyes and made an absolute fool of her. She was doing that just well enough by herself. They didn't follow her, she noticed, and felt a strange sense of gratitude. Back in the healers' hall, her room had already been stripped, but her book was still there waiting for her. She grabbed it, holding it against the locket, close to her heart, and fought to stay upright. All the air seemed to have left her body and she couldn't pull any more in.

'I don't know,' said a voice outside. One of the healers, she supposed. She didn't recognise it. 'You'd imagine most girls would be delighted to find out they were really a princess.'

'It must have been a dreadful shock though, if she really didn't know.'

'Do you actually believe that?' The first voice laughed. 'I don't think so. She knew. She had to. If Queen Aeryn really did raise her, she would have prepared her. I think it's an act. I wouldn't be surprised if she's just another fraud.'

'I can't imagine one could take in the Grandmaster himself. He's been notoriously hard on pretenders.'

'Yes, but this one's supposedly his bastard daughter, isn't it? Suits him, I'm sure.' And they laughed. Nastily.

Wren stood frozen to the spot, praying they would keep walking and not look inside. She didn't want them to see her, to know that she'd heard them. She just wanted the ground to open up and swallow her whole. That was what people thought of her then. That was what people were already saying.

Her only consolation was that if Roland de Silvius heard their gossip or heard about what they were saying, he'd probably pound them into the ground with his bare hands.

No, this wasn't happening, couldn't be happening. She had to get out of here. He just saw her as some kind of tool for power and control. Elodie had known all along. She couldn't trust him. The words in the book had been right.

Wren had thought it meant Finn but of course it didn't. She could trust Finn. But Roland was another matter altogether.

And now he wanted to put Wren on a throne to which she had no right, or no inclination. What would Elodie say?

No. Wren didn't even have to open the book to get the answer to that.

She had to leave. She had to get out of this place before it was too late and she was never able to do anything for herself again. She had to go now. She didn't even have much to take with her. Just the clothes on her back – not exactly practical for travelling, but the Seven Sisters weren't far. She just had to keep going. Or maybe she could find something else to wear. There had to be a store room somewhere.

Everywhere she went people would stare. Oh, some of them would try not to be too obvious. Damn it, they'd all report back to her so-called father as to what she was up to. She needed to get out of here fast.

But Lynette was waiting outside in the hallway. 'Oh good, there you are,' she said when Wren emerged. A sinking feeling dragged the pit of her stomach even further down. 'I'll show you to your quarters.'

'My quarters?'

'Well you can't stay here. The healers need the bed. I've set a room aside for you in my house, as your father requested.' She smiled gently. 'It must have been wonderful to meet him after so long.'

It wasn't. Not in the slightest. And he wasn't her father. He couldn't be. Just as Elodie was not her mother. No matter how much Wren had wanted it to be true. This was all some terrible mistake and she was going to have to get away before she could untangle it.

'Yes, wonderful,' Wren replied hollowly. 'Where is your house?' If it was nearer the walls she might have a chance. And a private house wouldn't be quite so guarded, would it? Oh, it couldn't be. She had to get out of here. As soon as it was dark.

But the thought of nightfall made her think of darkness and shadows and another chill swept through her. If they ever found out what she had done...

Elodie would understand. She'd be disappointed, sure, but Wren had spent her whole life disappointing Elodie. That didn't mean Elodie wouldn't help her fix it all again. That was what they always did.

Lynette wrapped her arm through Wren's and smiled, delighted with herself. 'Don't you worry. I'll make sure everything you need is ready for you as soon as we arrive in Pelias. I've lived in the court all my life until I married Yvain, and my mother was the most accomplished lady-in-waiting. It will all be fine, you'll see.'

As soon as we arrive in Pelias? Oh no. She couldn't...

'What about your husband? Don't you have a life here?'

Lynette just laughed. 'A life here in Knightsford? You're joking. Compared to Pelias this place is a farmyard. Yvain and I will travel back as part of your entourage. Your safety will take all priority for the knights from this moment on and as a Paladin my husband will not leave your side until you are back in the bosom of the Aurum. None of them will. We'll take such good care of you. I promise.'

There was nothing else for it. Wren closed her eyes and counted to calm herself. She was going to have to get out of Knightsford tonight. She would have to be as polite and gracious and as quiet as she could possibly be all evening. If she wanted to allay any suspicion she had to be as cooperative as possible. Lynette showed her to her house, a tall and gracious tower building overlooking the main gate, but more importantly far from the central garrison building. Her first bit of luck. Wren saw Lynette's husband, Yvain, only briefly, a man as tall as Roland and as fair as his wife. He bowed graciously to her and excused himself, saying he had to go and speak with Roland. Plans were being drawn up for her security.

Then they were alone.

Wren claimed she was sleepy at the first opportunity and made off to the bedroom appointed for her.

It looked out over the walls, towards the rolling hills, and most importantly of all it would be a cinch to climb out of compared to her tower home. Wren changed out of the gown with its many layers and found a simple tunic and breeches instead. The only shoes were delicate slippers, but she'd gone barefoot enough times. It was better for climbing anyway.

She waited until full dark, when the guards were barely visible anymore, and slipped out of the window.

CHAPTER 32

WREN

Wren had barely reached the ground when she was aware of someone watching her.

She reached out to the shadows around her and bid them come closer, pulling them up like a cloak. But before she could slip away, a hand closed on her shoulder, stopping her in her tracks.

Finn. Of course it was Finn.

He towered over her, his expression grim, his eyes stern. 'I might have guessed you'd do something like this. I was waiting out here, plucking up the courage to ask Lynette for an audience with you this evening. I didn't realise I just had to stand outside and wait for a princess to drop out of the sky.'

He tried to smile. Such a beautiful smile. It lit up his eyes and made her insides tighten. He was attempting to make a joke, trying to cheer her up. He wasn't very good at it. She doubted there was knightly training to cover it.

An audience with her. Was this going to be her life now? She couldn't bear it.

'I can't stay here,' she told him, pushing everything else aside. 'I just can't.'

His smile faltered into concern. 'He's your father.'

'Maybe. We don't know that for sure. Everyone seems to have a claim on me all of a sudden, from Roland to Leander.' She couldn't say 'even you', though she wanted to. It felt presumptuous, but the temptation was there. She didn't have to.

'Leander...' The name was a growl and she saw the loathing in Finn's eyes, fierce and dangerous. 'I thought... when he held you, when he threatened you, I thought I'd go wild. I *did* go wild. Everything I ever learned, all my training, none of it mattered. I killed those men without even a thought. I would have killed him too, and damn the consequences. I've never lost myself like that before. It was like a savagery inside me. As if I was becoming something else. Like the shadow kin or—'

'No,' she whispered, not wanting that to be true. Not her Finn...

'The shadow kin bite...'

'I purged that. You know I did. It's gone from you. There's nothing dark inside you, Finn.'

And yet there was, somehow. Something in his eyes, in the way he held her.

'You did something, Wren. It was like the whole Aurum burned inside me and I—I thought—' He closed his eyes in something so close to pain it made her ache inside.

'Thought what?' she asked when he didn't go on.

His eyes opened once more, staring at her, blue and glorious, blazing with intensity. 'I thought I'd been saved. That you'd saved me. That finally I was a true Knight of the Aurum. That after all this time, finally, I was safe. Don't you see? My bloodline, my heritage... it ties me to the Nox. But suddenly... it was gone. I don't know if what I'm feeling is real anymore. I don't know what you've done to me.'

'I'm sorry.' And still she didn't pull back, couldn't pull back. She leaned into him again and Finn took another step away. She knew she should let him go but that was impossible. Why couldn't she just let him be? Why did she need him so much?

'Great light, Wren,' he sighed. 'What's to become of us? I've taken vows. I'm meant to be a servant of the Aurum and you... you're...'

'I'm just me,' she assured him, even though she was aware that was a lie.

'No, you're not. I don't know what you are.'

A freak. A monster.

It crushed her inside, those words lingering between them. If he said it to her as well, if he used the same descriptions that Pol had used all that time ago, if he rejected her, she wasn't sure what she'd do.

Better to push him away, to leave him behind. Better to never give him the opportunity...

'I have to go,' she told him.

But Finn didn't move, didn't release her. 'And I can't let you.'

His hand stroked the length of her arm and she shuddered.

'Come with me.' That would work, wouldn't it? The two of them together, that would be all right. Maybe? It would take away the risk that they'd find out what she was, that the shadows answered her instead of the light. Without the strictures of the knighthood, without the questions about her birthright and what she was... They could just leave and run and never look back and—

'You're the princess. You're the daughter of the Grandmaster. You're—'

'Stop telling me what I am!' she shouted abruptly. Tears stung her eyes, and her throat tightened until she could barely get any other words out. 'Why does everyone have to tell me who and what I am and where I belong, when they have no idea really? It's not fair.'

For a moment he just stared at her and then he laughed,

softly, regretfully, his face transforming in that instant. Beautiful again, not strained and desperate. But still so sad and lost.

She shoved herself away from him. 'Stop laughing at me.'

She only managed to take about five strides when his hand closed on her shoulders, pulling her gently back around to face him. Her hands came up to his chest to shove him away so she could escape once more. But there was no escape now. His muscles tightened beneath her touch. And she wanted him. Needed him. The smile flickered over his sensual lips again and she leaned in, pressing her body to his. He backed up a little, surprised, seemingly reluctant to retreat but perhaps needing space all the same.

'We're both in trouble, aren't we?' he murmured.

Trouble. That was such a small word for it. If the knights found out... if he told them... But he hadn't said a word to give her away, had he? And it seemed like he might not know as much as she feared. How could he be like this with her if he truly understood what she feared? After all, he hadn't been there as she looked that thing in its endless eyes...

'What kind of trouble?' she asked.

'Infinite trouble. But I wouldn't be anywhere else, Wren.'

She still had both hands on his chest, palms flat. She ought to push him back, run while she could. Get out of here.

And suddenly she couldn't even manage that. She could feel the warmth of his body through the simple shirt he wore, and the movement of his muscles underneath. She could feel his heartbeat.

He growled something soft and dangerous and closed his eyes, seeking composure. 'What have you done to me, Wren?' The whisper came out hoarse and heavy with need.

'Nothing.' She knew that was a lie as soon as she said it. 'I didn't—I mean, I didn't mean to do anything.'

Great light she wanted him. Everything about him. She wanted to touch him and keep touching him, to kiss his lips and pull him to her. This wasn't natural. She knew that. It couldn't be. She tried to push him away again, this time determined, if not for her sake then for his, but there was nowhere left to go. His back had come up against the wall.

His hands closed around her waist, pulling her to him, firm, but at the same time so unbearably tender. As if she was something precious, something treasured. He hesitated, waited for her to move away again, to free herself and leave him.

When she didn't, he bent his head to brush his lips to hers and she let out a breath in surprise at the gentleness.

For a moment they just stood there, frozen together. His skin felt warm, his lips so soft. She lifted herself on her toes and his mouth opened to her.

And all of a sudden she was kissing Finnian Ward and she couldn't think of anything else.

CHAPTER 33
WREN

She wanted him.

That was all Wren knew, all she wanted to know. Just him.

She had done from the moment she had first seen him in the forest, wanted to make him hers, wanted to never let him go. It might not be logical, or even sane, but she couldn't deny it. He was hers. Somehow he always had been. Like he had been made for her.

Did it really work that way? The stories said it did but Elodie had always called that utter nonsense.

His mouth against hers, his tongue and lips moving in perfect harmony, drove all thoughts from her mind. She would do anything to protect him and the intensity of that feeling was terrifying. It was so unfamiliar and wild that she couldn't give in to her need for him just yet.

Because she had to know.

'Is it real?' she asked. 'What we're feeling?'

Perhaps she hadn't felt it from the very first time she saw him, but she had felt something. And once they were in the forest... in the darkwood... and... had it been real then? Was any of it real? He knew what she was, he had to. He had seen everything. Or nearly everything. And yet he was still here, with her, holding her, kissing her.

'It's stronger than anything I've ever felt,' he admitted. 'Like I'm being swept up in a flood, where the only choice is to let it take me with it. Do you understand? I don't know if this is something to do with the magic you used to save me or... or something else... I just don't know. And, Wren—?' He pulled her to a stop again, stared down into her eyes. For a moment he chewed on his lower lip, as if hesitating to speak. But the words would not be stopped. 'I don't care.'

Finn wrapped his arms around Wren, held her close against him, shielding her from everything. He'd protected her from the first, thrown himself into danger for her time and again. He was her champion, just like the Paladins and the knights from the old tales.

'What happened?' he asked. 'Back in the forest. What did you do?'

She pressed her forehead against his chest and closed her eyes. 'I was trying to heal you, to drive out the shadow kin's poison. But I don't know... it didn't work like I thought it would. The light... the light burned inside me and I think... I think I did something else. Changed you. So when Leander threatened me...'

'The bastard should never have even touched you.' The snarl was there again, buried in his otherwise gentle voice like a barb.

'He's your brother.'

'*Half*-brother. Different mothers. His a queen and mine... I don't know, a courtier, a servant, some other unfortunate who caught our father's eye. When Alessander recognised me as a son, my beloved brothers tried to drown me the very same evening. Joke's on them though, since Leander and I are the only ones still alive. And since he keeps trying to kill me at any available opportunity you can't say we're close.'

'How many brothers did you have?'

'Five. Alessander never did things by half and he delighted in setting us against each other.' His hand strayed to her hair, stroking it, running his fingers through it idly. 'It's the Ilanthian way, you know? Succession by murder. A delightful subject. We should talk about something else. Come on, let's go inside.'

She glanced around them. The courtyard was still empty and they were wrapped together in the shadows of the wall. Safe. Such darkness shouldn't feel so safe, but it did.

'I don't want to be a princess.'

'I don't want to be a prince,' he said, as if it was a joke. The problem was, it was true and there was nothing to be done about it. His fingertips traced a line down her jaw, to her throat, and Wren sighed, tilting her head back and leaning in to him again.

'What do we do?'

He turned solemn in a heartbeat. 'Wren, I can't let you run away. The kingdom needs you.'

That was it then. He'd keep her here and while part of her didn't care, or didn't want to care, the rest of her did. She needed to get out, to find Elodie and escape this nightmare. Which would mean leaving him behind.

It was like deciding to cut off her own hand. It shouldn't feel like that but it did. She reeled back, trying to put it into words.

'Finn,' she sighed, wishing for anything else. 'This place... these people... I can't...'

'Listen to me, come back. We'll talk to your father.' She winced as he called Roland that. She didn't want Roland as a father, not now, not ever. 'He'll listen to reason, I know he will. He's a good man, Wren. A kind man. He raised me. He... he won't give you up but he might...' And his words failed. Because they both knew that Roland de Silvius's duty to the crown was going to override anything else. She had understood that from the moment she had met him. His dismissal alone would have told her as much.

He served the crown.

Except once. When he'd fathered her with Elodie, if that was what had really happened. Everyone else seemed to think so. They'd both broken vows that night, obviously. Maybe he regretted it and everything since then had been to make up for it.

And here she was, living proof of his greatest failure, his deepest regret. Oh, her life just kept getting better and better. She couldn't do anything right, but then why would that be possible when she had been born from such a wrong?

But Finn didn't let her go. If he had, she was sure her heart would shatter into a million pieces.

She couldn't doubt his love and respect for his guardian. The man who referred to his bloodline as an *Ilanthian taint*. Roland did not deserve him. The very thought of it made her indignant on his behalf. But she couldn't tell him. It would break his heart. So she let him hold her.

'Besides,' he went on. 'You can't get out of the garrison tonight. The gates are locked and guarded. Roland has given the order that no one is to enter or leave. I'm pretty sure that includes you.'

He was good at giving orders, her so-called father. That much was obvious. He'd been quick to hand out orders to her as soon as she woke up and found herself trapped in this nightmare. She'd always dreamed of finding her father. She sorely regretted that now.

And when he found out what she was, what she could do, the way the shadows sang for her...

A freak, a monster...

'Where were you earlier? When I woke up?' she asked. 'Anselm was there but you'd gone.'

'At a debriefing. Being quizzed on everything that had

happened and everything about you. Don't worry, even I wasn't going to tell him what happened with the shadow kin. If they found out I'd been bitten...' He shook his head. 'And if they knew what happened at the camp...' His eyes darkened again, and for a moment she thought she saw little flecks of light dancing against the blue. 'I don't know what to do, Wren. I think we're both in a lot of trouble. Something in me has changed. I can feel it.'

She found the urge to apologise rising again and shoved it down ruthlessly. 'I couldn't let you die, Finn. I just—'

'Shush,' he breathed and kissed her again, silencing her.

They'd reached the door of the towerhouse. She hadn't even been aware of them moving, but here they were back where she had started. Finn opened it and they slipped inside and up the stairs. The house was quiet, the occupants all asleep now.

Finn didn't care what she might be. That meant everything. No, he couldn't mean that. He didn't care whether it was real or some enchantment. That was what he meant.

She didn't doubt for a moment that he cared for her. Which was part of the problem. She didn't know that she deserved it. She didn't know if it was real or something she had forced upon him.

But he seemed so sure.

Was it true? Had she done something to Finn so now he had no choice but to want her? Magic had that effect, she knew it. Hedge witches were very strict about its use for that very reason. Half the bargains with the darkwood she had ever heard about were made for love, or for lust, bargains made by people who didn't know the difference. People used magic to entice lovers, to keep them from straying, but for all the rumours of love spells she had never heard of anyone affected as powerfully as this. It was as if they had both lost their minds, as if a spell had been cast on both of them.

Wren reached the door of the bedroom assigned to her and

her hand stilled on the handle. Finn's arms still encircled her and every so often he found some new way to press a kiss to her, or a way to touch her skin that sent fresh shivers of need through her.

'What if you... what if you don't want this?' she asked. 'What if...?'

'Believe me,' he told her, blue eyes fierce and determined. 'I want this.' Then he seemed to pull back a little and doubt finally showed. 'But only... only if you do.'

'And if it's not real?'

'It has to be, Wren. I wanted you from the first but this... this is more. I came to care for you. This is like nothing else I've ever—'

She pulled him inside the room with her and kissed him to silence.

It had to be real, that was what he said and she believed him. She believed that too. It had to be. Because otherwise she was a monster, using magic to get what she wanted. Or they were caught in a tangle of enchantment from which they couldn't extricate themselves.

And part of her couldn't bring itself to care.

Kicking the door closed behind him, Finn reached for her again. If this was madness, or an enchantment, she didn't want it to end. She wanted him, only him. And every movement, every breath told her he wanted the same.

Wren slid her hands up his back, pulling out the shirt so she could touch the skin underneath.

'Tell me what to do,' he asked, his voice breathless.

She faltered, the words confusing her. 'What?'

'Tell me what you need. I don't want to hurt you, or... or...'

He looked for all the world a lost soul, desperate but also so very much in need of guidance. People looked like that when Elodie arrived to a terrible illness or accident, or to the birthing room. He shouldn't look like that. But at the same time it just made her want him all the more. How could she not?

Wren grabbed a fistful of his shirt so she could pull him towards her again. They toppled back onto the bed and he only just managed to catch himself on his outstretched arms so he didn't crush her completely.

She lay beneath him, breathing hard, trying to gather her thoughts.

'All right then,' she said at last. 'Undress.'

'Undress?' When she nodded, he complied, trying his best not to look like a green boy tearing off every scrap of clothing as quickly as he could. He pulled off his upper clothes and suddenly he paused as if unaccountably exposed in an entirely different way. 'Are you... are you sure?'

He stood there bare-chested, but being naked before her clearly didn't bother him. Was she catching a glimpse of something else?

Something inside him, something fragile and afraid. The fear that she could still reject him, that he'd have no choice but to put his clothes back on and slink away, defeated. Finn didn't seem like the type to go to bed with anyone less than willing. He wasn't like Pol and his ilk. How she knew that, she wasn't sure, but the certainty was there in her mind. He wanted her to be happy. He wanted to please her.

The thought sent a rush of pleasure to the core of her body.

'I'm sure, Finn,' she told him.

He pulled off the rest of his clothes more slowly and watched her with those beautiful blue eyes, as she took in his every movement, graceful as a dancer. When he'd finished and stood there somewhat awkwardly, waiting for her next command, she stood up and held her hands over her head.

'Now undress me.'

He took his time, indulging his desire for her. She squirmed when his fingertips brushed her skin, but he only did so accidentally. Well, maybe not entirely accidentally.

When they finally stood naked together, she rose on her toes and kissed his mouth again.

This time there was nothing else between them, nothing to hold them back. Her hands explored his shoulders, his chest, her clever fingers teasing his nipples until they tightened. He threw his head back and let her work her way further down his body. His abdominal muscles jumped beneath her touch, as hard as steel beneath his skin. Their lines guided her downwards.

'Careful,' he warned when she brushed her fingers up the length of his straining cock.

She pulled back. 'Did I hurt you?'

'No,' he laughed, a mixture of relief and desperation. 'You could never do that, heart. But too much and I'll spend before we do anything else. The things you do to me, Wren...'

When she touched him again, her name became a groan of need on his lips.

'Finn?' she whispered, hesitant now. She didn't know why. They were naked together, but now... now it seemed like something more intimate, more special. 'Kiss me?'

He looked down the length of her, studying her with an appraising eye. 'Where?'

'Everywhere.'

She blushed as she said it. But that was what she wanted.

Him.

Everywhere.

CHAPTER 34

WREN

Finn slid his hands up Wren's skin, teasing her, exploring her just as she had asked. She wanted this. But more than that... she needed it.

She felt delicate and beautiful beneath his hands.

He took his time, took every care as he touched her. Covering her in caresses until she wasn't sure she could bear it.

He bent to run his lips and tongue over her neck, shoulders, collarbones and down until he reached her chest. He knelt to claim one breast and then the other. She gasped out loud at the warmth of his mouth and the tingling sensation that lanced through her as he teased each nipple to hardness.

He caressed her skin with his teeth and tongue until she cried out and pushed her hips towards him instinctively. There was nothing else she could do, no words she could manage. There was only Finn, and his hands. And his maddening mouth.

Just hearing those little gasps and sighs she made seemed to drive him on into a new level of intoxication. He moved his hands to her back, to claw at her, pull her into him.

His tongue traced a line down her stomach and she trembled under his touch, burying her hands in his hair. At the same time his fingers continued their exploration, carefully designed to torment her. They followed her curves, round her hips, deliciously, deliberately... slow and inexorable. The anticipation was building, a moan already on her lips as he reached the top of her thigh.

As if he could sense it, he parted her legs and pressed inwards. One finger slid easily inside her and she gasped out loud, tensing against him. She wasn't sure what he did but a spear of pleasure took her breath away.

A rumble of triumph came from inside him, rippling into her skin everywhere they touched, and he moved so gently, coaxing her to trembling helplessness against him. Before she fell to pieces, he withdrew his hand.

'Don't you dare,' she whispered. When he would not give in to her, she pulled his face back to hers and captured his grinning mouth again with her own.

He returned the kiss passionately before gently pulling away. His hands tugged at her hips, burning against her.

'Lie down,' he told her.

Wren arched her eyebrow and smiled up at him. 'I thought I was giving the orders here.'

He turned his best glower on her instead. As if this was all a game. Perhaps it was.

'Lie down. Please.' He bit out the last word.

Wren sank back onto the bed with a soft laugh. As she reclined, he slid his hands slowly up her legs, until he reached the top, lingering there where her skin was most sensitive.

Slowly caressing her, he drew her thighs apart, delighting in her every reaction, drawing out her anticipation more than before. Wren moved restlessly beneath him with a desperation, her mouth open but only little gasps escaping, her hands still holding his head, stroking him restlessly.

But he resisted every urge to enter her and finally make

them one. Still teasing, still making her wait. Perhaps he knew already how she hated waiting for anything. Perhaps this was a new kind of torture he had devised. Instead, he trailed kisses where his fingers had been moments before. She tossed her head back when his tongue brushed her inner thigh, crying out as he continued higher. His fingertips brushed against the sensitive skin at the top of her legs and his tongue followed, toying with her now, smiling against her when she gasped or cried out. Finn pressed on, exploring her, drinking her in deeply, hungrily, until he found his intended target and focused entirely on her pleasure.

His tongue slid inside her, finding her core and sweeping it with long, inexorable strokes. His dexterous fingers were still at work as well, teasing, cajoling, tormenting...

Wave upon wave built inside her.

She couldn't stop it. She couldn't hold on any longer. She was lost in him, and when she came it was like losing a battle against the tide.

Her fingers burrowed into his hair, flexing against his scalp as she pushed up against him, calling out his name. Warmth washed through her, light and contentment, driving through her until she lost herself entirely.

Wren was glowing from within.

Not with pleasure, not with sweat. She was literally glowing, a living golden light moving beneath her skin. It reflected across the ceiling above her, his shadow silhouetted against it.

Finn lifted his head and gazed at her. Light reflected in his eyes, golden and bright.

'Wren?' he whispered, not afraid, not exactly. But the awe filling his voice made her body ache even more with need for him. She could see the desperation in his eyes.

'Come to me,' she said and he dragged himself up the length of her. It seemed to take eternity. 'Please, Finn.'

She reached out her hands to frame his face, staring up at

him to see a wonder as he hung there, poised to enter her. His cock throbbed against her skin and Wren lifted her hips towards him again as if in offering. She caressed his length, so carefully it was barely a touch, but even so she could tell it almost undid him right there and then. He gasped, swallowed down a curse and froze beneath her exploratory fingertips.

Two could play games of torture and pleasure, she thought.

He frowned, staring down at her.

'I want you, Finn,' she told him, her voice breathless and desperate. 'Inside me. With me. I want you forever.'

He frowned, hesitation written all over his expression. Didn't he believe her? How could he not believe her?

His voice when he spoke was a whisper. 'Even if I am a monster.'

A monster? He was glorious, beautiful. Everything about him. Nothing she saw in him could possibly be a monster. He was her champion. He was the truest heart she had ever known. Being a monster was her role. Didn't he realise that? She was the freak here. And if she had lured him in and trapped him...

But he had kissed her first. True, it had been in the dark-wood and he hadn't known what he was doing, and anyway he had probably thought she was a dream at that point. But the fact remained.

Was it wrong that she couldn't bring herself to regret it for an instant? None of it. Finn was her knight, her prince, her everything.

'You could never be a monster,' she told him and smiled as she pushed herself up on her elbows so she could press her lips to his. 'You're mine. I want you. All of you.'

For a moment it seemed he still held back, still struggled. As if he didn't quite believe her. She watched him swallow, his throat working like a ripple, and she licked his skin there, tasting salt. And desire.

Her hair moved, curling strands around his wrists on either

side, like black silken cords. She saw him glance down on either side, saw his eyes widen as the grip tightened, holding him there, binding him to her. Even the wild magic that flowed through her wanted him, the darkness and the light. Everything she was seemed determined to make him hers. To keep him with her forever.

He didn't pull away. His pupils flared wide with desire.

Finn plunged into her, filling her so swiftly, so completely that her cry escaped in a rush of air to break off the illuminated ceiling above.

She held him and cradled him, and came up to meet his every stroke. Her hair twisted itself around him, binding them together, and she arched her back to take him deeper. She pulled him to her and trapped him inside her, her body tightening around him again and again until another orgasm dragged itself from her.

Finn cried out her name as he tipped over the edge after her, his eyes closing tight as pleasure ripped through him. Through her.

He held her to him and kissed her skin over and over again.

She was lost in him, and it was wondrous.

She never wanted to be found again.

CHAPTER 35

FINN

Finn knew what he was, knotted with muscle and scarred, bruised from the beating he'd taken, but Wren didn't hesitate to explore him all night and his skin shivered with delight. Her fingertips were so soft, so gentle, and yet eternally demanding. Her hair tangled around him, holding him down until he was helpless before her. And he did not care.

She wasn't afraid, not of anything. She was fire and shadows, all the wonders of the magical world. Everything made sense with her in his arms. Finally. As if he had found some missing part of himself, something he needed to cling to forever.

Was it the effects of magic?

If it was, would he care?

What if you don't want this? she had asked him, giving him the moment he needed to turn away, to refuse her, to grasp the last thread of sanity available to him.

But not want it? He lived for it.

She'd said she wanted him too, but now his doubts rose again. What if this was too much for her, if his need had been too great? What if he had gone too fast or too far?

But Wren didn't seem to care.

And the light helped him. It was too easy to fall into her, her golden illuminations drowning him in delirious pleasure. Far too easy to give himself up in every way. And he never wanted to come back.

'You could never be a monster,' she had said in calm and solemn tones. 'You're mine. I want you. All of you.'

He desperately wanted to believe that, in the still of the night, her fingertips playing with the dusting of dark hair that ran down his middle.

Finn let himself fall into her again and again. All of him, body and soul. More times than he would have thought possible. There was nothing else he could do.

If it was an enchantment, what did it matter? It was everything he had ever dreamed of and he had no defence to counter it. If it was magic it had ensnared them both. She was everything. That was all he needed to know. She was darkness and light, hope and fear, pleasure and a longing so deep it was the twin of pain. He was lost in her and he couldn't bring himself to fight that, let alone care.

They lay entwined together as if they had always been this way.

Finn rolled on his back and Wren pressed her cheek to his chest, listening to his heart. Strands of her hair teased his skin like silken threads, binding him to her. It still clung to his wrists, wrapping around them like bracelets or manacles, marking him as hers, keeping him close to her. It ought to make him afraid, he thought absently. But it was a comfort instead.

But Finn knew he'd have to leave long before the dawn. If he was found here with her, Roland would probably have his hide.

That hadn't occurred to him before, and even now the thought was a distant thing.

You're mine. Those words had reverberated through him, words of power, of another kind of magic that meant something deep and eternal. He could feel the truth of it written on his bones, coiled up right at the core of him. Wren was his, and he was hers – that was all that mattered. Even if only for now.

Her breath softened as she drifted to sleep. He found himself just listening to her, matching his inhalation to hers, their heartbeats in time with each other.

He must have slept as well because, when he opened his eyes again, a figure stood over them both.

It wore a dark cloak and the hood was pulled up, but the moonlight coming through the open window opposite them framed it perfectly. Warily, Finn reached out for his weapon. Which wasn't there.

It was probably tangled up with his clothes on the floor, useless to him right now. Idiot. He should have known better. He always kept a blade to hand.

His movement woke Wren. She blinked as she half rose from his chest on one elbow. Her hair slid away from his skin, releasing him. Then she froze, staring at the same figure. At least he wasn't seeing things. That had to be positive, didn't it?

It was a woman, he realised. She reached up one slender, elegant hand, and let the hood fall down to reveal her face.

If Finn hadn't had Wren beside him he might have said she was the most beautiful woman he'd ever seen. Golden hair framed truly stunning features. Her skin had a warmth and vitality, was smooth of lines or wrinkles and her eyes were blue, bright with intelligence. She held her head very high, her neck long and elegant. When he narrowed his eyes he could see the traces of magic glittering at her fingertips.

'Elodie?' Wren murmured sleepily. 'What are you—?'

Finn's breath caught in his throat as if lodged there like a block of ice.

Elodie. Or rather Queen Aeryn... Enchantress, chosen of the Aurum, Queen of Asteroth... who had fled her throne and had hidden Wren away, stealing her birthright and forsaking her own.

Finn rolled out of the bed and grabbed the knife from the floor, bringing it up between them.

'Really?' Elodie said as if speaking to a troublesome child.

'I won't let you hurt her.'

She gave a brief and unladylike snort of laughter. 'And why would I hurt her? You, on the other hand... Oh, you I am going to hurt very much indeed. How dare you, spawn of Sidon? How dare you lay hands on her?'

The magic at her fingertips sparked with her anger.

'No!' Wren cried out. Her bare arms slid around his torso, her body flush against his. 'No, you can't. Don't touch him.'

Elodie scowled, ignoring Finn completely now.

'I don't know how you got yourself here and into this sorry predicament Wren, but I swear by the light itself if you don't let go of that boy I am going to—'

'Going to what? I did what you said. I ran. I got this far and I was heading for the Seven Sisters. I promise.'

Elodie flinched back, unexpectedly. 'The Seven Sisters? Why on earth would you go there?'

'You told me to.'

'I most certainly did not. You'd have to be an idiot to go there. Especially now. Who's been whispering in your ear? This Ilanthian bastard?'

Finn narrowed his eyes. Always the same insults, over and over again.

'No,' Wren protested, truly confused now. 'No, it was the book. Your book. Your writing. You said to come south.'

Finn tried to ease back, to put more distance between them

and Elodie. Wren wasn't making sense. There hadn't been anything in the book, had there? What was she talking about?

'I did no such thing. We had a plan, Wren. We always had a plan. Take to the deepest parts of the forest and wait. Why didn't you do that? You could have died. You could have been captured. And now we have to get out of here before Roland drags you off to the capital.'

She took a step forward and Finn moved to match her, still blocking Wren. He was knight-trained, a warrior and a killer all his life. Even with just his knife and his bare hands, he would be able to take out this slender woman. He had to protect Wren.

'Don't come any closer,' he warned her. 'The Grandmaster will want to talk to you.'

Her face froze for a moment, a mask of something like pain or grief. And then the scowl was back, deeper than ever.

'Oh, I'm sure he will, but that's not going to happen. Not now or ever.'

With the merest flick of her wrist, she threw something at him. Sparkling dust billowed around his face. He tried to jerk backwards, but it was too late. It filled his mouth and nose. In a moment it was inside him, inhaled on a gasp of surprise, scratching its way down his throat. Like sand in his eyes. He tried to wave it away with his free hand but it clung to him and everything blurred.

Wren... he needed to protect her. He needed... The world turned fuzzy and indistinct.

'Finn?' Wren said, trying to hold on to his suddenly failing body, her touch his only comfort. 'What have you done, Elodie? What's wrong with him?'

His legs lost their strength and folded beneath him.

No, this couldn't be happening. He had one job. Her. She was all that mattered. Wren was all... He hit the ground hard, the knife tumbling from his suddenly limp grasp. The room around him turned indistinct and their voices muffled.

Vaguely, he was aware of Wren trying to shake him awake, of Elodie picking up the knife in her oh-so-elegant hand. She fixed all her attention on Wren, ignoring him completely. Why would she? He was no threat to her now.

'Wren,' she said firmly, a maternal voice that was not to be argued with. 'Come here, little bird. Do as you're told and, I promise, I'll make it quick.'

Then everything slid to darkness.

CHAPTER 36

WREN

Finn's name died on her lips, as she watched him slip into unconsciousness.

He lay there, sprawled like a fallen tree. At least he was breathing. Not easily though. It came in fits and starts, laboured and then faint.

Wren turned her gaze on Elodie as if she no longer knew her.

Elodie advanced on her, knife in hand. She'd said she'd make it quick and all Wren could see was the exposed vein in Finn's neck, standing out as if protesting at all of this. He looked so vulnerable, helpless. She thought of Dancer, and Finn's mercy killing. Of the way he'd begged her to do the same when he thought the shadow kin would possess him. It was nothing of the kind.

Wren folded herself over him and pulled on all the darkness in the room, gathering it to her.

She'd use it, even if she wasn't sure how, even if she had to turn it against Elodie. She had done it before to protect him. And she would again. 'I won't let you kill him.'

Elodie shuddered to a halt, tendrils of shadow wrapping

around her like Wren's black hair. She gave a snarl of surprise and shook it off effortlessly. 'So that's what you think of me now? Thank you very much, young lady. Is this what you've been up to? Gathering dark magic? Very nice. Wonderful what you've learned from your new friends.'

She moved faster than Wren could have anticipated, grabbing Wren's hair, wrapping it around her knuckles and dragging her forward onto her hands and knees. The knife flashed between them, so close to Wren's scalp that she felt it like wind, severing the lengths of her hair as if they were made of the smoke into which they dissolved moments later.

Wren cried out as the magic she'd been building around herself fell away to nothing. Released from Elodie's grip, she fell back to Finn, still trying to protect him. Even if all she had now was her own naked body.

Elodie took an ominous step towards her, but her voice was tinged with regret now and didn't sound quite so terrible.

'I don't make a habit of murdering faithless knights, more's the pity. Or any great number of Ilanthian princes either, despite my reputation. Just the one and, honestly, he did that himself to spite me. Now get dressed, Wren. We have to go.'

Elodie hadn't been talking about Finn's life when she had said she'd make it quick, Wren realised with something akin to relief, but about her hair. Now it swung about her face, no further than the line of her jaw. And the magic it had let her control was gone.

She still didn't move. Not until she had answers. 'What have you done to him?'

'It's just a sleeping powder. He's fine. He'll wake up with a headache, that's all.'

The tightness in her chest eased a little. A sleeping powder. Nothing permanent.

'We can't just leave him here like this.'

Elodie picked up some clothes from the cupboard without

even looking at them and threw them at Wren. 'I assure you, we can and that's exactly what we're going to do.'

'But they'll find him here. They'll blame him.'

'I rather think that's his problem, don't you? I won't tell you again, Wren. Get some clothes on and come with me. It's too dangerous to be here. We need to get back into the forest as quickly as possible. Where it's safe.'

Safe. That was a joke.

'The forest is crawling with Ilanthians,' she told Elodie, but the hedge witch just gave another dismissive snort.

'Correction. It *was* crawling with Ilanthians. Between the knights bumbling around and my own efforts there are significantly fewer of them. The forest and I have a longstanding arrangement. They run fast when startled. If they're lucky.'

That was sobering. What had Elodie done? Her magic was powerful, and the forest constantly bent to her will. Wren only knew half of what Elodie could do. If that.

And if Elodie was really the queen of Asteroth, perhaps Wren didn't know her at all...

'And Leander?' Wren asked. Part of her dreaded hearing the answer, no matter what it was. He'd been... right up until he'd turned on her, he'd been... charming. She shook her head, trying to clear the muffled feeling that settled on her when she thought of him.

'They really got their claws into you, didn't they? That family.' She turned such a look of pity on Wren that she shrank back in shame. 'Great light, Wren, didn't you listen to anything I ever said? Ilanthians are witchhunters, all of them. Their princes are the worst of them. They will do anything to trap you, anything.' She cast a scathing glance at Finn. 'Now, are you finished? Come on.'

Wren pulled on Finn's clothes. Right now she didn't have a lot of choice and it was going to be more practical than any of the gowns. Barefoot would have to do. She tightened the belt around her waist and looked up defiantly at Elodie.

'Where are we going?'

'I already told you. Back to the forest and then far away from here.'

'But you told me to go to the Seven Sisters.'

Elodie paused in gathering her magic like strands of gossamer. She stared at Wren.

'When?'

'In the book.'

Elodie threw her head back in frustration. 'What bloody book, Wren? I don't know what you're talking about.'

Wren grabbed it from the bedside table and thrust it at her. 'Your diary. This book.'

Elodie froze, staring at it. Then she snatched it out of Wren's hand. 'Where did you get this?'

Someone knocked on the door and a concerned voice sounded. 'Princess? Are you quite well?'

Elodie let out a string of curses and, shoving the book into the pouch at her belt, grabbed Wren's wrist. Her grip was like iron and she hauled her to the window. The knocking became a banging, the careful inquiries shouts of alarm.

Moonlight shimmered, a spider web stretching out with Elodie at the centre.

'Hold on to me,' said Elodie and wrapped her cloak around Wren, holding her tight. The words Elodie spoke were other-tongue, but such a stream of them as Wren had never heard. They shook their way through her body, wrenching all the remaining power from her, dragging the shadows from the room around them, from the night itself and bending them to Elodie's will.

The door burst open, and Roland stormed in, followed by Yvain and several servants with lanterns. For a moment the Grandmaster just stared, dark eyes wide, locked on Elodie.

Wren felt the other woman suck in a breath of alarm, and then she frowned. A dark, determined expression.

Just as Wren had inadvertently done in the forest when she called the darkness, Elodie now did the same in reverse, pushing back the night to suck light from every available source to power her spell. Light flared all around her, light so bright that Wren had to clamp her eyelids shut to avoid blindness, while the others shied back. The light of the Aurum blazed through them both, blinding and terrible. It scoured its way into Wren's skin, winnowed through her flesh, like lightning, ripping along her veins and driving the shadows away.

Someone screamed. Wren realised only later that it was probably her.

And then they were somewhere else.

Somewhere full of light and flames that danced against their skin, a sickening aura of colours spiralling around them, somewhere in between. Wren's stomach twisted in on itself and her gorge rose, ready to vomit. It hurt. Everything hurt. She tried to pull away, but Elodie just held on to her with an implacable grip.

As abruptly as it had appeared the light was gone and Wren dropped to the forest floor on her hands and knees, throwing up everything she had eaten earlier in the day.

Elodie sank down to sit behind her, watching her closely. It was excruciating, as if Wren was still a child to be watched at every turn. But all the same, the feeling of Elodie's hand on her back, right between her shoulder blades, was the only comfort she still knew. This was a touch that had cared for her all her life, nursed her through illness and comforted her since she was an infant.

When there was nothing left to bring up, Elodie handed her a small flask of one of her tinctures. Much as Wren wanted to tell her to go and burn herself alive right now, she grabbed the little vial and drank its contents, because no one made cures like Elodie did.

Elodie produced a pair of boots from the pack she carried and handed them to Wren, who couldn't exactly reject them. Not if Elodie meant her to walk, which she clearly did. Wren pulled them on and wrapped her arms around herself, feeling the black fabric brush against her, inhaling the scent of him. At least she had that.

'Better?' Elodie asked after a long silence.

'No,' Wren lied. She had a million questions. Not least, what had Elodie just done to her? How had they got this far away from the garrison?

Unfortunately Elodie had questions of her own, and she got there first.

'What did you think you were doing with Finnian, Wren? Using him like that. It's... it's despicable. How could you?'

Wren didn't understand. '*Using* him?'

'He didn't stand a chance against your magic, did he? Right from the first moment he saw you, I suspect. I thought I taught you better than that.'

'I didn't force him.' She would never do that. But that was what she had been worried about, wasn't it?

Wren knew magic was not a thing to be turned on people, never to be used to take away free will. She hadn't even been sure it was possible until Elodie said that. She hadn't known what she was doing, it was an accident if she had. But Elodie seemed to think Wren was capable of anything all of a sudden.

'You wouldn't have had to. He's besotted. Anyone can see that. You used the Aurum to save him, didn't you? I felt it in the air and the earth. After that, he wouldn't have stood a chance against you. Your magic winds through him. You have to be better than that.'

Oh that was enough. Elodie had no right to talk like that.

No right at all. Wren was living proof of that. 'Like you were with Roland?'

Elodie surged to her feet, blood draining from her face. 'You have no idea what you're talking about.'

But Wren had seen the look they exchanged in that instant before Elodie had worked her magic and whisked her away. She'd seen the love, and the agony, and the rage. No one felt that much if they didn't care. No one felt that much if everything had not gone horribly wrong somehow and there was too much guilt and blame to bear.

'Don't I? It's the reason I'm standing here, isn't it?'

For once, words failed Elodie.

She stood there, mouth opening and closing while nothing came out. Then she turned away sharply. 'No. You have no idea.'

'He's my father.'

'No he is not.' She bit out every single word.

'Really?' Wren pulled the locket from her neck and hurled it at Elodie, who turned at the last possible second to snatch it from the air. Her hand closed over it and shook as she pulled it in against her chest as if it was the world's greatest treasure. 'What's that then? He certainly thinks so. Don't lecture me, Elodie. Not anymore. Not when you left him thinking you... that *both* of us were dead. You're all he thinks about, even now. You were all he wanted to know about when he questioned me. Just you.'

To Wren's horror, Elodie's eyes glistened with sudden tears. 'You spoke to him?' Her voice came out thin and stretched, as if it was a torture to ask.

'Yes.'

'How... how is he?'

She sounded like something had just knocked all the air from her lungs. And Wren saw it then, stark, written all over her face. Elodie still loved him. More than loved him. Adored him. And she'd walked away and broken him. Twice now.

'What did you do? Tell me. What happened? How are you the lost queen?'

Slowly, Elodie wrapped her arms around her body and seemed to diminish, folding in on herself.

'I'll tell you what I can. But we need to leave this place before they come after us. And they will come after us. Asterothian and Ilanthian alike. They want our magic, Wren. They want it more than anything. They want to enslave us both and use us. I will not let that happen. Not again. That's why I had to leave Pelias, and that's why we had to hide for so long. It's why we have to run now. As fast and as far as we can.'

'Where?'

'I can't leave the kingdom, but it's a big kingdom, Asteroth. The mountains perhaps. In the south. It's sunny there. You'll like it.'

Wren doubted that very much. She hated sunshine.

'What about Finn?'

'Finn will be fine. He's a Knight of the Aurum. Without you there, his life will right itself and he'll be back on the path intended for him. He'll be safe again. They might even accept him as a Paladin now after what you did to him. Who knows? They want a new one badly enough.'

'And with me there?'

'With you there...' Elodie let her head fall back and sighed to the stars overhead. 'Wren, my love. I know his line, I know what's in his blood. I saw it all. If you're there, the darkness will take him. I can't explain how or why. I can just tell you that it will. Leave him to serve the Aurum. It's what he wants. Now come on. I need to prepare, to gather my strength again if I'm to work another path of light so soon. And we are still too close to Knightsford.'

But Wren dug her heels in. 'No.'

'Wren, we don't have time for this,' Elodie said in that stern tone that always ended up with things going her way.

Not this time, Wren told herself. 'You can't make me come with you.'

'Can't I?' The look was a threat, a warning, and Wren felt her skin go cold. Because Elodie could. Of course she could. There was very little Elodie could not do.

'You wouldn't.'

Elodie shook her head. 'I'm sorry my love. I wish you'd cooperate but so be it.'

And with that a silvery web of light fell all around Wren, trapping her in an instant.

CHAPTER 37

ELODIE

When Elodie had been a child the world had handed her everything. She lived in a palace, and she was the apple of her father's eye. There was nothing he would not do for his little princess. She was already pretty, but those who tended her made her beautiful. Every single day. And she was not just beautiful but brilliant as well. They took her gifts and made them wonders. She was tutored by the greatest minds, she trained with the most skilled warriors, and she was loved. Loved by everyone. Her family, her courtiers, her people.

When she first saw the dark-haired son of a country knight, skulking around the kitchens having been sent on a fool's errand by his new superiors, she'd known in an instant that he was the man she would love. Maybe not in the way adults knew such things, but she knew he was meant for her. When others mocked him, a fire burned in her. She didn't understand why they couldn't see Roland as she did, why they dismissed him.

And Roland, her beloved Roland, had fought and struggled and made his way from the bottom right up to the top. He was her champion by the time she was seventeen, her lover by the time she was twenty, but always he was her everything.

He's mine, she had said. And never had words been more true. Heart and soul, they belonged together.

Right up until the moment Evander of Ilanthus arrived.

The prince was handsome. No one could deny that. Charming and courteous. Everything a prince should be. The brother of a king, sent on a mission of reconciliation, to seek a marriage that would form an alliance.

Roland looked heavy-set and inelegant in comparison. He wasn't schooled in scholarly works like Evander, and he couldn't dance. Or wouldn't. He got embarrassed and she would tease him. It was done with love but later she realised that he was sensitive about it and regretted every time she had laughed.

Evander courted her with the utmost care, set out to seduce her as only he could. And she fell for it. Idiot that she was, she let herself believe in the wrong fairy tale, in the wrong handsome prince. She agreed to the marriage.

Her father was old, her mother dead and her kingdom waiting for Queen Aeryn to have an heir. The Aurum needed her line. She had duties. Each time she took the vows of a new Paladin, the flames burning behind her, the light filling her, she knew people worried that she might be the last. The royal blood of Asteroth passed only through the female line. The Aurum awakened only when a queen sat on the throne, ignoring even its chosen Paladins and the maidens who tended it. Without her, there was no one.

It was only on the night of the wedding she realised she had made a terrible mistake. Her handsome prince became a beast the moment the vows were exchanged. There was no true love between them. He was of the line of Sidon, used to ruling, born to subjugate witches to the service of the Nox. And that was all she was to him. Another witch. Another uppity woman who didn't know her place. He didn't mean to be a consort, he told her. He had been born to be a king, but for the accident of being second born, and that was what he would be in this relationship. If she knew what was good for her she would make sure never to cross him, never to disobey him and never, ever to look at another.

Of course she told him what he could do with his demands. She told him in no uncertain terms, defiant and furious.

Evander hit her. No one had ever hit her before, not like that. She'd learned to fight, and in the training ground things happened. But this was different. The humiliation was so much worse. As she struggled up from the floor of their bridal chamber, still in her wedding finery, he opened his breeches, pulled out his dick and told her to get her mouth to work.

When she recoiled he had grabbed her by the throat and—

The door had burst open and Roland had saved her. Roland, who had always been there, always so kind to her, her Roland who she had cast aside. He saw her at her worst, degraded and pathetic, and his only thought was to rescue her.

He'd drawn his sword and advanced on the prince.

'Kill me and you invite war,' Evander had snarled. 'My people will fall on you like a tidal wave and destroy everything you hold dear.' And he was right. Because he was still a prince and he was under her protection. If Roland killed him, if she allowed that, there would be war and so many people would die.

Perhaps it was what Evander wanted, she thought later. Perhaps that had always been his plan.

'Don't, Roland,' she'd said. 'He's not worth it.'

Roland had carried her to safety. He'd cared for her. And she had finally realised what love meant, what it looked like in the real world. She finally knew he loved her in every action, with every movement, and that, like the fool she was, she had taken him for granted.

Later, much later, she'd stood in the chamber of the Aurum with blood covering the marble. Evander lay lifeless before her, having taken his own life to summon the Nox. As his empty eyes stared in triumph at the darkness bearing down on her, Elodie had known only one thing. She didn't do this to save herself, or her people, or even her kingdom. She did it to save Roland.

It was like she summoned him. Because he always came when she needed him. He always had. And always would.

'Elodie?'

The door had stood open and Roland ran towards her. She could feel the air shivering. The shadowy figure formed of dark magic rose from the shadows and the blood, twisting, transforming, seeking out the thing that would defeat Elodie, her greatest fear, her greatest weakness, and she summoned all the power at her command, draining the Aurum to defeat it. It would kill him. It would kill them all.

Elodie flung out her hand, and with it a force of magic, not at the Nox, but at Roland. She hurled him back from the door and felt his look of shock and betrayal like she was being stabbed in the heart.

So be it, she thought, and slammed the door between them. He was safe and that was all that mattered. Her Roland was safe.

Elodie had given herself up to destiny with a smile on her face.

But destiny had other ideas.

HERANDAL'S THE FALL OF THE HOUSE OF SIDON

Princes of the line of Sidon have always been sworn to the service of the Nox. Some say it is written on their hearts, that it flows in their veins with their royal blood. It is said that spilling blood royal of Sidon will summon the Nox's incarnate form, a dark goddess in her full power.

In each generation one will die, sometimes willingly, sometimes not.

Even disincarnate, the Nox is always hungry. And the princes will always obey.

CHAPTER 38

ELODIE

The notebook was worrying. It reeked of dark magic. The pages seethed with it.

From the moment she had grabbed it from Wren in the bedroom, from the moment her fingers had touched the leather cover, it had reached out to her. Elodie could feel it tucked away in the pouch she carried at her belt, little threads of magic probing her consciousness, trying to see how it might use her. Oh, it shied back from her the moment it realised who and what she was, when it noticed her noticing it, but the energy was still there. Still looking for a crack, seeking out a weakness.

The sentience attached to it chilled her. It recognised her and she recognised it, somehow. Like a ghost, or a memory. Like hearing a voice from the past. She would have lit the damned thing on fire there and then, except she knew it would take more than natural flames to destroy it.

They stopped to rest soon after midday, filling the canteen with water from the stream and sitting in the shade. Elodie had almost gathered enough strength to work the travelling spell again. She'd decided on the southern mountains. She could picture the place perfectly, a lake surrounded by high crags, desolate and isolated. Somewhere they could start again. The problem was, every time she felt almost strong enough, that power drained away. Not entirely but enough to stop her casting the next travel spell. Perhaps she was just exhausted. She had done too much in a short time. But there was still so much to do.

Wren still wasn't talking to her above what was necessary. Which was fine. She'd raised Wren on her own. She had seen every adolescent tantrum the girl was capable of, which had been not so very dissimilar to every toddler tantrum, truth be told. More words, no doubt, much more swearing. Letting her spend time in that wretched village had always been a mistake but she'd read that children needed the company of other children and so it had seemed a good idea at the time. She had never had that herself, apart from Roland. So she should have known better. Besides, Wren had never been like other children.

How could she be?

The sulking now was silent and cold, and it hurt to have it turned on her, but Elodie calmly told herself it was no worse than she'd seen before. Wren would get over it, eventually.

Threads of magic wound about Wren's body, holding her to Elodie's will. If Elodie squinted she could see them still, like gossamer. It was an old spell, and one that she hated using.

But sometimes there was no choice. Which was also the point of the spell. For all Elodie's talk of free will and never using magic to subvert it, when she needed someone to just do as they were told, she had that option. She used it now and hated herself for doing it to the girl. But there wasn't time to reason with her. Of course maintaining the spell meant it was taking longer than she would have liked to gather up the strength to work the travelling spell. But so be it. If, in the end, she got Wren to safety, she would make it up to her. Eventually. Wren would forgive her. She had to believe that.

With nothing better to do, Elodie took out the book and opened it. The pages inside were blank. She flicked through it, looking for some trace of the words Wren had insisted were in it, these so-called messages from her, telling her where to go, how to meet up.

There was nothing.

'Where did you find this?' Elodie asked.

Wren looked over at her then. She had been staring into the trees as if listening to something far away, her hands playing with the ragged ends of her now short hair. Elodie hated cutting it. Wren's hair had always been so beautiful. But it was also unnatural and, left too long, it invited disaster. Magic had to be controlled, measured. She'd thought she'd taught Wren that, but the moment they'd been separated, the girl had apparently forgotten everything. Or maybe Finnian of Ilanthus had stolen her wits.

'In your room. In the chest.' She grunted out the words grudgingly and Elodie ignored the resentment. This was for the best.

That was exactly where she would have hidden something like this – something precious, something dangerous – but Elodie had never seen this book before. Oh, it looked like something she would have owned, long ago. It carried the mark of the Aurum, embossed into the fine leather, and the pages were a lush creamy paper, heavy with cotton fibres. They whispered as they turned and felt smooth as skin beneath her fingers. It was a pleasure to hold.

Except... except there was nothing pleasurable about it. The whole thing made her flesh crawl.

Reluctantly, because she needed answers, she held it out to Wren. 'I can't see anything in it. Show me what it says.'

Wren eyed her suspiciously for a moment and then snatched it out of her hands. She opened the book wide, holding up two pages as clear and unblemished as new fallen snow. 'There.'

'There's nothing there, love.'

Wren frowned, her brow knitting together in puzzlement as she studied the pages herself. 'Yes there is.'

'What does it say then? Read it to me.'

Wren's eyes moved over the empty page as if she was reading, or at least trying to read. But instead of speaking she frowned even more deeply and her mouth moved slowly, like a child trying to sound out something she couldn't understand.

'I don't... I don't get it,' she said at last. 'The words aren't our tongue but... they aren't othertongue either. I thought...' She looked up then, meeting Elodie's steady gaze. She looked worried, as if she was finally coming to grasp the seriousness of all of this. 'I thought I read it earlier. It was a diary. Or at least it seemed like one. About when you were young but every time I tried to read it... it changed. It became a warning.'

Magic then. Well, Elodie had known that much. This just confirmed the details. A thing of magic tuned somehow to Wren alone. Elodie had really been hoping for something else. She ought to have known better than to hope, even for a second. Because that thing, whatever it really was, had not been in her possession and should not have been among her belongings. If it had been she would never have left it for Wren to find.

Darkness rolled off it in waves. The touch of the Nox, its power, ghosts of the past, malicious and determined. It sent chills through her.

'What is it, Elodie?' Wren asked at last.

'That, I don't know. What do you see now? What's it saying?'

'It... it says I shouldn't trust you.' Her voice shook. 'It says you're lying. And that I should go to the Seven Sisters.'

'I think, my love, that's the last place you should go.'

'Why's that?'

Because the book bound with dark magic was telling her to go there, of course. And because Wren was... well, Wren was what Wren was, but Elodie couldn't tell her that. She'd promised herself right from the start. The less Wren knew about her origins the better. Nothing had happened to change her mind about that.

'The Seven Sisters is an old place of ancient magic. Part of the first magic. Before the Aurum brought us order and light, there were lots of stone circles and people went there to draw on the powers of darkness and light. Like the stone circle in the darkwood at home.'

'There's a stone circle in there?'

Elodie smiled. Even now Wren didn't know as much as she thought she did. 'Right in the heart of it. It's where pacts are made, where people die.'

Wren frowned. 'Where I found Finn?' It was a whisper, perhaps an admission. It made sense, but this entanglement got worse and worse, Elodie realised. The further she could keep Wren from this boy the better. They needed to move soon. The Sisters were too strong and something – something truly terrible – had its eye on Wren. Perhaps it always had. Now, it was luring her in. And perhaps it had help.

'Probably. Maybe it used him to draw you there. Maybe he was just unlucky. Maybe you both were. It's old magic, magic bounded by the stones, sunken deep into the ground, reaching for the stars. Most of them have been destroyed, or co-opted. The chamber of the Aurum itself was built around one such circle. But it was one dedicated to the great light already. Others... others bend in a different way.'

Which was an understatement, but she didn't want to terrify Wren. She needed what little cooperation she could still get from her.

'But if there are answers there, about me, about us and what we have to do...'

Elodie shook her head firmly. 'It's too dangerous, love. Even if it wasn't a vortex of magic, it's wide out in the open. The knights will no doubt look for us there. As will the Ilanthians if they're still circling.' And they were. She knew they were. Leander would not give up that easily. Not if he suspected the truth about Wren. Or even a fraction of the truth. 'And I believe… I believe that book wishes no good for you.'

It felt strange to talk about the thing like it was sentient. But that was how it felt, she realised. She wished she knew what it was, and now she saw it back in Wren's hands she wished she hadn't let it go. It felt wrong, and if it was somehow communicating with Wren that was wrong too. Dangerous.

The problem was she was also relieved to let it go, not to have it anywhere near her anymore. The strange sensation of slowly being drained of energy had started the moment she'd taken it from Wren. And now it had stopped. That couldn't be good. She needed every scrap of power she had to protect them, and to get them away from this place.

But Wren didn't seem impacted at all. The thing was trying to communicate with her. Clearly. Elodie shivered, her nerves on edge. She had to believe in Wren, that she had raised her right. 'You're my little bird, remember? I'm just trying to look after you.'

To her dismay, Wren dropped her gaze to the pages again and she frowned. For a moment she didn't say anything, but the words found their way out all the same. Wren had never been able to keep anything from Elodie, and that, Elodie thought, might be their one saving grace.

'It says… it says you're lying.'

Elodie laughed. She had told so many lies over her life that sometimes she wasn't sure what was the truth anymore.

'I'm sure it does. But you know me, Wren. I will do anything and everything to protect you, no matter what the cost. Even if you hate me for it. Now, time to move on. Put that thing away and don't pay it any mind. We'll find a way to deal with it later.'

They would have to. Some kind of spell to unravel the enchantment on it. Elodie didn't want it getting its nasty claws any further into her little girl.

But Wren wasn't a little girl anymore. She was a woman. With a woman's body and a woman's heart, and a mind of her own. The spell of binding might hold her now, but in the end... in the end Elodie would have to release her, and pray Wren would forgive her.

Elodie had to admit, she was no longer sure that was a given and, somewhere deep inside, her heart was breaking at the thought.

But right now, there was no choice. No choice for either of them.

CHAPTER 39
WREN

The little threads of magic chafed against her body, not quite painful, because Elodie would never intentionally cause her pain. She knew that. But Elodie always believed she knew what was for the best and was determined to get Wren to safety. So that was that.

The fact that she gave Wren no say in the matter didn't seem to occur to her. Nor did the utter hypocrisy of her accusing Wren of using magic to take away Finn's free will – which she definitely had not done – while doing the very same thing herself.

Her thoughts rumbled beneath the surface. She couldn't do anything to stop herself obeying. Had Elodie done this to her before? When she was younger maybe? She couldn't recall and that itself was a worry. The outrage of it all made her want to scream but she couldn't. All she could do was walk when Elodie wanted her to walk, and sit still when Elodie wanted her to sit still.

How dare Elodie do this to her? How dare she abduct her and drag her off against her will and tell her it was all for her own good?

She had always been like this. Always.

But, Wren was no longer a child.

So she answered Elodie's questions and tried to work out how to get herself out of this.

When Elodie quizzed her on the book and handed it back to her, an idea spiralled up from inside her. Like a spark of rebellion from the bonfire raging at the pit of her stomach.

Maybe Elodie was not as smart as she thought she was. Or maybe she was just too trusting.

The first of the lines of Elodie's magic that held Wren broke, and a shadow wound its way out of the pages of the book, up through the other lines, moving them aside.

Music whispered to her, words that weren't quite real, weren't quite understandable. She strained to listen as she walked, to understand. The song was there, but muffled by Elodie's enchantment. But the more she concentrated, the clearer it became.

It was only a matter of time until Elodie felt strong enough to cast her spell of transportation again, and then she'd drag Wren off to the other end of the kingdom to start over. If Wren didn't get out of this soon, she was going to be so far away from this place that she'd never make it back. She knew Elodie. She did not do things by half.

The book seemed to be the answer. It was magical, and it was trying to help her. She lingered behind Elodie and took it out, trying to read it as she walked. Again, the swirl of words and letters seemed to make no sense at first, until, at last, they resolved into something legible again.

The writing didn't look like Elodie's this time. Clearly that deception was at an end. It didn't matter, Wren decided. Now she knew it wasn't Elodie, she'd just have to be a bit more wary, that was all.

Come to the Seven Sisters, it said.

Sure, she thought, as easy as that.

And as soon as she thought that, another word appeared, one she didn't know. It was othertongue, but not in any form that she knew. The power radiating from it made her stumble and, when Elodie turned to look at her, she snapped the book shut.

'This will have to do,' Elodie told her and held out her hands.

The strands of her spell still lingered enough that Wren had no choice but to reach out and join hands with her.

'Please don't do this,' Wren whispered, but Elodie just tightened her grip and began to murmur the words of othertongue as she had in Knightsford. Light swelled around them, blinding and terrible, setting every nerve in Wren's body on fire. She tried to pull back, to tear herself free, but she couldn't. All the same, she struggled, panic sweeping through her.

She had to get out of this. She had to make Elodie stop.

Come to the Seven Sisters, the book had told her, and it had given her the means to do so. If she was just brave enough to do it.

The book sent out a final flicker of shadow and Elodie's spell holding Wren shattered.

Elodie's eyes opened wide as she felt it come apart, locked on Wren's face as Wren, unable to do anything else now, fixed her mind on the stone circle. She didn't know what it looked like but she tried to conjure up an image and something sprang into the forefront of her mind, like she had picked it out of the air. Tall standing stones in a ring, seven of them, ancient and cold, wreathed in darkness. Nothing grew in the middle. It was empty. The image wasn't a comfort, and it didn't feel like an escape. More like a trap.

Elodie had told her not to trust it, that it wasn't safe, but Wren hadn't listened. The book had given her a word, had forced it on her, and that was the word she said now. She had to. It fell cold and hard like iron from her lips, instead of the sweeping song she usually associated with othertongue. Even as she said it, she knew she had made a terrible mistake.

For a moment everything seemed to freeze. In Elodie's eyes, Wren saw the dawning horror spread through the blue of her irises like storm clouds.

'What have you done?' Elodie whispered, and her voice, always so sure and certain, always so strong, quavered in horrified disbelief.

CHAPTER 40

WREN

Something dark and endless enveloped the both of them, ripping them out of the path of light and slamming them back to the ground with a crack like a lightning strike. Light flared, bright and blinding, and then darkness swept in behind it.

Wren rolled slowly onto her back, every part of her protesting. She stared up at the cloudless night's sky, the moon high and the stars clear and bright. And, as she brought her gaze down lower, she saw the stones rising in a ring around her, tilted in towards her like the teeth of some great beast rising from the dark earth. Elodie lay a little further off, at the edge of the circle, very still, a crumpled heap.

Shapes circled them, moving, sliding from shadow to shadow. Not human. Wren knew that in an instant. There were shadow kin gathered all around them, clinging to the edge of the stones, stalking their newly arrived prey.

What had she done?

'Elodie?' she called. But Elodie didn't move. Wren forced herself up onto her feet and stumbled across the space between them, half running, half crawling, until she reached Elodie's unconscious form. 'Elodie, I'm sorry. Please... please, wake up.'

'Well,' said an all too familiar voice from the darkness. 'This worked out better than expected, didn't it, little bird? I hoped to snare you. I didn't for a moment imagine we'd get her as well. Well done, my darling. You're everything I hoped for and more.'

Leander leaned on one of the standing stones as if he hadn't anything better to do with his life. As Wren watched, his remaining men fanned out around the stones, keeping clear of the swarming shadow kin but cutting off any possible escape, even if she was lucky enough to make it that far.

And to flee now, she'd have to leave Elodie behind, so that wasn't about to happen.

What had she done?

Leander walked towards her, brushing one of the shadow kin back when it drifted too close to him. It obeyed his thoughtless gesture instantly, like a dog well-trained by its master. Who or what was he? A prince of Ilanthus who could command the dark fragments of the Nox? Wren's mouth went dry and her throat tightened.

'I couldn't have imagined my little book would work so very well. It was more of a whim to leave it there for you. I'd thought the queen would have taught her daughter better than that, but it seems she was remiss in a lot of areas, wasn't she? Too many secrets to keep, that's her problem. Always has been.'

His book. So they must have been his words all along. Telling her not to trust Finn, not to trust Elodie, to run away, to hide, to come here. Confusing her, frightening her. Playing with her.

Great light, she was such a fool.

Wren grabbed the book from her side and hurled it at him, aiming straight for his head. Leander laughed as he snatched it out of the air, petting it like something precious. 'Now princess, we're really going to have to do something about that temper of yours.'

'I'm not a princess,' she told him.

'Oh I think you are. More than a princess. You're something very special indeed. I can smell it on you. And when we're wed, you're going to be a queen, and more. Ilanthus has a special crown waiting for you.'

'Wed? I'm not... There is no way I'm marrying you.'

Leander shook his head as if dealing with a child. 'Take them both,' he told his men. 'We've got a lot of preparations to make but this is as good a place as any. Strong and old, powerful. The earth itself is stained dark and I can feel the veil at its thinnest.'

The shadow kin drew back and his men rushed in. They didn't look as certain of any of this as he did, but to argue was clearly to invite instant death. They seized Wren, pulling her back from Elodie, and then dragged Elodie clear of the stones. In an instant, chains snapped closed around Elodie's unresisting arms, the same dark metal that seemed to glow with a black and blue nimbus with which Leander had imprisoned Finn.

Finn, Wren thought desperately, what would he say now if he could see her? That she was a fool who had brought this on herself, that she should have stayed where she was safe, that she shouldn't have trusted anyone let alone Elodie. Oh and he would have some choice words to say when he knew she had been acting on the suggestions of his own brother.

The guards brought Wren to Leander, releasing her to stand before him at the edge of the circle. He smiled at her, such a beautiful but terrible smile.

'I prefer your hair longer,' he said, but he reached out to stroke the short length all the same. His touch was so gentle, like Finnian's had been, and Wren fought to suppress a sob. He frowned and, unexpectedly, his voice gentled. 'Don't be scared. Once we're finished here, my love, you'll never be scared again. I'm going to make you so strong, so powerful, no one and nothing will ever be able to hurt you. You'll see, Wren. You'll thank me.'

'Leander, I don't know what you think is going to happen but I—'

He shushed her, his hand closing on the back of her head, his thumb stroking her cheek. She couldn't move, couldn't escape him. He pulled her close and kissed her lips, his mouth warm and devastating. Her body went limp in his grip, helpless, and then his words – the words he spoke even as his lips brushed against hers, as his breath played against her skin – reached her ears.

It was a song. It was othertongue, and she recognised every terrible word. Her mind translated it as if it was her native language now. She had listened too well, and it had taught her to understand.

It was Leander's voice, but not just his voice. It was many voices and they were all bent on one thing. It was the song in the trees, the music that had come out of the darkwood.

Come, oh divine darkness and be made whole once again. Come to your servant, supplicant before you here, where the veil is thin and your prison walls are weakest, come to the vessel that once was yours. Come and be mine, and let me be your servant forever.

She pulled herself back, ripping herself free of him and colliding with one of the stones in the ring. Reversing course, she stumbled back into the circle of the Seven Sisters. The stones took on that same darklight, the blue-black glow shimmering over their surface like the shadow-wrought metal binding Elodie's magic. The moonlight grew horribly bright overhead and the ground trembled underneath Wren as a web of magic spread out beneath her feet. The air filled with a humming and she saw the shadow kin whirling through the sky above her, their eyes aglow like the stars. So many of them, too many of them, gathering together to form one terrible mass.

The world seemed to pause around her, the air itself expectant.

'What have you done?' she shouted at Leander.

'Just one more thing needed,' the prince of Ilanthus called back to her, his voice carrying over the rushing air and swirling darkness. 'We still need that final ingredient to restore the Nox. Millennia ago my forefathers offered her a sacrifice, a tradition we have kept faithfully generation after generation, royal blood to be spilled for the goddess. Until now. My father failed. I will not.'

Royal blood? He couldn't mean his own. Even Wren could see that.

He wasn't the only member of the House of Sidon, was he? But Finn was far away, back in Knightsford. Safe.

Leander drew his sword, brandished it like a talisman before her. Blue-black light glinted along the edge, shadow-wrought, the blade of a prince blessed by a dark goddess.

'Did you think he loved you, little one? Did you think a girl who grew up isolated in the forest, raised by a witch of our most hated enemies, would naturally engender the devotion he showed you from the start? He couldn't help himself. And now he's here to die. Not for you, little one. For her, for the Nox.'

And Finn Ward stepped up to the edge of the stone circle, armoured, sword in hand, his face blank and his eyes ablaze.

CHAPTER 41
FINN

A bucket of freezing water woke Finn, coughing and spluttering... and naked.

The events of the night surged back into his memory and, before he could catch his breath, another bucket of freezing water struck him, knocking all the air from his lungs again.

'What did you think you were doing?' Roland roared at him.

Hands seized him, dragging him upright, and he almost wished they would just leave him there to die. Because anything would be better than facing his guardian right now.

Wren was gone.

Wren.

Great light, what had he done?

There had been more shouting, a lot more. He had no words of explanation, no excuses to give. Wren was gone, Roland had seen Elodie take her, and all that had been left was Finn unconscious on the floor of the girl's room.

Roland's daughter's room. The girl spirited away by the traitor queen, the love of Roland's life. And Finn had done nothing to stop them.

His life was over. Or it should have been over. But even

though Roland was armed with Nightbreaker, the Grandmaster's sword, they had just dragged him back to the barracks, in full view of every curious eye peering out at the disruption to the quiet night, and thrown him into his room.

'Get dressed,' said Anselm, not unkindly. Anselm never did anything unkindly. It wasn't in his nature. He was Finn's closest friend. Perhaps the only one left now. 'He'll want to see you. There's every chance—'

'That he'll dismiss me,' Finn finished. 'If I'm lucky that's all he does. He can't send me home, but there are some very secure prisons he has the keys to.'

'Well, quite. What were you thinking? I mean, she's pretty Finn, but...' He scraped his hand through his hair. 'What *were* you thinking?'

Finn had no answer for that.

Thinking? He hadn't been thinking, had he? She addled his brain and had done from the first. Wren just had to look at him and he was lost. That was the problem.

Alone in his room he dressed himself in the uniform that he suspected very shortly he would have no right at all to wear. He'd go back to being just another royal hostage and Roland, who had been a far better father than his own father could ever have been, would disown him entirely. He was a disgrace and he had disgraced the Grandmaster, Wren and everything the knights stood for.

Outside, thunder rolled through the night's sky. He heard the commotion before he realised what was happening. And then Anselm was back. He opened the door without hesitation.

'Change of plan. You're needed. We're all needed.'

'What's happening?'

'We're under attack. Shadow kin, a veritable army of them. Move it, Finn. Every able-bodied man is called to arms. Even those in disgrace.'

Shadow kin? They had to be looking for Wren. Her light

could drive them away, destroy them. So, naturally, they wanted to destroy her, especially now she was back with her father. They must have known somehow and massed together to destroy her before she could reach the Aurum.

Training took over. It was more than second nature; it was his first instinct. In the scramble to don armour and gather weapons, he saw Roland, grim-faced and still angry, handing out orders to all and sundry. But they faced something far worse than Finn's stupidity right now. Theirs was an argument for another day.

Argument, Finn thought. There was no argument. He'd betrayed Roland's trust. Even if he hadn't already suspected who Wren was, the moment he'd known for sure he should never have touched her. But by then it had been too late.

Logic told him he couldn't have fallen in love with her so quickly, but there was no other word for his feelings towards her. She was everything.

At least she wasn't here for this. Elodie would keep her safe, get her far away. And when Knightsford fell, there would be stories told about the last stand made there by the garrison, a handful of Paladins and those knights who never got to make their vows before the Aurum.

Because it would fall. He knew that.

Outside the walls, an ocean of shadow kin rose from the forest, from the depths of the darkwoods, more of them than had been seen since the last days of the war, when the Nox was destroyed and the world tore itself apart. They were coming for Knightsford, coming to take Wren.

It was a small comfort to know that Wren, his beautiful Wren, wasn't there.

Holding Knightsford for as long as possible would give her more time to get away, and he'd take as many of them with him as he could. That was all he could do for her now. Fight hard, die well. So be it.

Finn mounted the horse and joined his brothers-in-arms as the gates opened to let the knights out. Roland led them, followed by Yvain. Anselm fell in beside him. Finn lowered the faceguard of his helmet and drew his sword.

They waited in total silence for Roland's signal, and then, when it came, plunged out through the gates to meet the tide of darkness that roared out of the night.

Battle raged around him and, the next thing he knew, he was deep in its heart. The enchanted blades shimmered with the Aurum's light as they tore through the shadow kin and sent them screaming back into smoke and shades. But the shadows were many and, in the darkness of the clouded night, they were at their most powerful.

The knights flanking him fell back, but he pushed on, determined to keep up with Roland who had charged right into the thick of things, as usual. His guardian had always led from the front, even when he shouldn't. Not as Grandmaster.

But no one could inspire men like Roland de Silvius. His soldiers were devoted to him, because he always protected them. And Finn was no different. Roland had always protected him, even when no one else would. Roland might hate him now, and Finn could hardly blame him, but that didn't mean Finn didn't have his back.

A wall of darkness rose around Roland's white horse and for a moment Finn lost sight of him. He pushed forward again, calling on the great light and the Aurum for protection. Deep inside him something answered. As he charged into the darkest part of the battle, the light with which Wren had healed him surged up again. It blazed along his veins and burst out into the night, illuminating the nightmares into which he rode. Shadow kin recoiled from him, screaming, and his blade made lines of fire through the air, banishing them with something even brighter than the blessings laid on the other knights' weapons.

Roland's horse was down, shadow kin feasting on it, and for

a moment Finn thought his heart had stopped. But then he saw the armoured figure stagger to his feet, Nightbreaker still in one hand and a knife in the other. Roland had lost his helmet but he was still fighting. Finn reached his side just in time to drive back the biggest of the monsters bearing down on him, circling around his guardian and using his own mount as a shield.

He reached down and pulled Roland up behind him. The Grandmaster was bleeding from numerous wounds but nothing took out Roland de Silvius. He nodded to Finn and gritted his teeth, holding on with one hand while still brandishing Nightbreaker to defend them both now. Finn turned his horse's head back towards the bulk of the knights. Safety in numbers, he reasoned. But even as he dug his heels in and the poor creature carrying two of them in armour strained to take them to relative safety, something closed around his body, something dark and strong, so much more powerful than any shadow kin he'd ever faced.

'Finn!' Roland shouted, as he was dragged off into the mass of shadow kin. Tendrils wrapped around him. Not vines this time, not unless vines were larger than a warrior's forearm and could crush bone. Tentacles bound his legs tight and closed over his face, smothering him. He felt Roland's hand close on his arm, desperate for purchase against the armour and finding none. Grabbing the gauntlet, he tried to cling to Roland but the force surrounding him was too powerful. It ripped them apart. The horse went over screaming and kicking, Roland somewhere underneath it, and even as he called out his guardian's name, Finn felt the light blazing in him give way to something else. Something dark and terrible like a poison rushing along his veins from the place where the shadow kin had bitten him. Here, in the embrace of its family, he didn't stand a chance. Everything dark and endless, all the rage and all the madness roiled up inside him, pushing reason and light aside.

He lost himself inside it and all that was good and light, all that he valued and cherished within himself, burned away to ashes.

CHAPTER 42

FINN

Finn came back to his senses on the edge of the stone circle, not so very far from Knightsford, head still spinning and clogged with darkness. He could still hear the sounds of battle far behind him, but he was not alone. Far from it.

Shadow kin whirled overhead, sealing off escape, huge things, far larger than any he had seen before. Not that he could have run anyway. His body moved like a marionette, something other manipulating him. Finn struggled to regain some semblance of control of his own body again and pain ripped through him, tearing at every nerve.

Wren stood in the circle, alone and afraid, her eyes so very wide. She stared at him like he was some kind of monster from her nightmares. She looked so small, standing there, while the shades of dark magic whirled around her.

On the far side of the circle he could see the figure of Elodie. She was manacled in shadow-wrought metal shackles, and slumped there, unmoving. He remembered the agony of their touch on his own skin. Perhaps she was lucky she was unconscious.

'Finn? Look out!'

Her cry was the only warning he got as Leander attacked. Instinct brought the sword up to deflect the killing blow and Finn ducked aside, rolling with the momentum and coming back up in a defensive position to block another strike.

'I thought you'd never get here,' his brother snarled at him. 'What took them so long? I would have thought you'd want to hasten to her side.'

'You sent them? The shadow kin? Why?' He'd seen men fighting and dying, men he lived and trained alongside, his friends and brothers-in-arms. He'd left Roland back there and who knew what might have happened to him. And Leander had sent that army of shadows? To bring him here? This couldn't be happening.

'You're needed, little brother. You have a duty to perform. Or did you forget that too? The one thing you were born to do?'

Leander's blade sliced through the armour. It shouldn't be possible but shadow-wrought steel could cut through nearly anything. Finn felt it bite into his skin underneath. The leather jerkin took the worst of it, but nothing could protect him from that blade except to avoid it. He parried the next blow, his own sword of Aurum-forged steel the only thing strong enough to block it, and tried to retreat. But his brother just came after him again.

Leander had always been the better swordsman. He relished that. No matter how hard Finn trained, Leander was always better.

Another cut, another slash and Finn went down onto one knee, trapped between the stones, which sucked away any protection the Aurum could still give him. Precious little now. He could feel the vestiges of the Nox threading their way through him with each cut, his body aching and mind blurring. Slowing him down, draining him of strength, wearing away his will to fight.

Give up, it seemed to sing to him, and he longed to obey.

Rest and be at peace at last. Accept the inevitable. You were born for this. Born to die.

He almost believed it.

Then Wren shouted his name. He turned, desperate to reach her, to save her, to do anything for her. Inside his mind light ignited again, her light, or the light she had given him. His one strength, his one remaining hope...

In the stone circle, she was pulling shadows from everywhere to join with her will, a terrible darkness welling up beneath her and massing overhead. She stood in its centre, a focal point and nexus. The key to whatever was happening here.

No, not the only key. The stones had a part to play. And so did he.

You were born for this, born to die.

Leander's sword burst through his chest, the armour tearing like paper. Finn stumbled and dropped to his knees, staring at the point, surprised to find it there.

It didn't hurt. That was the strange thing. In a weird, distracted way, he knew it should but there was no pain. Nothing hurt. The cold that spread through him stole away all pain, all feeling. And doubt. And fear.

Wren let out a wild, keening cry, the shock of it making her release the hold she had managed to maintain on all the magic in her, and the darkness rushed in on them both. Even as his eyes dimmed, he saw the darkness beyond darkness flood through her. The way the light had filled her when she saved him in the forest, when she had driven the poison of the shadow kin from his flesh and purified his blood. But now darkness took its place, a darkness so deep it was like a new kind of light. Glimmers of blue and violet raced across her skin like marsh light, luminous and terrible dancing flames that came out of nowhere. Wren's eyes were fixed on him, wide and terrified, desperate, and all he could do was stare at her, into the endless depths of them. He couldn't see any difference between pupil and iris, nor indeed any trace of the white. All was black and empty. Windows into the void beyond.

Her hair billowed out, growing longer by the second, lush and dark. The hair he had buried his hands in, wrapped in the silken strands, the hair that teased him and tormented him. It moved like she was underwater, or as if it had a life of its own. Perhaps it did. He had realised her hair reacted to magic, or reflected its use. He didn't know the way it worked, but he'd seen it grow and seen her powers grow with it.

It had enchanted him from the first, he realised. Just as she had.

And now as endless dark magic flowed through her, channelled through the ground, drinking down his sacrificial blood and focused by the stones bearing down all around her, lightning flashed overhead and he saw her as she truly was.

A dark goddess. The one to whom his life was forfeit, one who already owned him body and soul. And who now collected her due.

The one thing he was born to do, Leander had said. To die for her. That was the only reason he was alive in the first place.

'Finn,' she whispered but her voice was everywhere. On the wind, in the earth, raging through the stone above, reverberating through the stones. Singing in his blood, beating with his heart...

The Nox reached out with Wren's slender hand, her fingers no longer trembling, reaching for him, and at her command the darkness filled him as well. Her darkness, endless, limitless, lit from within with the complete opposite of light.

CHAPTER 43
WREN

No. This couldn't be happening. He couldn't die. Not Finn. The panic and the rage swept through her, stealing her breath. Her chest felt like bands of that horrible shadow-wrought metal were clamped around her and her head swam.

Wren threw herself across the open space within the stone circle, half falling, her hands digging into the soil until she reached Finn's body.

He lay so still, just sprawled there on his face, and beyond the stones she saw Leander, watching intently, leaning on the sword like it hadn't just killed his brother.

No. Not killed. Finn couldn't be dead. She would not allow that.

As she dropped to her knees, he took a single, shuddering breath and she saw the gaping wound, torn armour front and back, the blood seeping into the dark and hungry earth... and she knew.

Wren gathered him in her arms, lifted him against her body.

He blinked, but he didn't seem to see her.

'Wren?' he whispered all the same. He knew she was there. That was something. It had to be.

'I'm here. I'm here, don't move. Don't… great light, don't leave me. Please Finn don't… don't leave me.'

He tried to smile. The darkness flooded his eyes like clouds in a stormy sky. 'I may not have a choice.'

'I won't let you!' It came out in a snarl of sound, something savage and alien to her.

'If anyone could stop this,' he whispered, his voice growing faint. 'It would be you.'

And his eyes closed.

His blood was on her hands, on her clothes. It burned on her skin.

He was wrong. She wasn't strong enough. But she knew someone who was.

'Elodie,' Wren yelled, desperate now. 'Elodie, please. I need you. Please!'

But Elodie couldn't help her. She was in chains, her power smothered by their shadows. Wren didn't even know if Elodie was still conscious. Or alive. Even if she was, there was only the two of them against all Leander's men, and the shadow kin he had summoned.

And all around her she could hear the song again. Leander circled the outside of the stones, still singing out in othertongue, and the Nox joined him in so many harmonious voices in this world and beyond. She hated him, loathed him. How could he do this, and to his own brother? Oh there was no love lost between them, but to do this…

Wren couldn't let Finn die, not like this. She had to try. Gathering what light she could in her mind, she poured it into Finn's poor broken body, trying to heal and knit it back together, seeking out anything that might help her. She didn't know what she was doing. She worked entirely on instinct, trusting her heart to lead her.

But the light was gone too quickly. All around her was darkness. Who knew what hour it was? Where had the moon gone?

It was if shadows had closed in around them, cutting them off from any source of illumination she might use. The night seemed to have lasted forever.

And part of her feared it would now, that it would never end.

'Wren,' Elodie called out weakly, her voice shaking. 'Wren, just hold on. Don't do anything stupid. I'll find a way. I'll find—'

Leander was on Elodie in an instant. He struck her hard, sending her down onto the ground with a terrible crack, his fist still clenched. He didn't use the sword, and for that Wren thanked the light. But he wouldn't, she realised. Not for Elodie. He wanted her to hurt. He wanted her to know she had failed.

Strange, how transparent the prince was to her now. For all his charm, all his machinations, all his treachery... she could see him for what he was.

Leander turned towards her, meeting her horrified gaze with his own unswerving one.

'You know what you have to do, Wren, my love. If you can save him he's yours. But only if you can save him. I'll let you all go. If he lives. So go on. Make him live, princess.'

The mockery in his voice made her recoil. But she'd show him. She had to show him. Even if he didn't keep his word, she couldn't let Finn die.

With no light to help her, she had no choice. If she was going to save him there was only one way to turn. She reached out to the shadows instead.

Elodie cried out her name, just her name. A warning. A denial.

And then Wren was somewhere else.

The darkness pressed in on Wren from all around, crushing her, like a candle flame deprived of air. It was vast, endless, and all of its attention was fixed upon her.

The voice, when it sounded, was like a rumble of thunder. It rolled through the air with the storm and shook its way into her body.

What are you doing, little vestige? Why do you defy me?

Wren felt herself drop to her knees, helpless. Why did she defy it? Because she had to. She knew what it was. Deep inside her, she knew that this was the Nox and, if she let it, it would consume her entirely.

'You belong here.' She forced the words out and it was like tearing strips of skin from the insides of her throat. 'You don't belong in me.'

The Nox laughed, the laugh of a young woman, her own laugh perhaps. It shook her to the core. *In you? No, you have it all wrong. You belong in me. Come home, little one.*

It pressed down on her again, trying to force her open like an oyster, something like a knife sliding into her mind to twist it apart.

You're mine, little one. Part of me. You came from me. Surely you always suspected that. I'm your mother.

'No. Elodie... Elodie's my mother...'

That thief? The tone turned vindictive and vengeful. *She stole you from me when I was weak, took you away and hid you. For years she hid you. I sent all the remaining fragments of my power looking for you but to no avail. She made a bargain with the old magic in the forest to hide you. But here you are now. And so is she. When I'm free, we are going to do such things to her. We're going to tear her apart a piece at a time. Now, stop fighting me. You belong to me.*

It was lying. It had to be lying. And yet everything suddenly made sense. Why Elodie hid her away, why the darkness responded to her the way it did, why the fragments of the Nox and the shadow kin flocked around their home... looking for her.

It couldn't be true. But the moment it was said, Wren knew

somehow that it was. That some vital part of her had come from this thing and that it meant to take her back.

Wren screamed but there was nothing she could do, nothing that would stop it. She was trapped and the Nox was inside her, around her, everywhere. She felt it fill her and for one last moment she struggled, clinging to her own consciousness by her fingernails.

She had to hold on.

I can save him for you, the Nox whispered.

CHAPTER 44

WREN

Wren didn't mean to let go. She couldn't help it. That offer, that suggestion, startled her and she was lost. Finn was dying. Somewhere, in her helpless arms, Finn was dying. His blood burned on her skin and his eyes stared sightlessly at her face. And she was going to lose him forever, before they had even begun to discover what they might really have.

Another voice reached Wren, distant and faint, no more than a sigh, so different from the Nox's insidious whisper. A voice she knew...

'*It's a trick, my love. A lie. Hold on. Just a little longer.*'

It sounded almost like Elodie. But that was impossible. Elodie was out there – somewhere – on her knees, in chains, helpless and in Leander's power.

Some tiny part of Wren that still remained reached out to the voice and found a sliver of light still cutting through the shadows. No more than a glimmer, but it was there.

Her mother.

Only Elodie had never called herself that.

It didn't really matter one way or the other if Elodie had actually given birth to her. She had raised her, taught her to walk, to read, to reason, to think for herself. She had been there when Wren had taken ill and nursed her through it. She'd been there when Pol first broke her heart. She had always been there. Caustic and fierce, short-tempered sometimes, but still there. Holding her, helping her, guiding her to the light. Always to the light.

We are witchkind. We will live free or die.

'Elodie,' Wren sobbed and felt ghostly hands touch her face, stroke her skin with love and care. The same hands she had known all her life. The ones that brought her through fever, and pulled her out of nightmare, that drew her in for a kiss, that brushed her hair so gently...

She heard a whisper. Little more than a breath. But it was there.

'*Just a little longer. Look to the sky, little bird. Look to the east. Now.*'

Wren's eyes snapped open. Everything was dark and cold. But she was back, the stones looming over her, the shadows pressing close. Finn lay too still, staring at the sky overhead without seeing it.

Look to the east?

Wren turned her head, fighting to do so as the Nox tried to stop her, forcing her own body to obey her. She looked over her shoulder, as above the treeline, above the distant hills, the first light of dawn began to stain the sky.

Light. New light. A fresh day. It spilled over the treetops like liquid gold, its honeyed tones illuminating the world as the sky turned a kaleidoscope of colours. And with light came power. Elodie's power, tied so intimately to the light of the Aurum.

'Now, Wren!' Elodie shouted out loud and her voice shook the sky.

She'd been biding her time, Wren realised, waiting for that light and the surge of magic it would bring. Elodie had always been powerful, but Elodie with something to fight for could not be contained.

Except by one thing.

The manacles still held her, dampening her magic. It was the only thing keeping her in check.

Wren could see the threads of the Nox's magic that permeated the metal. That was how they made such things, wasn't it? It had to be. She could see it, feel it, sense it. It made sense. The Aurum's blessed steel such as Finn's sword was its opposite, its counterpoint. This metal had been blessed by a dark power now lost to the Ilanthians. The manacles, the chains, Leander's sword... they all stood out to her now and she could see their function and their purpose, could see the things that made them what they were.

It was so easy to reach out with her mind, with the magic buried deep in her blood, and pull those threads. It took almost no effort at all. The shadows embedded in the metal so long ago answered her, just as the shadows had always answered her. Willingly, immediately, like well-trained dogs.

Wren reached out and pulled away the power of the Nox threaded through the chains.

Elodie, bathed in the light of a new day, lifted her head, and met Wren's gaze. She smiled. Wren couldn't remember the last time she'd seen Elodie smile like that.

'Stay where you are, my love,' she said without raising her voice, but Wren still heard her. They were connected. They always had been. 'I'll just be a minute.'

And a pillar of light blazed in the place where Elodie had been.

Leander yelled orders at his men as the shadow kin recoiled.

Elodie, or the figure made of living fire that had been Elodie, rose to her feet. The manacles still swung from her hand, open now, just pieces of metal. As Wren watched, Elodie ran her hand down the length of steel. The othertongue that spilled out of her was a song, triumphant and terrible. A blessing. Beneath her touch the metal transformed, flowing like water, illuminated from within like a flame, and became a sword.

She moved like a dancer, and any who danced with her died.

'Come then,' Elodie shouted at Leander. 'This is what you've wanted. Isn't it, you stupid boy?'

Leander raised his own dark sword and stepped into the stone circle, bearing down on Wren instead.

'I'll kill her,' he warned. 'It might just as well release the Nox. We don't know. And then what will you do, your majesty?'

'I'll kill you all,' Elodie promised grimly in return. It was no threat. More like a promise. 'Make no mistake, Leander. I'll kill everyone here for her. It will not even be the first time.'

His remaining guards threw themselves towards her, trying to stop her advancing, to protect their prince.

'Wren?' Finn whispered. She pulled him against her chest, holding him close. He was still alive. There was that. She had that much. Finn was somehow still alive. She just had to keep him that way.

'Close your eyes,' she told him. She needed to protect him from this. It was all she could do for him now. But Finn didn't obey her this time. Instead she felt him move, even though moving had to be an agony. She wrapped herself around him, but he just pressed something hard and cold into her hand.

His sword.

Wren moved based on instincts alone, or perhaps guided by the magic that filled her. She brought the blade up before she could think about what she was doing. It intercepted Leander's blow, turning it aside. The impact sent shudders down her arm and she almost lost her grip entirely.

Still trying to hold Finn and keep him clinging to life, or at least force him not to die, Wren couldn't keep control of everything. Leander came at her again and, this time, othertongue spilled from her lips, in an attempt to drive him back. The sword in her hand grew bright and terrible.

Another roll of thunder sounded, nearer this time, and she smelled the sweet sting of the oncoming storm, crackling in the air. The sword raised on high, she reached for the light. Light had always defied her. Always so difficult to control, always a trial, but now she realised it was just the opposite of the darkness.

And if she could command the darkness to go, light took its place.

Leander staggered back as light like a beacon burst from the stone circle, far brighter than anything she had seen before. It didn't hurt this time. It was just the other side of her power. Not something to fight but to embrace. And to use. She knew what she had to do. The light flowed over her skin, but it drenched the man in her arms like a summer rain storm, illuminating Finn inside and out. It threaded its way along his veins and rippled through his skin, seeking out his wounds and forcing him back to life.

The earth shook. Wren felt it as the light subsided, trembling beneath her, as the Knights of the Aurum rode into the clearing to join the fight.

The sword was too heavy, the strain too much. She let it fall and wrapped herself around Finn, holding him close, filling him with what light she could still muster, drawing out the darkness that had threatened to take him. It had nowhere to go but into her, but that was all right. She could deal with it. She could keep it safe.

But she couldn't fight anymore. She had to hold on and hope someone else would save them both.

What else could she do? Her strength was gone and it was taking everything she had to keep Finn alive.

The Nox laughed in the back of her mind and pressed its advantage again. She had forgotten it. And now she had nothing left to defend herself with from its renewed assault. It flung itself at her with a vengeance.

CHAPTER 45
ELODIE

Elodie fought as she had not fought in years. There had been no need. But she had lost none of her skill.

With the light of the Aurum blazing beneath her skin she moved like lightning. She barely noticed the faces who fell before her. Later, she knew, they'd come back to her. In her nightmares, or in the dark of the night when she couldn't sleep at all. But for now, for this moment, they were blurs.

All but Leander's. He looked too like his uncle. Too like Evander, who had hurt her and betrayed her. Who had betrayed everyone.

Perhaps they should have expected it all along. It had been a last-ditch attempt at peace, but she should have known it would never work. Her handsome prince had used it as a trick, a cunning plan to get inside Pelias, into the chamber of the Aurum and do his worst. A suicide mission perhaps, but Evander had never cared about that. He would have done anything to bring Elodie to her knees.

She hated him. Still hated him with a fire that never ceased, a fire she turned on his people now. It would have been too easy to lose herself in its blazing fury, let the Aurum fill her and be its instrument again, its hand on this earth. But there was a purpose to her action and she clung to that. She had to reach Wren, had to protect her. She had to stop this.

The prince – not Evander, Elodie reminded herself, but barely any better – retreated from Wren as the girl drew on more magic than Elodie would have thought possible and drove him out of the circle. This endless power belonged to Wren now, to her and the Nox. The two of them were working together, the magic entwining with her and wrapping itself around Finn. Wren was focused entirely on the man she held, the man who should have been long dead in any other circumstances.

But Wren wasn't having that. Finn was hers. Body and soul. Perhaps he always had been. Light poured through her, a light so bright, and it anchored him to the world, to her.

Her Wren. So brilliant, so powerful, so impossibly stubborn. Elodie realised that she had never been more proud. Her Wren, still holding firm, still clinging to the light, still determined not to lose anyone she loved.

And it was love. There was no way she would be able to do it otherwise. Not even the Nox could work a wonder like that.

I knew it, Elodie wanted to shout in triumph. I knew I was right about her.

Horses thundered around the clearing, the Knights of the Aurum riding to their rescue. Her knights. The Ilanthian troops still standing broke to run. Shadow kin turned on their would-be rescuers, a swarm of darkness and malevolence. No, not this time, not when she could do something about it. Elodie raised a shield of light over the newly arrived knights, incinerating any of the dark creatures who came too close to them.

She had to look for him. She couldn't help herself.

Her Paladin...

And on the far side of the clearing, across the circle of ancient stones, she saw him. She couldn't fail to recognise him.

He had been in her dreams for more than twenty years. He had once been her everything. Roland shouted his commands as he always had, clear and precise, and moved like the warrior he had always been. Entirely present in the moment, focused completely on his troops, his role, on the battle. He and his mount seemed to be one being, moving with one mind. A killer, and a champion, and everything she had ever wanted.

She almost stopped in her tracks, staring at him.

The impact to the back of her body sent her down in a heap but the light still shielding her deflected the worst. Leander aimed a kick at her head that she rolled to avoid. As much of a little bastard as Evander ever was then. It figured. She was up on her feet again before he could strike a more dangerous blow.

'You finally crawled out of your hole then,' he hissed at her. 'It's never going to be safe for you again, understand? I'm going to make you pay for everything.'

His retreating men shouted for him, but he didn't move. He wanted her dead, she knew that. He wanted to kill her himself.

Like he would have half a chance of that.

'Run away, little boy,' she told him, swinging her sword nonchalantly into position. 'Go home and lick your wounds, and don't come back. Don't ever come near what is mine again.'

'Yours?' he sneered. 'Is that your claim now? She's going to be mine. She's going to beg me to take her. The Nox will see to that.'

'The Nox is broken and banished. Your goddess is nothing now.'

At that he laughed, actually laughed. Like she was an idiot, standing there in front of him. This child, this boy, laughed at her.

'Queen Aeryn of Asteroth,' he said with a sneer, drawing out each phrase in mockery. 'Heading back home to the chamber of the Aurum, in the Sacrum itself. With little Wren beside her. What could possibly go wrong?'

Elodie narrowed her eyes, trying to work out what he knew, how he could possibly know. No, she told herself. I was right. All these years, I've been right.

Roland stepped towards them, and Leander backed up, a little less certain faced with two of them. Slowly, he shook his head.

'What are you going to do, either of you? Kill me and it will be another war. Ilanthus will fall on you like a wave.'

'Your uncle said things like that once,' said Elodie. 'He died too.'

Leander grinned at her, that maddening, mad smile of the line of Sidon. 'You murdered him.'

Elodie was about to answer but he wasn't exactly wrong. Her protest failed. Evander had died and war had come, a war from which she had fled. There was so much to plead guilty to here. She didn't know where to start.

'He's right,' said Roland, his voice a deep rumble behind her. Elodie didn't dare turn around, couldn't. She told herself it was because she didn't want to take her eyes off the prince, but that wasn't entirely true either. 'He's their crown prince. Let him go.'

'He's broken the Pact,' Elodie said. 'He shouldn't be here. He should never have come after Wren.'

'Elodie,' Roland murmured. 'He isn't worth it. Let him go.'

For a moment she wanted to ignore him, wanted to scream and run the little bastard through. But she couldn't move. Just like so long ago, when Evander had used the same threat, she knew he was right. Kill him and everything would fall apart. Show mercy and maybe, just maybe, there was a chance... if not to avoid war then at least delay it. For a time.

Slowly, she let her sword arm drop and nodded. Hating him. Hating herself. Hating Roland.

Leander didn't need to be told twice. He broke and ran, vaulting onto one of the Ilanthian horses and tearing off to the north. His men, those still alive, fled with him. Just like that, the battle, such as it was, was over.

Suddenly, Elodie felt a million years old, her arms weighed down and her body wrung out. She let the sword fall from her hand, thudding onto the grass, and its light finally dimmed to a faint glow. The use of so much magic, even if it had come naturally to her with the dawn, left her drained and aching. It had been too long. She'd forgotten how hard it was, especially afterwards.

The urge to just drop to her knees right there in the mud and pass out was powerful indeed. And then, she realised, she had another problem as well. One much worse.

A shadow loomed over her. But it wasn't a creature of the dark. It was so much worse than that.

Oh no. Not this. Not like this.

How could she face him again, after so many years? What could she say?

She turned slowly, longing to just run instead. And looked up.

Roland de Silvius, older, a touch of silver in his black hair, a few lines on his face, but the same man. Towering over her. The same as he ever was.

Mine, her treacherous heart whispered inside her. *He's mine.*

His lips moved, as if numb or as if he'd had a blow to the head, leaving him almost senseless. The way they always did when he said her name. Her true name. 'Elodie?'

Not like this, she thought. It couldn't be like this. She had to go. She had to run. She needed to get Wren and run. They could still make it if she...

She backed away and saw Roland's brow furrow. He knew, she realised. But then he had always known what she was thinking, sometimes better than she did. And behind that confusion she could sense his anger, his pain. She couldn't face that.

It was her fault. It was all her fault.

A voice cried out, one full of anger and fear. 'Don't touch him! Don't you dare—let go! I have to—you'll kill him.'

Wren!

Her attention snapped away from Roland and straight to the girl. Two no doubt well-meaning knights were trying to help her with Finn but Wren wouldn't see it like that. Even now Elodie could see the flow of power between them, the way the girl had tangled herself with the life essence of the young man she clung to. And she was right. If the idiots tore them apart, they'd break the spell. They would kill him. Nothing was keeping Finnian alive except for Wren's erratic magic.

Their eyes met and Wren's face fell to desperation. 'Elodie! Help!'

The newmade sword was still at her feet. She could fight her way out if needs be. Their weapons were old in comparison. Hers was newly forged Aurum steel, made from the manacles but purified by the light she'd poured through it. It was strong and beautiful, a blade for a hero. Not for someone like her. But all the same she would use it, even against him, even against her own knights, and she would escape.

But it would mean leaving Wren when Wren needed her most.

And Elodie knew, with a cold and terrible realisation, she could never do that. Not under any circumstances.

How could she have even dreamed that was possible after all these years?

Elodie abandoned the sword and sprinted into the stone circle. It was dormant now, the magical power engendered by the darkness drained away with the dawn, leaving only traces behind. She could still feel the potential rippling through the ground and the air. It shook through her, stirred up by Wren's use.

The two knights stared at her in abject horror. They were

young, so very young. They looked like boys. 'Get back from them, you idiots. Are you trying to get him killed? Stand down.'

They glanced over her shoulder and she was certain that, behind her, Roland caught their eyes and nodded in that slow grim way of his.

Still, they hesitated. Probably more out of fear than anything else. They'd seen what she'd done. They might even suspect who she was.

She didn't want to think about that. It was a problem for later.

'I won't say it again. Get away from my daughter!'

The world seemed to freeze around her and tears stung her eyes, vicious little pinpricks that tormented her. Wren looked up at her, the girl's dark eyes glistening, and she held out a hand.

Her daughter... her child...

Elodie dropped to her knees, wrapping her fingers around Wren's and pressed her other hand to the wound in Finnian's chest, willing the flesh to reknit itself, and the internal damage to heal. She even forced the shredded metal to get out of her way so she could heal him.

It was a working of pure force, without subtlety or charm. She didn't have time for that. The light flowing through her came from the old magic itself, threading through the earth and the sky, the light that fuelled the Aurum and allowed her to work wonders. The boy was already touched by it. Wren had chosen him over and over, and she had all but anointed him already. He was more of a Paladin than half of the men standing around them. Perhaps more so than anyone but Roland himself.

What that might mean, Elodie didn't want to think. An Ilanthian, of the House of Sidon, Evander's nephew... blessed by the Aurum, light flowing through his veins like quicksilver. It was an anathema to everything she believed in. And yet, here she was.

When Elodie was done, and the light faded, Wren rested her face against her chest, sobbing so quietly. As she released Finn, Elodie wrapped her arms around the girl, holding her close like she used to when Wren was tiny and the nightmares had been the worst.

'It's all going to be all right, little bird. I promise,' she murmured, not even able to believe her own lie. But she had to say it. She had to say something. 'It's going to be all right.'

When she looked up, every man there was gathered around them. They dropped to their knees, heads bent, and Elodie knew what was coming next.

Roland was the only one still staring right at her, fixing her with that dark and endless gaze, the one she had once fallen into and never really found her way out of.

Then slowly he drove the point of his sword into the ground and dropped to one knee before her.

'Long live Queen Aeryn of Asteroth,' he said, and the knights all took up the cry.

Elodie hung her head and hugged Wren close. *My daughter*, she had said, for them all to hear. *My daughter*. And Roland had heard her too.

The one thing she had never wanted to happen. And here she was.

Finally trapped back in her nightmare of twenty years ago. And this time she didn't even have Roland to support her. Not anymore.

This time, Roland was her captor.

CHAPTER 46

WREN

The worst part, Wren decided, was sitting there in the infirmary. How Finn had done it while she had been unconscious, she didn't know. But he slept easily, his chest rising and falling slowly, and she could almost believe that it had all been a nightmare, that she hadn't seen that same chest torn open by the black blade of Leander's sword, the armour curling away like the flimsiest tin. That she hadn't felt Finn's hot blood on her hands, or heard the Nox make its promises and threats. That she hadn't felt him die.

That she hadn't forced him back to life.

Because that was what it had felt like. She'd refused to let him go. She'd held him to her, and tangled him with herself and everything she was to keep him with her.

It had almost been too late. If Elodie hadn't come to her aid, it would have been. Her strength was already draining away. The light wasn't an innate part of her and only her desperate need had let her use it at last. She would have lost him. And, with him, everything that made her whole.

The ability had already gone. But the darkness was still there. The Nox had claimed her, named her as part of it.

It wasn't true. It couldn't be.

She was Elodie's daughter. She'd heard Elodie herself say it.

Everyone had.

Including Roland.

Beforehand, the voices in Knightsford calling her princess had sounded almost sarcastic. Because while they thought she *might* be Roland's daughter by the queen, that was still all rumour and hearsay really. Now it was confirmed. And her father's identity didn't seem to matter so much anymore.

Queen Aeryn was back, and she had called Wren her daughter in front of countless witnesses of unimpeachable character. No one was going to naysay that, even if there was talk of the queen going on trial.

Some whispered that there would be an inquisition and a thousand punishments looming over her when they returned to Pelias. She would face the judgement of the Aurum and if she failed she would die. Elodie had abandoned her throne. She'd plunged the whole kingdom into war. She had vanished for twenty years. They hated her.

All whispers though. Voices had a nasty habit of falling silent if they caught sight of Wren, or realised she might be there. That she could be listening. And she couldn't help but listen.

If Elodie was executed, what would become of Wren? Roland intended to put her on the throne, she was sure of it. She couldn't bear that thought. She wasn't ready. She wasn't the right person to wear a crown, not any crown. Especially not the crown of Asteroth. What would the Aurum do with her? It would look inside her and see... what?

Elodie came to check on Finn later in the day. Or so she claimed. Since Wren had refused to move, it was also the only way Elodie could check on Wren. She fussed quietly over them both. She sat down and was about to engage Wren in some kind of painful conversation when Roland arrived at the door as well.

He froze when he saw her like some kind of startled deer.

Given his size, age and gravitas, Wren would have smiled, if the pain in the air between the two of them had not been so palpable.

'Oh, I'll…' he stuttered helplessly. 'I'll come back.'

Elodie rose to her feet, hands clasped before her, eyes downcast. She refused to even look at him for more than a second. 'No, I'll let you see to your ward. Come along, Wren.'

Wren, of course, didn't move. No one did. Instead, Wren reached out for Finn's still hand and wrapped her fingers around it where they belonged. Pointedly.

'He would have died without Elodie,' she said. 'I couldn't have saved him alone.'

Roland's nostrils flared just a little. 'He shouldn't even have been there.'

'And he wouldn't have been if it wasn't for me,' Wren finished for him sombrely. 'I know.'

'Don't you dare blame her for it,' Elodie cut in, that strange deference vanishing in an instant in Wren's defence.

Roland's voice came out clipped and sharp. 'I don't.'

No doubting who he did blame then. Elodie straightened her back. 'I should be going.'

'You aren't *going* anywhere.'

Elodie rolled her eyes in a most un-Elodie-like way. She sighed heavily. 'To my room, Roland. That's all I meant. Is that acceptable to you, Grandmaster?'

She swept by him and he turned as if to follow her, like he was drawn on an invisible string. Wren didn't miss the expression of longing on his face, but Elodie did. Perhaps she couldn't bear to see it.

'We leave in the morning,' he called after her. 'Be ready.'

Elodie didn't deign to reply.

'I'm not leaving Finn,' Wren told him.

Roland sort of folded into the other chair. He looked tired, all of a sudden, and far older than his forty or so years. 'Why am I not surprised that you're as stubborn as she is?'

Wren fixed him with a deliberate glare. 'As stubborn as who?'

He caught her meaning and gave a brief snort of laughter, almost the same sound that Elodie made when she was amused but didn't want to admit it. For some reason it made him sound human at last. 'You are my child, after all.'

Wren shrugged. 'I've gone from no one wanting to claim my parentage to everyone, all of a sudden. It's a bit much.'

And as for everything else he must have seen in that stone circle, the magic, the darkness...

Finn's hand tightened on hers and she turned – Roland, Elodie, her dubious parentage and the dark magic that came so naturally to her completely forgotten. He gazed up at her with an unwavering gaze.

'Wren? Are you... are you all right?'

The sound that came out was more a strangled sob than an answer, but she nodded all the same, and bent to kiss him.

Roland cleared his throat uncomfortably and Finn almost levitated off the bed when he realised where his guardian and commanding officer was. Wren pushed him back down and glared at her erstwhile father. Strange, to call him that. But it seemed she needed to get used to it.

'Sir, I'm sorry, I—' Finn began, babbling away, torn between apology and explanations he couldn't hope to give.

Roland held up a hand for silence and Finn obeyed. Too well-trained, Wren decided. But Roland's voice was unexpectedly gentle when he finally spoke.

'We will discuss everything later. For now, I just want you to get better. We're setting off for Pelias tomorrow. Will you be able to make the journey? The healers say there is nothing physically wrong but if you—'

'No,' said Finn. He still had not released Wren's hand, she realised. 'I'll be ready. I'll come with you.'

Who was that for? she wondered.

Roland stood again. 'Very well. I'll let you talk then. I need to—' He lifted his eyes to the window. Beyond it, in the garden, Wren saw Elodie sit on a bench and bury her face in her hands. You'd only be able to see her from here. The bower was draped in flowering wisteria, hidden from view from anywhere but here. 'Excuse me.'

And then he was gone.

Finn was silent for a while, slowly sitting up and trying to work out if and how his body was still whole.

'What happened in the stone circle?' he asked at last. 'I saw... I don't know what I saw. But Wren... was that the Nox?'

She nodded slowly, dreading the expression he might wear at that revelation. But Finn just pulled her into his embrace and held her close. It was more than she had hoped and the relief made her weak.

'Tomorrow we leave for Pelias,' she whispered, unable to hide her fear. 'And everything is going to change, isn't it?'

'Yes,' he said at last. 'I'm afraid it is. But I'll be there with you. I promise.'

At least there was that.

CHAPTER 47

WREN

It was going to take several days to get to Pelias. The knights moved like a living shield of metal around Elodie and Wren. They were constantly surrounded.

Every night it seemed they had to stop in someone's estate or castle. There were banquets and discussions, crowds of people gathering on the edges of the towns and villages to see them pass. The word had gone out that the queen had been found.

If she was honest, Wren would have bolted back to the forest at the first opportunity if it was not for Finn. She suspected Elodie would have been only two steps behind her. But Roland was not letting his queen out of his sight. The constant coldness between them was only making things worse.

It was almost a relief to finally see the city. Almost.

Pelias clung to the edge of the ocean, white and shining in the sunlight, blue tiled roofs and golden domes making it a striking view from a distance. Wren caught her breath when she saw it and beside her, on his own mount, Finn grinned easily.

'Beautiful, isn't it?'

She could only nod. She had never seen anything like it. What could possibly compare?

'Welcome home,' he said.

Home. What a strange concept. Pelias had only been a word before, a distant place out of stories. And now it was home.

Trumpets sounded as they entered the city gates. For all the grim whispers about an inquisition and a trial, Elodie's people seemed ecstatic to see her. They threw flowers from above and thronged the streets. But all the time Elodie rode like a statue, straight and tall, her eyes fixed on the distance. Roland wasn't much better.

Thankfully, no one here really knew about Wren yet so she just followed behind them, safe for now, or so she hoped. Anselm and Finn flanked her, having been given orders by Roland to guard her, no doubt. Although she thought Finn would have been there anyway.

They passed through internal fortifications and up spiralling streets until they reached the palace. A huge white stone of a building, a keep so old no one knew of its origins. As they dismounted, an older woman appeared, grey-haired and birdlike, but on sight of Elodie she gave a cry and ran across the courtyard, embracing her like a long-lost child.

'Lady Ylena, her aunt,' Anselm supplied. 'Your great-aunt, I suppose.'

'I suppose,' Wren said, feeling very lost. It hadn't occurred to her there would be other family members here. Not that the woman seemed in the slightest bit interested in her.

On the other side of the courtyard huge wooden doors decorated with gold swung open and twelve women dressed in white seemed to glide out. They also surrounded Elodie and the foremost of them bowed her head curtly. It wasn't exactly deferential. In return, Elodie nodded in much the same manner.

'Who are they?'

'The Maidens of the Aurum. They live in there, in the Sanctum. It opens only in two places—this courtyard and the Sacrum itself, where the Aurum burns. They'll be leading the trial. She might have been one of them in another life.'

Wren hadn't known that. She hadn't even suspected it, but she supposed Elodie had to have learned magic somewhere. She glanced at Finn but he had that same fixed expression, which meant he was holding something back. She knew him too well now, she realised.

'What happens next?'

But it was Anselm who answered. 'Next? We rest. We eat. We definitely wash.' He mimed holding his nose and she had to laugh. Thank the light itself for Anselm, she thought. His answering smile was somewhat rueful. 'Next, your life really changes. I'm sorry Wren.'

So was she.

For the rest of the day, she had been pampered like some kind of prize hound, offered a dizzying array of ridiculous gowns from which she had selected only the simplest, and had been kept away from Elodie at all costs.

It was grating and Wren had had enough.

Someone insisted on putting a coronet on her head, befitting her station apparently. A simple enough circlet, given the other monstrosities on offer, she decided, but it felt so strange, her hair pulled up around it to hold it in place. Too heavy. Out of place. Strands of her hair caught on it, wrapped around it.

All Wren wanted was to tear everything off but that was going to take too long, and there were far too many hands ready to stop her. The first moment she had, as soon as their backs were turned, she slipped out of her door. There had to be somewhere she could be alone, even if just for a while.

The ladies-in-waiting were already talking about the great feast being prepared for her, how her father – what a strange concept – would want to present her to the regents' council, and let the nobles greet her, to let her learn her place in the court. It was like being a child and she really did not take well to that. She was a grown woman and knew her own mind. She even contemplated using some choice words of othertongue to get rid of them. Or, failing that, some old hedge witch charms might do the trick.

But then what would they all say? They'd blame Elodie for that too, no doubt. Look how she raised the girl, they'd say. Look at the monster Elodie made.

Except they didn't call her Elodie. She was Queen Aeryn here, and any brief mention of her true name, or her possible fate at all, was hushed and fraught with tension. They didn't know what was going to happen to her either. No one did.

The door opened noiselessly and Wren closed it just as quietly. There was no guard, probably because there was no way she would be able to get out of the keep on her own. The moment the gaggle of women in there realised she'd gone, they were going to come after her. Maybe the ladies-in-waiting were the real guards. They were certainly fanatical enough.

She didn't even know what way to go. The place was a maze. She was in the safest place they knew, the stronghold of the Knights of the Aurum, the palace of the royal family of Asteroth. They didn't need to guard her.

But Finn was waiting for her. He unfolded from his place against the wall in the shadows and Wren had to smile to see his easy grace. This was not what she had expected. It was better.

'Running away again?'

'If I actually could, I would,' she answered, truthfully. She'd give just about anything to get away from here. But that would mean deserting Elodie and Wren would not do that. Not again. Especially not now when everyone seemed set against her. 'Where's Elodie? They won't let me see her. And they won't answer any questions.'

He nodded slowly and took her arm, leading her down the corridor as if they were just going for a stroll. Perhaps they were.

'She's with the maidens. Preparing for her trial. It isn't going to be easy, not on anyone. They loved her and if she did truly betray us all—'

Wren was so sick of hearing about Queen Aeryn the traitor.

'She wouldn't. Whatever happened, she had reason. I know her.'

His voice turned serious. 'She's lied to you all your life, Wren. Did you ever think about that?'

Of course she did. But she didn't want to say that now. It felt ungrateful somehow. If Elodie had lied, well, it was to protect her. From all of this. Wren understood it all too well now. She'd do anything herself to get out of this. She just wished she could tell Elodie that. Forgive her. Let her know that in one way, even if only the one, she had done the right thing.

Finally finding out who she was, where she came from, who her parents truly were... that had always been her dream. She had never thought it would turn out to be such a nightmare.

At least she had Finn. She leaned against him, and he slipped his arm around her shoulders.

'What will happen? At the trial, I mean?'

Wren wasn't even sure why she asked. She didn't want to know what would happen if they found Elodie guilty. She could guess and that was enough.

'She'll be presented to the Aurum. It will decide.'

'A *fire*? They're going to let a fire decide? How does that even work?'

He laughed and his hand brushed against her arm, sending

shivers through her. 'Come on, you know it's not just a fire, Wren. It's... it's alive with magic. It's linked to Elodie, and through her to all of us. It is light incarnate. You felt it running through both of us. You used it to save me.'

Had she? Sometimes she wasn't so sure. She had used something. Yes, she had felt the light, the burning, blinding, brightness of it, but she had also felt the chill and soothing touch of its antithesis, the dark.

'Can you... can you show it to me?'

It wasn't that Finn squirmed, he'd never do that. But he shifted a little uncomfortably. 'We're not meant to just wander in there. It's a holy place. But... if we're quick and quiet... all right then. Come with me.'

CHAPTER 48

WREN

They didn't exactly hurry on their way. A moment with Finn was not to be squandered because, now they were in Pelias, those were already becoming rare and precious. Every so often Wren stopped and kissed him, as soon as they were both sure they were alone.

The temptation to just find an empty room and pull him into her arms was even stronger than she had imagined.

Later, she thought, later. After the presentation to the council and the feast, and whatever other horrors the royal court had planned for her. She'd take him back to her ridiculously large quarters, dismiss anyone still there, and they could make love. She had to have something to look forward to. So long as they found a way to lock the door, because she was not comfortable with the way people just kept bustling in and out of her private chambers. But she would find a way. The lure of Finnian Ward was too strong. Just walking alongside him, entwined with him, made her feel all kinds of things she was certain princesses were not meant to know about.

But she wasn't really their princess and she never would be.

It all had to be a terrible mistake. Everything she was told her that.

Finn opened a discreet door and led her along a rather plain corridor. It was almost a shock given the lavish surroundings elsewhere, and, she had to admit, a massive relief to step inside.

'Servants' corridor,' he told her with a grin when he saw her confusion. 'The keep is riddled with them. It's like another world.'

Interesting. She filed that piece of information away in case she needed it later. She'd find out where the rest of these passages were.

They climbed an equally plain staircase hewn from the white stone of the hill on which Pelias stood, and then, finally, Finn opened another door.

The chamber beyond was enormous. She stepped through, gazing up in wonder. Everything was the same white marble. On the floor it had been polished to a mirror sheen, veins like golden threads running through it. It was like standing in a cave made of ice, and had clearly been carved out by many hands over many years. Above them the dome arched high overhead, and carvings decorated the walls, depictions of kings and queens, of great battles, of lovers, of families, of tragic deaths and newborn children. But in all the scenes the symbol of the Aurum repeated. A flame curling into a circle, eternal and powerful, a vortex of pure light. There were no windows, she realised, no natural light at all.

All illumination came from a flame, constant and ever moving, in the centre of the huge room. And around that flame rose a group of seven standing stones, each larger than a human being, rough and unpolished, in stark contrast to everything else here, the most natural thing in this unnatural place.

'Like the Seven Sisters,' she murmured, bemused.

'I'd never thought of that, but yes,' Finn admitted. He looked uncomfortable with the thought.

Carefully, Wren approached the flame. It was confined to a well-like structure in the centre of the stone circle, and it moved constantly, dancing before her. It was almost the same height as she was. That didn't seem to vary. Almost human-like. She felt like it was watching her as much as she was watching it.

Without thinking, she passed inside the circle of attendant stones and reached the low wall surrounding it. In the depths of the flame she could hear something, she was sure of it. Distant and faint, but so alluring. A song, perhaps, a lullaby, something she knew, although she couldn't name it. But that song, that tune... it had been with her all her life.

Wren reached out a hand towards the flame and she felt it welcome her, draw her towards it, the song growing louder, more distinct.

Finn grabbed her shoulder and pulled her back, the action sending a shockwave of alarm through her, and she turned into his arms.

'You can't touch it. It's sacred.'

'But I—' What could she say? That it wanted her to? That it was calling her? No, those were the words of a crazy person and she didn't want Finn to look at her like she was mad. 'I'm sorry, you're right. Maybe we should go.'

But she was there in his arms, pressed against him. And she didn't want to go anywhere. Finn was gazing into her eyes as if he couldn't see anything else and she watched the startling blue of his irises reflect the flame behind her. He was beautiful, she thought. More than beautiful. He was everything, all she wanted.

She kissed him and felt him resist for a moment before melting against her, that desperate, dammed-up desire they both felt breaking free again. He buried his hand in her hair so he could cradle her head, his mouth claiming hers. Wren's voice gave a whimper of need as she pulled him against her.

The stupid coronet they'd insisted on making her wear, no

doubt in some effort to make her short hair look more regal, slipped free and clattered onto the marble floor behind her. The sound startled them both and brought them back to where they were. Somewhere they should not be.

About to defile a sacred place, she thought. Probably. She really was a terrible princess. Why did no one else realise that?

Finn pressed his forehead to hers and sighed, giving her a rueful smile.

'Perhaps we should go somewhere else,' she said, with a degree of hope for the first time in days.

'I think that's an excellent idea.' He let her go and retrieved the coronet. It was, she thought, pretty enough for something so ridiculous, a slender circlet of white-gold wire, woven like the branches of a tree in which tiny gems sparkled with the wintry light of the chamber. Whoever had picked it had noted the contrast with her hair's colour and used it accordingly. The ladies who had dressed her were experts in the court after all. They wanted a princess and that was what they would make of her, whether she cooperated with them in the endeavour or not.

The weight of that settled on her shoulders, even as Finn settled the coronet reverently back on her head. His fingertips brushed against her hair, then down the sides of her face.

'There,' he said fondly. 'Back to being a princess.'

Not what she wanted to hear at all.

But as he stepped back to admire her, he seemed to freeze, his eyes widening as they fixed on something else behind her. Where the flame was.

'What is it?' she asked, confused.

Finn wasn't staring in wonder or affection now. He wore a look of something very much like horror.

'Finn?'

She started to turn but he just grabbed her arm and started pulling her after him, away from the Aurum, away from the stones, back towards the little door to the servants' corridors.

'We have to leave. Right now.' There was a note of alarm buried in the unexpected commanding tone.

'What do you mean? What's going on?'

Wren twisted back, unable to tear herself free of his grip, but just enough to see the flame of the Aurum transform with the same blue-black hues that had suffused the metal of Leander's sword. Illuminated with the light of the Nox.

PROPHECY OF AELYN THE FIRST

When the Nox is scattered across the land,
Sidon's walls come down.
When the Aurum sleeps in silent flames,
Pelias gives up its crown.
When shadows take the Aurum,
the Nox will take the throne.
When the Nox is crowned in the Sacrum,
the lost queen stands alone.

A LETTER FROM JESSICA

Dear reader,

I want to say a huge thank you for choosing to read *A Touch of Shadows*. If you did enjoy it, and want to keep up to date with all my latest releases, just sign up at the following link. Your email address will never be shared and you can unsubscribe at any time.

www.bookouture.com/jessica-thorne

Writing *A Touch of Shadows* has been a wonderful adventure in its own right and a story I've wanted to tell for a very long time. I'm so excited to be able to bring each part of it to you with Bookouture in quick succession. It's going to be a rollercoaster.

As always I want to thank my agent, Sallyanne Sweeney, my lovely editor Natalie for her insight and enthusiasm, my writing friends of the Naughty Kitchen, and here in Ireland, Sarah Rees Brennan, Catie Murphy and Susan Connolly. Writing is a solitary pursuit, so having people who understand the chaos is a bonus.

And speaking of general chaos, my family are always there for me. And Pat is still my hero.

I hope you loved *A Touch of Shadows* and if you did I would be very grateful if you could write a review. I'd love to hear what you think, and it makes such a difference helping new readers to discover one of my books for the first time. You can get in touch on social media or through my website.

Thanks,

Jessica Thorne

www.rflong.com/jessicathorne

facebook.com/JessThorneBooks
instagram.com/Jessthornebooks

PUBLISHING TEAM

Turning a manuscript into a book requires the efforts of many people. The publishing team at Bookouture would like to acknowledge everyone who contributed to this publication.

Audio
Alba Proko
Sinead O'Connor
Melissa Tran

Commercial
Lauren Morrissette
Hannah Richmond
Imogen Allport

Cover design
Mary Luna

Data and analysis
Mark Alder
Mohamed Bussuri

Editorial
Natalie Edwards
Sinead O'Connor

Copyeditor
Rhian McKay

Proofreader
Faith Marsland

Marketing
Alex Crow
Melanie Price
Occy Carr
Cíara Rosney
Martyna Młynarska

Operations and distribution
Marina Valles
Stephanie Straub

Production
Hannah Snetsinger
Mandy Kullar
Jen Shannon

Publicity
Kim Nash
Noelle Holten
Jess Readett
Sarah Hardy

Rights and contracts
Peta Nightingale
Richard King
Saidah Graham

Printed in Great Britain
by Amazon

48297437R00169